W9-BMQ-290

"Are you from around here?"

Jolie could feel Matt Dawson assessing her as a possible threat to his son. Saw it in the way his arm came to rest protectively on Charlie's shoulder. And she liked him better for it. "I'm Jolie Maxwell. I guess I'm your only neighbor up here. I understand you're from Chicago."

Nodding, he took her hand, releasing it as if he didn't want to prolong the contact a second longer than necessary. His intent gaze never wavered. "Are you from Montana?"

Nice handshake. Warm, firm, decisive—her fingers were still tingling long after she'd stepped back. "My family's been here for generations, but I've lived in California since college. The Maxwell family ranch, Walking Stones, is thirty miles away."

Shoving his fists into his back pockets, he surveyed the snowy mountain peaks surrounding them. "Must've been hard to be away from all this."

Jolie's thoughts drifted. Last Halloween her brother, Bobby, had nearly killed himself and two of his friends while driving drunk. And a month later, her father had suffered a heart attack and refused to even consider his doctor's advice. No surprise there— Robert Maxwell's stubborn independence was legend.

She'd missed the mountains, all right, but there were *much stronger* reasons for coming home....

Dear Reader,

A Montana Family, set in the shadows of the Crazy Mountains, is a book that touched my heart. I love exploring issues surrounding family relationships—old wounds, old regrets, the forging of tenuous new bonds despite nearly insurmountable barriers. And above all, what it means to receive the gift of unconditional love.

For the three Maxwell sisters, growing up with a powerful, emotionally distant father shaped them into very different people. For Jolie Maxwell, that meant leaving her beloved mountains and making a new life for herself far from the family's Walking Stones Ranch. It's taken years for her to realize just what she's been missing…and now she hopes to reclaim all that she lost. When she meets her new neighbor and his children, she finds far more than she ever expected.

I hope you'll read the other two books in the Big Sky Country trilogy, and will enjoy meeting all the inhabitants of Paradise Corners. It would be lovely to hear from you. I can be reached online at:

www.roxannerustand.com
www.superauthors.com

Or by mail at: Box 2550, Cedar Rapids, Iowa 52406-2550

Best wishes, and happy reading!

Roxanne Rustand

Books by Roxanne Rustand

HARLEQUIN SUPERROMANCE

857—HER SISTER'S CHILDREN
895—MONTANA LEGACY
946—THE HOUSE AT BRIAR LAKE
982—RODEO!

A Montana Family
Roxanne Rustand

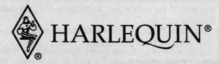

TORONTO • NEW YORK • LONDON
AMSTERDAM • PARIS • SYDNEY • HAMBURG
STOCKHOLM • ATHENS • TOKYO • MILAN • MADRID
PRAGUE • WARSAW • BUDAPEST • AUCKLAND

ISBN 0-373-71008-9

A MONTANA FAMILY

Copyright © 2001 by Roxanne Rustand.

This edition published by arrangement with Harlequin Books S.A.

® and TM are trademarks of the publisher. Trademarks indicated with ® are registered in the United States Patent and Trademark Office, the Canadian Trade Marks Office and in other countries.

Visit us at www.eHarlequin.com

Printed in U.S.A.

ACKNOWLEDGMENTS

With many thanks to the following people
for their invaluable assistance:

Joan Harding, M.D., for her generous gift of time
and medical expertise.

Kathy Ross, DVM, for her time, advice and reference
materials on the four-legged residents of Paradise Corners.

Diane Gates
of the Montana Investigations Bureau,
Division of Criminal Investigation,
for her information on current latent fingerprint technology,
and the procedures followed in her state.

Any errors in this manuscript are mine alone.

DEDICATION

For Larry, Andy, Brian and Emily, as always.

And to my brother Glen...with fond memories of childhood
trips to the mountains and a certain strawberry shortcake.

CHAPTER ONE

WHEN SHE LEFT Montana at the age of seventeen, Jolie Maxwell swore she'd never move back. It had taken sixteen years, an advertisement and the death of Wendell Hill to prove her wrong.

Shivering into her down jacket, she drifted idly back and forth on the porch swing of her newly leased cabin and breathed in mountain air so sharp and pure that her lungs ached with it.

Peace. No roar of rush-hour traffic, no arguments coming at her through a condominium wall. Only the occasional sharp whistle of a marmot on the rocky slopes rising above the cabin, or the distant bugle of elk broke the silence.

Grinning, she surveyed the clearing surrounding the cabin, carved from twenty fenced acres of dense pine and aspen. Late-March snow still gleamed in the shadows of the trees like heaps of whipped cream. A late-March breeze rustled the aspen leaves. Absolute heaven.

A long, furry neck stretched over the porch railing. Velvety lips flapped. Bright eyes studied her with interest. The neck and head extended farther, like a horizontal periscope, until those lips wiggled against her nape like a couple of fuzzy fingertips.

"Dolly!" Jolie laughed as she scooted out of range.

The llama hummed in response, its large, liquid black eyes watching Jolie with interest. Then suddenly she lifted her head and stared at the edge of the clearing.

Leaves rustled. A twig snapped.

Dolly snorted, spun around. Then took off at a gallop toward the sounds with her head high and ears pinned back. Her companion, Sadie, a nearly blind ewe, bleated piteously and trotted several steps in pursuit before pulling to an ungainly halt.

The llama hated dogs and coyotes, and right now some terrified four-footer was probably fleeing through the underbrush at the sight of such a bizarre creature barreling in its direction.

The moment Dolly disappeared into the brush, something—or someone—screamed in fear.

Jolie launched to her feet. The porch swing swung wildly as she took the deck steps two at a time and hit the yard at a dead run. What on earth would a child be doing way up here?

At the edge of the timber, Jolie paused. She heard nothing—no movement, no sound of a llama crashing through the brush. No squeals or snorts or cries of human terror.

And then she heard a faint sound. *A whimper.*

Shifting direction, she sped through the ghostly pale aspen and prickly spruce fronds, sweeping branches aside with her upraised hands.

She found Dolly beside a tumble of Volkswagen-size boulders near the fence line, her ears pricked forward, her head lowered. She was humming at something hidden in the rocks.

The llama definitely wouldn't be offering comfort to any four-legged predators. Jolie approached slowly, patted Dolly's fluffy back in greeting, then moved closer.

Wedged between the boulders, as tightly as he could manage, was a boy—maybe nine or ten—his head tucked down and arms wrapped around his upraised knees. He was clearly expecting to die.

"Hey there, buddy. My friend, Dolly, is sure happy to see you."

The boy opened one brown eye, then the other, and looked up at her. Tear tracks glistened through the dirt on his face

"She's a llama," Jolie continued easily, offering him a smile. "Did you hear her humming? She's worried about you."

He darted glances between Jolie and Dolly, clearly afraid to trust either one.

"My name's Jolie. I moved into that cabin over in the clearing two days ago. Who are you?" When he didn't answer, she studied him for a moment, then cocked her head. "I'll bet you're...one of the woodland fairies who live around here."

Some color came back into his pale cheeks as he rolled his eyes at her. "Am not!"

"One of the elves?"

"Charlie."

"Ah." She gave him a measuring look. "And where did you come from, Charlie? You're almost three miles from town."

He scrubbed awkwardly at the drying tears on his face, then scrambled to his feet. "We just bought the brick house down the road. We're from Chicago."

"I didn't know that place was for sale." The rambling old lodge stood a mile downhill from her cabin, and had caught her eye the first time she passed. It had to have a spectacular view of the mountains from its west windows.

Charlie took a wary step forward to touch Dolly's nose, but the llama shied away, lifting her head above his reach.

"Does she bite?"

Jolie laughed. "She doesn't like her face touched, but she's never tried to bite me. She's very curious and likes to investigate anything new. That's probably why she followed you.''

Despite the chilly day, he wasn't wearing a jacket, and he'd shoved the sleeves of his sweatshirt up to his elbows.

Looking down at a number of scratches on the boy's arms, she frowned. ''What happened there, buddy?''

''I sorta fell.''

''On the rocks, I'll bet.''

He flushed, dropped his gaze. ''When I climbed over the fence to get back here.''

''You must have come up through the woods. There's a cattle guard in the road that's a little easier.''

''I...I was exploring.''

''Can I take a look at your scrapes?''

She gently took his hands and turned his dirt-smudged arms over. The scratches were long, and several were still lightly bleeding, but there were no deep lacerations that would require sutures. ''You need to get cleaned up. Are you up to date on your tetanus shots?''

He shrugged, then winced as she touched a bruise over his wrist. ''Ouch!''

''Sorry.'' She released him and rested her hands on her hips. ''We should get you back to your mom so she can take care of this. Want a ride down the road?''

''I don't have a mom anymore.''

''Oh. Well then, your dad?''

Charlie scowled. ''He isn't home.''

Jolie stared down at the young child and felt anger rising in her chest. What kind of father let his child roam these rocky foothills alone?

She'd seen far too much abuse and neglect at her clinic in Los Angeles, and during the alternate weekends she'd worked in a hospital emergency room. Kids who ran free late into the night were at great risk in a city. Up here there were other dangers—bears and coyotes and timber rattlers…

Suppressing a shudder, she beckoned to him. "Come with me, and I'll take care of your battle wounds, okay?"

Dolly followed as they walked back to the cabin. The ewe fell into line as they passed her. Now and then Dolly bumped gently at Charlie's shoulder.

"She's not as mean as I thought," he marveled, stopping to give the llama's neck a hug when they reached Jolie's cabin. "How come you got her?"

"She came with the cabin. So did that sheep." Jolie nodded toward Sadie, who was now grazing industriously on the winter-brown grass of the clearing.

"We didn't get anything that cool with ours," he retorted with a glum look, plopping down on the porch steps. "Just mice in the closets and an owl that likes to sit on the roof."

Jolie smiled. "The guy who owns my cabin is now in a nursing home over in Cody. He used Dolly to guard his sheep against coyotes."

"Coyotes?" He looked at the llama with new respect.

"She'd have a hard time dealing with a pack, but one or two she could handle. Wait here. I'll get some things to clean up your arm, and then we'll get you home."

A moment later, Jolie returned to the porch with a basin of warm water and a package of gauze squares, then slipped on a pair of protective gloves. Charlie flinched as she began gently cleaning the dirt and dried blood on his arms.

To distract him, she continued talking. "The old man's family didn't dare sell this place or his best friend, Dolly. They didn't want to risk breaking his heart. And since llamas get really lonely, they had to keep Sadie. The family still brings Mr. Walters up here, now and then. Until I moved in they had to come up to feed her every day. Now llama care is part of my rental deal."

Patting his arms dry with a series of clean gauze squares, she sat back and studied the damage. All superficial, just as she'd thought. No imbedded debris. "Does your Mom...er, your Dad ever use any sort of antibiotic cream on you?"

He gave her a wary look. "I guess."

"You can do that at home, then, but the main thing is to keep this clean."

She surveyed him from head to foot and couldn't help but grin. From his tousled hair and dirty face to his floppy tennis shoes, he looked like a modern-day Huck Finn who would have trouble staying clean and out of trouble for more than five minutes at a stretch. "You might want to keep some adhesive bandages over the two deeper scratches for a few days, okay?"

He nodded.

Dolly had been watching with interest, blowing at the back of Charlie's neck and ruffling his hair with her muzzle. She lifted her head abruptly and spun around with her ears pricked forward.

From down the road came the distant sound of a man's voice calling Charlie's name. A deep voice filled with unmistakable worry.

"Oh, no," groaned Charlie. "I'm in *big* trouble."

"Let me guess. That's your dad—and you didn't leave him a note saying where you were going." From the look on the boy's face, his dad wasn't going to take this adventure lightly. Jolie pictured a scowling, angry man who wouldn't waste a second on his son's explanations.

Of course, not every father was like hers. *Thank God.*

Charlie shifted uncomfortably. "Uh...thanks. I better go." Like a shot he jumped to his feet and started for the rocky lane leading out of the clearing. His dad appeared before he'd gone a dozen yards.

Given Charlie's unkempt appearance and lack of supervision, Jolie had envisioned his father as someone far different from the man who strode into the clearing.

Instead of a beer belly and week-old stubble, this man was clean-shaven, a good six-foot plus, powerfully built. Jeans. A green plaid flannel shirt with cuffs rolled back, revealing muscular arms.

He gave the llama only a cursory glance, pinning his full attention on his son. At first glance he appeared intimidating, his stride and the set of his strong jaw suggesting an intensity that didn't bode well.

But as he came closer, she could see that his features weren't twisted with anger. Instead, his dark eyes were filled with relief and frustration.

"Charlie!" He stopped in front of his son and looked down at him, resting one hand on the boy's shoulder. "Where have you been?"

Charlie studied his feet and kicked a tuft of dead grass. "Just exploring," he said in a small voice.

"Your sister is back at the house in case you show up there and I've been looking for an hour. Do you have any idea—" His voice broke off as if he'd said these words a thousand times before and knew just how futile they were. He lifted his gaze to Jolie's, then glanced at the cabin behind her, and his eyes narrowed. He looked back to her. "Matt Dawson. We've just moved in to the other place on this road."

"So Charlie said." She could feel him assessing her as a possible threat to his son. Saw it in the way his other hand came to rest protectively on Charlie's shoulders. And she liked him better for it.

His wavy black hair and strong jaw were simply a very attractive bonus.

She offered her hand. "Jolie Maxwell. I just moved up here, too, so I guess I'm your only neighbor. Charlie says you're from Chicago."

Nodding, he shook her hand, releasing it as if he didn't want to prolong the contact a second longer than necessary. His intent gaze never wavered. "Are you from around here?"

Nice handshake. Warm, firm, decisive... The palm of her hand tingled long after she'd stepped back. "Dad's ranch is thirty miles away, but I've been in California since college. My family has been here for generations."

He seemed to relax at that. Shoving his hands in his back pockets, he surveyed the snowy mountain peaks above them. "Must have been hard being away from all this."

Jolie's thoughts drifted back to last Halloween, when her brother, Bobby, had nearly killed himself and two of his friends while driving drunk, leaving his best friend paralyzed.

And the week after Thanksgiving, when her father had suffered a heart attack. According to the family, he still had intermittent chest pain but refused to even consider his doctor's advice. No surprise there—Robert Maxwell's stubborn independence was legend.

She'd missed the mountains all right, but there were stronger reasons for coming home. "After Christmas one of my sisters faxed me information on a job opportunity, and I figured it was...time to move back."

Matt's gaze fell onto Charlie's forearms. "What on earth happened to you?"

"Nothing."

"Charlie—"

"*Really,*" he said quickly. "Jolie cleaned it off and she says it's okay."

"Well...not exactly," she murmured. "He needs to find out when he last had a tetanus shot."

"I can see where he might forget about that." A dimple deepened in Matt's cheek. "He's never met a doctor he liked, but he *is* up to date on all his vaccinations."

Glad she hadn't mentioned her profession just yet, Jolie bit back a smile. "Let's hope his aversion to doctors changes soon."

The man really had the most beautiful eyes. Warm brown with gold flecks, fringed with lashes she would have killed for in her younger, maybe-I'll-find-the-right-man days.

But those days were long gone. The guys she'd dated had either been attracted by her medical degree and earning potential, or had drifted away when they discovered her professional dedication and long hours made them feel second best.

The quest was no longer worth the bother.

"Thanks for helping my son." He squeezed Charlie's shoulders gently. "What do you say?"

Charlie mumbled thanks, his head bowed. "Can I come back to see Dolly?"

Matt stared at the llama grazing a few dozen yards away and gave a strangled cough. "Dolly...*llama?*"

His barely suppressed laughter charmed Jolie clear to her toes. "I swear I didn't name her. She came with this place."

Charlie looked back and forth between the adults, clearly mystified. "Well, can I come back? Please?"

"Only if you ask permission first." Matt's gaze met and held Jolie's. "*And* if it's okay with Ms. Maxwell."

A warm sensation curled around Jolie's heart. An hour ago she'd been savoring the absolute peace and quiet of her secluded retreat. Now that silence no longer seemed so appealing. "Of course it's okay. I enjoyed meeting you, Charlie. You remind me of my kid brother when he was young."

But such boyish innocence was long past for Bobby Maxwell, she admitted to herself as her new neighbors waved and turned for home. He'd been just four when she moved away to college, and he'd grown into a wild, troubled young man whom she barely knew.

The llama bumped her nose against Jolie's jacket pockets, begging for crackers. "Sorry, Dolly. I'm all out."

Back at the cabin, she sat on the top step of the porch and dropped her chin in her hand to watch Dolly and Sadie graze. Thinking about her family invariably made her feel melancholy.

Just a month ago, after her sister Thea's Valentine's Day wedding reception, Dad had been distracted, agitated when she'd tried to discuss her plans to move back to Paradise Corners. When she and Thea had tried to approach him, concerned about whether he felt okay, he'd uttered a profanity and stomped out of the room. Bobby had seemed equally tense, and had peeled away in his pickup moments later.

Another day, another argument between their father and their brother, Thea had guessed. Bobby's restrictions to stay on the straight and narrow never lasted long, and Dad's heart failure made him tired, less capable of dealing with his wayward son, but they were still two of a kind.

Robert fought acceptance of his failing health as hard as Bobby fought the idea of facing his responsibilities. Stubborn, independent Maxwells, both of them—qualities that could spell success or lead to disaster.

Jolie was looking forward to starting her new medical practice in a small-town atmosphere where everyone knew each other and friendships ran deep. But more than that, this past winter she'd realized that her family needed her.

Whether they'd ever admit it, or not.

ON MONDAY MORNING Jolie brushed the hair out of her eyes and leaned on her broom, studying the pile of dirt and debris at her feet.

Shortly after Christmas, the Paradise Corners Town Council had advertised for a doctor in a number of newspapers across the country. With her long work hours, she'd missed seeing the advertisements. Her sister Thea hadn't.

A fax of the ad had come from the family's Walking Stones Ranch the next day, accompanied by Thea's brief note urging Jolie to come out for an interview. The advertisement had boasted:

A clean, modern clinic. The only medical practice within forty-five miles. Friendly people and the most beautiful country on earth.

Modern clinic was stretching the truth. *Clean* was a complete fabrication. After two days of hard work there was still an awful lot to do.

Jolie had seen the facility during a brief visit the weekend of Thea's Valentine's Day wedding.

The heat hadn't been turned on and the lights were dim. After a long discussion with the council, there hadn't been much time to explore the place before rushing back to the ranch. Now she suspected that had been the city council's plan.

There hadn't been any time for a more thorough look after the wedding, either, because she'd had to leave for the Bozeman airport at dawn the next morning.

Still, the place wasn't bad. The waiting room was large, with a receptionist's window opening into an office area. Down a short hall were two exam rooms, a small lab and an office. At the back was a bedroom, apparently for a doctor working late hours, though in the days before strict hospital coding, it might have been used for an occasional overnight patient.

The clinic was dark, musty, and offered minimal storage, but with a little work it would do. She took a deep breath. Today, the last of the dirt. Tomorrow, painting.

Through the open windows and door facing Main Street came the chatter of schoolkids walking home. Pickups and stock trailers rattling by. The bawl of cattle being hauled through town in semis. Now and then passersby stopped and peered in the windows of the clinic.

She felt a prickle of awareness at the back of her neck. Looked over her shoulder. And discovered a middle-aged couple standing just inside the front door. Neither one looked friendly.

"Hi there," she said easily. "Beautiful day to be outside, isn't it?"

The woman's sharp features grew even more pinched. With a snort she pivoted toward the street. Her companion scowled. "Council shoulda looked a mite longer before bringing a Maxwell in here," he muttered.

Jolie stared at him. "Excuse me?"

"No matter what you think, not everyone thinks the Maxwells walk on water. And now we've got you instead of some doc who might have actually *cared* about people here. It's a damn shame." With a sound of disgust he turned and walked away.

Her earlier optimism dimmed as she watched the couple reach the sidewalk and continue toward the center of town. The man's vigorous gestures and the vehement shaking of the woman's head telegraphed more than mild dislike.

Jolie sank into one of the uncomfortable wooden waiting-room chairs facing the doorway. It wasn't hard to imagine that her domineering, powerful father had made a few enemies, but surely this couple's attitude couldn't be widely held…could it?

A four-wheel drive black Ford pickup cruised slowly past on Main Street, and Jolie stared after it. *Matt Dawson.* His tanned arm was crooked on the open window at his side. Sunglasses obscured his eyes.

She sighed in appreciation of one devilishly handsome man. *Stay clear,* an inner voice warned her.

As if she needed warning.

At the sound of more footsteps coming up the walk, she rose, feeling oddly guilty for taking the brief rest. After a cursory knock on the door frame, two council members stepped inside.

Marge Wilson, barely five feet, but a good two hundred pounds to Wayne Forman's six feet of gaunt sinew and bone, thrust a big platter of cookies into Jolie's hands and beamed at her. "Welcome to Paradise Corners, dear."

Wayne held a large potted peace lily. He glanced around, then moved forward to set it on an end table. Studied it. Then rotated the pot a quarter-turn so its giant pink bow faced out into the room.

"Thanks so much." Jolie placed the cookies on the receptionist's counter and gave her future office space a wry look. "Paradise Corners might be paradise on earth, but this clinic has a ways to go."

Pursing her lips, Marge scanned the room. "Old Doc Grimes had a strong practice here for decades."

Yeah, but he's long dead and so is his practice. Most of the dog-eared patient folders in the cabinets were from the 1940s, when he'd first started practice, through 1995—the year he retired and subsequently died.

Since then several young doctors had stayed briefly and left. For a while, a clinic in the next town had tried sending out physician's assistants for routine care, but the building had been empty for the past year.

Little consistency and outdated records meant there was no viable practice to take over. She would be starting from scratch. "I imagine people will be happy to have local medical care again," Jolie said tactfully.

"That's why we advertised," Wayne agreed. "Too hard for some folks to make the trip to Billings or Bozeman in the winter. Too far in an emergency. Even when we have to airlift people out, a local doctor can help a great deal on this end."

"A man and woman stopped by a few minutes ago. They didn't seem too happy to see a Maxwell taking over. A paunchy guy in his forties, a grim woman with short dark hair."

Marge and Wayne exchanged a quick glance. "Your experience and education are perfect," Marge soothed. "And your references were outstanding. You'll do fine."

Jolie's niggling doubts flared into true concern. "Is there anything I should know? The community…"

Stepping forward, Wayne gave her a hearty clap on the back. "We're *all* glad to have you here, and hope you'll decide to stay on after our agreement is up. You could buy or lease this building. Put down roots. Paradise Corners is a wonderful place to raise a family."

Both he and Marge started for the door.

"Wait a minute."

Wayne kept going. Marge stopped and turned around, a wary smile on her weathered face. "What, dear?"

"How many doctors were interested in coming here?"

"Oh, my. We had a great number of calls and letters."

"No…how many actually came out here to look over the clinic?"

"You were certainly the very best."

"How many?" Jolie persisted gently. "I'd like to know."

Marge sighed. "We had three who came out."

This was like pulling teeth. Though she already knew the answer, she wanted to be sure. "And how many wanted to take over?"

"Only the best. You."

"So even if there *was* local feeling against the Maxwell family, you didn't have a choice."

"We wouldn't have brought in just anyone." Marge reached out to lay a hand on Jolie's arm. "The committee thought you were ideal. You have the right background, and you have family in the area." She hesitated. "It's none of my business, but I'd guess you haven't been in close touch with people here for a while."

An understatement, at best. Her closest childhood friend, Gwen, now practiced medicine in Billings, but they hadn't seen each other since high-school graduation.

"Walking Stones Ranch is a good thirty miles away. Thea, Cassie and I were home-schooled until high school, so we didn't get to know people in town very well, then I went straight to college after graduation. The town has grown, changed during the sixteen years I've been away. I haven't seen many familiar faces."

"Well, don't you worry. Things will work out just fine." Marge lifted a wrist and glanced at her watch, then bustled toward the door. "I've got to get back to school for a teachers' meeting," she said briskly over her shoulder. "Call me if you have any concerns."

As if calling you would mean getting a straight answer. Jolie stared after her in bemusement, then picked up the broom and began sweeping again.

Calling the ranch had been futile, too. She'd phoned twice, left messages on the machine, but spring calving always kept them busy night and day, and no one had returned her calls.

Some homecoming.

Back in Los Angeles, she'd dreamed about the close sense of community that existed in small towns. The feeling of belonging. Everything that had been missing from her life for years, though she hadn't even realized it until Wendell Hill died early last December.

He'd been a patient of hers. Crowds of concerned friends and relatives had maintained a constant vigil at his bedside throughout his last three weeks. Though nearly destitute, he'd been deeply loved. Watching the outpouring of affection and concern for him, she'd realized that few people in her life would even notice if she disappeared.

So far, things hadn't changed much. She was back in Paradise Corners, and her most significant conversations had been with a ten-year-old boy and a llama.

She surveyed the waiting room, imagining it filled with children and moms, and the elderly stooped over their canes. Then she wistfully remembered Thea's beautiful wedding to Deputy Sheriff Rafe Rafferty. A perfect couple—deeply in love. What more could anyone ever ask?

She'd shed tears of joy for her sister that day. And later, when she'd headed back to California alone, perhaps even a few for herself. *Foolish dreams, useless wishes,* she'd reminded herself firmly. Marriage and family probably weren't in her own future.

But whatever was missing in her personal life, her profession provided a deep sense of satisfaction. She would make a positive difference in the lives of people in Paradise Corners.

And that would just have to be enough.

CHAPTER TWO

LILY DAWSON GLARED at her younger brother. If desperate, heartfelt wishes meant anything, she would be back in their old neighborhood instead of this stupid town. And Charlie would have turned into a frog years ago.

"Come on, Charlie!"

Instead of cooperating, helping her escape, he plopped down on a bench in front of the elementary school. "Just 'cause you're fourteen doesn't mean you're the boss. Dad said to wait here."

"He'll see us on the sidewalk downtown," she hissed, grabbing his arm. "Come on!"

"Ow!"

The crowd standing around in front of the middle school across the street seemed to turn around as one and look straight at her. One of the taller boys snickered.

Lily wished she could beam herself to any other spot on the whole planet. Today had been their first day of school. She'd never wanted to move. Starting school at the end of March was like moving to another world, where people spoke a different language and had bonded together against any aliens that might turn up.

The humiliation of all the stares and whispers in every class had been bad enough. Tripping as she walked out at the end of the day, dropping her books at the feet of the three most gorgeous boys in school, had been a hundred times worse.

And now Charlie was making her feel like an even greater fool. "I...I'll buy you something downtown. I've got ten dollars in my backpack," she pleaded. It was meant for her lunch ticket, but she'd been too nervous to approach the lunch ladies at noon. Not knowing what to do—afraid of looking stupid—she'd just sat at a table in a corner by herself.

Remembering her own clique of friends back home, she knew they'd been just as cool to newcomers and made things just as hard. Being on the other side hurt a lot.

"Do you want a sundae? A hamburger? You know Dad is always late. *Please.*"

At *sundae* Charlie was on his feet. By *hamburger* he was already at the end of the block.

Her cheeks burning, Lily started after him. They'd walked the entire four-block length of town before she realized something truly awful about Paradise Corners. They hadn't passed one fast-food place. Not a single ice-cream store. Not even one theater. Like, people actually *chose* to live here?

Charlie stared up at her, then looked down the rest of Main Street. It trailed through the town, turning into a highway that led past scattered bars, a few gas stations and a big grain elevator.

Almost every vehicle parked in town was a pickup truck with a gun rack across the back window and a big dog waiting like a sentinel on the front seat.

"What do people *do?*" he whispered. "There's nothing here!"

A wave of dizziness washed through her and made her go weak. Her stomach hurt. She was tired and really thirsty, and now they had to trudge all the way back to the school if Dad didn't happen to drive past and see them. A lump the size of a tennis ball filled her throat.

But...a fourteen-year-old girl did not sit down and cry.

Not with cars driving past and other people walking along the dusty sidewalk. Not with a pesky brother who would tease her to death about being a big baby. *Oh, Mom, I wish you were here…*

But her mom had died long time ago, and Lily was trapped at the end of the earth.

"Hey, look," Charlie said, his voice rising with excitement. "Over there! It's the llama lady!"

Across the street a woman in old jeans and a denim shirt bent over some straggly flowers in front of a white building. She tugged vigorously at some weeds, flung them over her shoulder, and then reached down for more.

Barely looking for cars first, Charlie darted across the road. A car jerked to a halt a good twenty feet away, but from the look on the elderly driver's face Charlie had just taken ten years off her life.

The woman sat frozen in her car, hands white-knuckled on the steering wheel long after he reached the other side.

"Charlie!" With a quick wave at the poor woman, Lily ran across the street after him. She snagged his jacket collar and hauled him to a stop on the sidewalk. "You need a leash," she snapped. "Either that, or iron bars."

He twisted out of her grasp and made a beeline for the lady in blue jeans. "Hi!"

She turned and shaded her eyes with a gloved hand. "Why, hello there. Are you just getting out of school?" She shifted her attention to Lily and smiled. "I'll bet you're Charlie's sister."

Lily nodded awkwardly, unable to think of anything to say.

"This is Jolie," Charlie announced. "She has the really cool llama, and the sheep. Remember? I went up the road and saw her last week."

"That got us both grounded." Lily scowled at him. "Thank you very much."

The lady gave her a sympathetic look. "Do you keep track of your brother while your dad works?"

"Like anyone could. C'mon, Charlie. We need to get back so Dad can find us."

Stubbornly shaking his head, he moved to the door of the building to peer inside. "Is this a store?"

"A clinic. It's been empty for a while, so there's a lot of work getting it ready."

He looked up at her in awe. "Are you a *vet?*"

The corners of her eyes crinkled. "Nope, I'm a people doctor." She chuckled at his crestfallen expression. "I'll bet that doesn't sound as exciting to you as horses and boa constrictors."

Tuning out their conversation, Lily watched three girls walking down the street together, their arms slung over each other's shoulders. She'd seen them at school. They were popular girls, who had the right clothes and wore more makeup than Dad would ever let *her* wear. One said something and the others dissolved into laughter.

That big lump was back in Lily's throat as she remembered her own friends back home, who were still having fun every day after school.

"Lily?" The llama lady was looking at her with an expression of concern. "You look a little pale. Do you want to come inside and sit down?"

"We gotta go," Charlie announced. "Before my dad thinks we're lost again and gets mad."

"I was never lost. You were," Lily retorted, embarrassed.

"Would you two like a can of pop? You can take it with you." She turned toward the clinic. "I'll be right back."

Heading down Main Street came the unmistakable sound of Uncle Ed's pickup truck backfiring. The color of rust, with loose fenders that rattled and a big dent in the passenger door, it was the ugliest thing Lily had ever seen. Uncle Ed had loaned it to Dad yesterday so he could pick up some building supplies.

Mortification swept through Lily as she glanced the other way and saw the trio of girls stop to look over their shoulders.

The truck pulled to a creaking halt right in front of the clinic. Lily felt heat rise in her cheeks as three pairs of eyes swiveled toward her when Dad climbed from behind the wheel and strode up the sidewalk. Two of the girls laughed, then they all continued on their way.

Dad didn't look happy. "Why weren't you two down at the school? I waited fifteen minutes, then I started looking for you two. I—"

Jolie stepped out of the clinic. When she saw Dad's expression, her stride faltered, but Lily had to give her credit—she recovered fast.

"Hi there. I'm afraid I was chatting with your kids, and kept them from meeting you," she said easily, handing Lily and Charlie each a frosty can of root beer.

"I *hate* it here," Lily muttered under her breath. "We belong in *Chicago,* not this boring—"

"Manners," Dad said quietly.

"Why did we have to move?" She knew she sounded like a three-year-old, but all Lily could feel was pure misery, a swamp of despair.

"I think it's cool! We can get horses and ride in the mountains," Charlie piped up. "And there's skiing and bears."

"I hope not at the same time," Jolie said dryly. She gestured toward the small, one-story building behind her. "Want to see the clinic?"

Dad shook his head. "Another time. I need to get this

truck to my brother's place so he can run to Billings for some equipment.''

''We have to…ride…in that thing?'' Lily closed her eyes. With her luck, half the kids from school would still be in town to see her. They'd think her family was too poor to own a decent car.

No one in their old Chicago neighborhood would have been caught *dead* in something like this. She would have argued further, but Dad gave her The Look and she knew there would be no point.

With her chin raised, she stalked to the truck and tried very, very hard not to touch its battered exterior as she climbed in after Charlie.

Tonight she would start writing letters to every friend she had in Illinois. Surely someone, somewhere, would take her in.

''THIS WAS THE BEST meal I've had in a year.'' Matt leaned back in his chair at the dining-room table and gave his sister-in-law a smile of appreciation. ''Thanks for inviting us over.''

''Nina's the best cook in the county,'' his brother agreed, giving her rear an affectionate pat as she walked past him toward the kitchen, empty serving dishes in her hands. ''I thank my lucky stars for her every day.''

''I do like a grateful man,'' Nina retorted as she nudged the kitchen door open with one hip and sidestepped through. Small, thin, her youthful mahogany-brown hair at odds with the wrinkles at her eyes, she'd always been an outspoken bundle of energy—the opposite of her laconic, easygoing husband.

The ceiling above them shook. Footsteps thundered across the floor. ''I'll go check on those kids,'' Matt muttered, starting to rise. "At this rate you aren't going to have a house left."

"Hell, no. Just sit yourself down." Ed Dawson lifted his coffee cup and waved it in the general direction of the ceiling. "If my two haven't come through the floor yet, then two more buffalo up there won't matter. We've got things to discuss."

Matt hesitated, then relaxed in his chair and studied his older brother. Ed was forty-five, just ten years older than Matt, but he looked like the far side of fifty with that gray streaking at his temples and the extra thirty pounds of belly. "Any response to our advertisements?"

Ed shrugged. "It's still off-season for new construction around here. Remodeling jobs have been steady all winter. Enough to keep the home fires burning."

"What do you have lined up?"

"A gift shop up in the foothills scheduled for the end of April. A new home to start mid-June. That gives us a month for a kitchen over in Fairfax and a—" he smirked "—designer smokehouse."

"A what?"

"You know—California yuppies, not too concerned with cost? They want it to match the house."

Starting a new construction business involved a lot of risk, and Matt had invested everything he owned in this move. Given their rocky relationship in years past, working with Ed might be the biggest challenge of all. "Things are looking good, then?"

"Yep."

Nina backed through the swinging door with a loaded tray in her hands. "Here you go, guys."

She poured more coffee and passed out slabs of warm blackberry pie smothered in homemade ice cream—sheer heaven on a plate.

Matt grinned. "Thanks, this looks wonderful. Should I call the kids?"

"They had theirs in the kitchen already. Blackberries and this carpet just don't mix. Believe me." She set a carafe of coffee between them, then zipped into the kitchen. The woman never, ever sat still.

Ed forked up a chunk of pie. "Like your new place?"

"Great view, privacy, but it needs work. I knew that going in, though."

After wolfing down his pie, Ed shoved the empty plate toward the center of the table and lifted his coffee cup. "You ever go back, just look around?"

Matt didn't have to ask what he meant. "Never."

Ed grunted.

Some things were worth remembering, some were best forgotten. Only in fragments of dreams did Matt ever see the house back in Chicago where he and Ed had grown up— the place where they'd managed to survive by knowing when to disappear and how long to be gone.

The irony was that while Matt had never touched a drop of alcohol, Ed had followed the old man's footsteps. Fortunately, during the last five years he'd managed to stay dry...or so he said. Matt hoped it was true.

"I hear you got a new neighbor up on Coyote Hill." Ed casually hooked a booted foot over the opposite knee, but there was an edge to his voice that hadn't been there before.

"Surprised me. The place was empty when we were looking at property."

"Seen her?"

An image of Jolie Maxwell flashed through his mind as Matt finished the last bite of his pie and laid his fork across the plate.

Not just pretty, she was more than that, with all that strawberry-blond hair and those big blue eyes—or were they green? When she smiled, her face transformed into downright beautiful. And he'd bet that under those loose clothes she had curves in all the right places.

Not that it mattered. With two kids, a new business and all the trouble he'd had dealing with Barb's death four years ago, the last thing he needed was another woman. Low-risk and alone was the best course from here on out.

"I met her. She seemed nice enough. Charlie tells me she's a doctor." *And remember it, too, because she's not your type. She might as well be from another planet, with those degrees on her wall and that kind of money in the bank.*

Ed eyed him with suspicion. "You *liked* her?"

Had he said that aloud? Surprised, Matt set down his coffee cup. "She was friendly to the kids."

"Don't matter. She's one of Robert Maxwell's daughters," Ed said with finality.

"So?"

"You didn't read those newspapers I sent?"

Matt shrugged. "The real-estate ads, mostly."

"No one dares cross him. They say he's run more than one business into bankruptcy just out of revenge."

Matt suppressed a smile. "Maybe in the Old West. But not now—"

"Believe it. He's had most of the officials around here in his pocket for decades," Ed retorted. "I heard that he tried fixing his daughters up with wealthy ranchers and real influential people over the years, but his girls refused to cooperate—more power to 'em. Just save us a lot of grief and stay clear of Dr. Maxwell. Our business doesn't need any trouble."

"I'm not looking for any." Still, the idea of some pompous old rancher with a royalty complex rankled. "It's hard to believe Jolie comes from a family like that, though."

Nina appeared at the kitchen door, her arms folded and eyes glittering with anger. "The Maxwells are the law unto themselves. If Boss Maxwell dropped dead tomorrow, there aren't many who would shed a tear. And that son of his—" Her voice broke.

"Nina," Ed said quietly. "Everything will be okay."

"Will it?" Her voice rose. "Ask my nephew Danny. Ask his parents." She shook her head slightly and shifted her gaze to Matt, as if she suddenly remembered he was there. "I...I'm sorry."

She whirled and disappeared through the door. Seconds later they heard her footsteps dash up the stairs.

"I don't understand."

Ed scowled. "That Maxwell woman comes from money—*big* money—and a father who'd rather steal your last dime in a business deal than say hello. Her brother recently proved that a guy can get away with anything short of murder if his dad is Robert Maxwell. Steer clear of her— she's nothing but trouble."

JOLIE HAD HOPED to open the clinic by the first of April. Stubborn plumbing and a leak in the roof delayed the big event until the following Monday.

The big event was a bit anticlimactic, she acknowledged, surveying the empty waiting room from the doorway. But once people arrived, they ought to be reasonably impressed, especially considering how dreary the building had been before.

New paint—eggshell white inside, a soft yellow outside—had made an incredible difference. A fresh coat of wax brightened the aging vinyl flooring, and bright prints of children and rural scenes graced the walls.

The budget granted by the town council had been limited, and Jolie couldn't afford any major aesthetic changes. Not when this might be a less-than-successful venture. But if the practice grew, and someday she bought the building...

Stepping into the waiting room, she tested the dampness of the soil of a lush pink azalea sent by the Paradise Corners Chamber of Commerce, then swept back a lacy curtain with her hand and looked out at the street. *I wish you could have seen this, Mom. You always said I would make my dreams come true.*

With a sigh, she retraced her footsteps and sat in the swivel chair at the front desk.

An ivy plant in a wicker basket sat on top of the file cabinet. Its card read *Best wishes from all of us at Walking Stones Ranch.*

Jolie knew life was hectic out there right now—two men short and dealing with the usual round-the-clock chores of checking herds, dealing with obstetrical emergencies, doctoring sick calves, hauling feed, breeding mares.

Her sister Thea had called one night after midnight, sounding exhausted and distant. No wonder—she and Rafe were living in his house at the edge of town until their home could be built on Walking Stones property. She probably only caught a few house of sleep each night before having to make that thirty-mile trip back out to the ranch. "Come out to see us sometime," she'd said. "Or we'll come to see you."

But no one had made the trip into Paradise Corners for a social call, and Jolie had been working around the clock herself, trying to get the clinic ready on time. Or maybe that was just an excuse to avoid going out there...

When the small bell tinkled above the front door she nearly jumped out of her chair. Hand at her throat, she stood and found a harried girl of maybe nineteen with a blanket-covered baby carrier on one hand and a diaper bag in the other.

The mom glanced uncertainly at Jolie, then scanned the empty room. "Uh...is this Dr. Maxwell's office? I read the notice in the paper, but maybe..."

"You're in the right place." Jolie walked out into the waiting room and smiled at her. "I'm Jolie Maxwell."

"Maria Ramirez. And this is my son, Benjamin. He's three months old," she added proudly. She dropped the diaper bag onto a chair and lifted the blanket, revealing a tiny face streaked with tears. He was sleeping now, but obviously he'd had some major complaints a short time earlier.

Jolie brushed her fingertips gently across his soft cheek. Cool and dry. His breathing was even and quiet, no noticeable wheezes or congestion. "What a beautiful little boy. How is he doing?"

"He wasn't feeling good yesterday. I thought he had just a mild cold, but he was up all last night. As soon as I put him down, he started to scream. He wouldn't eat, he wouldn't even let me sit down to rock him. I've been walking with him almost nonstop. He finally fell asleep on the way here."

Jolie mentally ran through the most likely possibilities as Maria filled out a new-patient information sheet. Ear infection. Strep throat. Colic. Too young for teething. Intolerance to the formula—

"Is he on a bottle?"

Maria shook her head as she handed back the completed form. "Nope, never."

"Any diarrhea? Vomiting?"

"Nope."

"What about fever?"

"Last night, he was up to a hundred degrees, so I gave him a dose of liquid Tylenol. It seemed to bring down his temperature, but he was still just as cranky."

Once they reached the second exam room, Jolie gave the

mother a sympathetic smile. "I hate to wake him, but we'll need to undress him down to his diaper."

With efficient movements Maria undressed the sleeping baby. The moment Jolie gently positioned the otoscope in his right ear, his eyes flew open. Little arms flailed as he arched his back and gave a piercing scream.

"Poor baby," Jolie crooned as she checked the other ear. After listening to his lungs and palpating his abdominal area for tenderness, she checked his temperature. Not high, at 100.2.

Maria held him steady and murmured comforting nonsense to him, but his heartrending sobs escalated with every passing minute. "Can I pick him up now?" Her voice trembled.

At the clinic in L.A. Jolie had learned to watch for subtle signs of parental neglect or worse, but this mother hovered close to her child and, despite her obvious exhaustion, was on the verge of picking the baby up to comfort him whether Jolie was ready or not. A good sign.

"Of course."

When she picked him up he immediately clutched tightly at her shirt, as if he couldn't get close enough to her. A sob shook through him. He stared at Jolie, his eyes wide and wet with fresh tears.

After writing a progress note in Benjamin's new chart, Jolie set her pen aside. "His lungs are clear, his throat is a bit inflamed. He does have quite an ear infection—more so on the right. Has he ever been on antibiotics? Had any trouble with them?"

With one hand Maria dug into the purse she'd dropped on the counter and withdrew a spiral notebook. She flipped it open to show Jolie a page listing the dates and details of several mild illnesses. "The erythromycin seemed to bother his stomach, but the others were okay."

A good, *caring* mom, despite her own youth. Jolie calculated the dosage for amoxicillin and wrote a prescription, then explained the times and amounts. "You can continue the liquid Tylenol. He should be feeling better by tonight. If he isn't, you can call me and I'll take another look."

"I just want him to feel well. Having a good night's sleep will do us *both* good." Maria bundled Benjamin back into his snowsuit and gathered her things. "It's great having a full-time doctor here again," she added fervently.

Jolie reached out to smooth a hand over the baby's downy hair. *So soft, so sweet.* Was there anything more precious? Just the scent of a clean baby always touched a melancholy chord in her heart. She held open the front door. "I'll be here."

Halfway out onto the landing, Maria turned and smiled. "I just want you to know. No matter what anyone says, I'm real glad you're here, and I think you're a *great* doctor." With a cheery wave she headed up the sidewalk.

Her words still rang in Jolie's ears long after Maria and Benjamin disappeared from view. *No matter what anyone says...*

What had she gotten herself into?

HIGH ON THE HILLS overlooking Walking Stones Ranch, Robert Maxwell pulled his horse to a stop.

The incredible view of the mountains rimming the ranch on three sides, and the endless vista of rolling grassland to the east, had always filled him with a sense of satisfaction. Now he felt only the roiling anxiety that had set in after Bobby's accident last October, and had escalated with the passing months.

The charges against his son had secretly terrified Robert. The Aiken boy's injuries and the looming multimillion-dollar lawsuits were enough to raise his blood pressure. But he had lawyers to deal with those types of problems.

The Wheeler girl was entirely another story. When her greedy, conniving father showed up at the ranch at the end of Thea's wedding reception last month, Robert had quickly ushered the man into the office at the back of the house. Abe hadn't expressed a shred of true concern for his daughter Megan, but he'd made it clear that he was after money, and a lot of it.

Now Robert looked over to where Bobby had stopped his horse. "Tell me again what you told me the night of Thea's wedding."

Slouched in his saddle, Bobby stared at the mountains rising to the west. Only the flick of a muscle in his jaw indicated that he'd even heard.

"Did you make that girl pregnant, or not?" Robert demanded. "A man has to have honor, son, or he's worth nothing. Honor, and a sense of responsibility."

Bobby didn't answer.

"I haven't said a thing about the Wheeler situation to anyone else—not even your sisters. But something like this won't stay secret long. We need to deal with it."

"Why? Wheeler's just an old drunk."

Robert had intended to stay calm. To discuss the issue in a businesslike manner, to get at what he suspected was the truth, and then work on a way to take care of it. But Bobby's insolent tone set his teeth on edge.

"Because, you young fool, if you slept with that girl, then she's carrying a Maxwell," Robert said through clenched teeth. "Doesn't blood mean *anything* to you?"

Bobby jerked a shoulder. "Yeah...we messed around." His gaze slid away. "But she could've gone off with someone else, too."

The muscle twitching in the boy's temple and the guilt

written on his face told the story that he wasn't man enough to tell.

"Our lawyers contacted Abe, but apparently the girl has moved out and is refusing to cooperate. She says she doesn't want help from us or anyone else. It might take a court battle just for testing to prove who the father is."

"So then we're okay."

"Okay?" Robert roared. "For once in your life, show you're a man, instead of some kid who can't keep his pants zipped and nearly kills his friends by driving drunk. You've screwed up way too many times."

Bobby flinched. Gathering up his reins, he wheeled his horse sharply away.

"It's time for you to grow up—hell, you're already nineteen. You said you were ready to take on more of the ranch operation. So far, I haven't seen any evidence. And if that's your child, you need to take responsibility. Is that clear?"

"*Crystal,*" Bobby bit out. Nudging his horse into a lope, he headed across the ridge and disappeared down the other side toward the herd they'd spotted earlier.

At least he didn't hightail off in the other direction. That's progress.

Last year, after Robert's heart attack, the boy had made bedside promises to grow up and start shouldering more responsibility at the ranch. He hadn't followed through. As always, Bobby had a short memory when it came to anything but his own pleasure.

Robert's horse sidestepped impatiently, wanting to follow, but he held the gelding back. A trio of hawks circled high overhead, drifting on thermal currents. The lands of Walking Stones surrounded him, as timeless, as much a part of him as his own flesh. A legacy of pride, of accomplishment, of possession.

Taking over an empire like this one required a great deal

of guidance, a lifetime of knowledge only Robert could give. The irony was that Thea would have embraced the opportunity. Bobby ran from it like a colt high-tailing it up into the hills to avoid a saddle.

But whether he liked it or not, Bobby had to start accepting the responsibilities handed down to all the firstborn Maxwell sons for generations. Robert's health was failing— he'd suffered a heart attack a few months ago—and the pressure in his chest sometimes made it nigh impossible to breathe. He couldn't hang on forever waiting for the boy to grow up.

And soon it would be too late to guarantee the future of Walking Stones Ranch.

CHAPTER THREE

THE NEXT MORNING, Matt stood at the front bumper of his pickup with a bouquet of wildflowers in his hand and studied the clinic. *Damn.* Jolie had seemed like just a girl next door when they'd first met. Not some doctor with a handful of degrees after her name.

But no matter what this might look like to anyone in her waiting room, this visit was duty not flirtation. She wasn't his type—hell, he didn't even have a type anymore. After Barb's death, he'd eventually tried dating again, but his abiding sense of betrayal to her memory had made it impossible. Nothing—and no one—had ever felt right.

Jolie was a neighbor, and she'd been nice to the kids. So he needed to be neighborly and wish her well in her new practice.

With heavy footsteps he approached the building, then walked into the empty waiting room. *Not bad,* he mused, surveying the obvious face-lift. Cheerful colors, plants, *new* magazines on the end tables.

He approached the receptionist's window and tapped on the bell. Maybe he'd just leave the flowers with an employee. He and Ed had plans to go over…

Jolie came from a back room. Dressed in trim black slacks, a silky peach blouse and a thigh-length white lab coat, she hardly resembled the jeans and sweatshirt–clad woman he'd met before. Now her hair was twisted up in some sort of fancy knot on top of her head, and small gold hoops glittered at her ears. Uptown. Definitely uptown.

As far from South Chicago as a guy could get.

"I just wanted to drop these by for your new clinic." He cleared his throat as he handed her the flowers. "And as apology for my son's behavior. He and I had a discussion about trespassing on other people's property."

"They're just beautiful. Thanks—this is so thoughtful of you." After an awkward pause she added, "Would you like a tour?"

He should have declined, but when she set the flowers on the counter at the receptionist's window and motioned him to follow her, he couldn't bring himself to refuse.

She smelled like lilies after a rain—a light, delicate scent that drew him to her as she led him around the clinic.

At the door of her office he inadvertently brushed against her. When he reached out to steady her, touched her elbow gently, he saw her eyes flare wider. Masculine satisfaction rippled through him. *So she's not unaware of me, either.*

"So…what do you think about my office?"

"Nice desk. Good lighting with those south-exposure windows. That old paneling ought to go."

She tapped a forefinger against her full lower lip. "Sheet-rock instead, do you think?"

"All of the old paneling in this building should be replaced."

She laughed. "I can just imagine what the city council would say. The town owns this building and the council has balked at most of my requests thus far. I think they've seen too many young doctors come and go."

She led him through the rest of the clinic, stopping here and there to get his opinion on remodeling projects. He tried to keep his attention on the tour and not the guide, but glimpses of the silky blouse beneath that lab coat sent his imagination soaring. Soft silk...silky skin...

The floor joists creaked as they moved down the hallway. Water stains darkened the ceiling of the lab. The cupboards in there were battered, with doors hanging slightly askew on old hinges.

The back door locked with a push button on the door handle and a cheap surface slide bolt that any self-respecting vandal could break through in a split second.

The thought made him uneasy. She could come in some morning and find the place destroyed. Worse, she wouldn't be safe here, late at night.

"So when are you getting to the rest of this work?" He ran a hand along the sash of a double-hung window, where years of condensation had softened the wood. "Medical clinics are prime targets, so you need better security."

"You're right. My brother-in-law, Rafe, is the local deputy sheriff, and he stopped by yesterday. He said the same thing." She braced her hands on her hips and surveyed the room. "Maybe the hardware store would have locks of some kind."

He tipped his head toward the door. "With that big glass pane, another lock wouldn't help. You need a new door."

"I agree, but the town won't go for that. Nobody really wanted this building to begin with. Old Doc Grimes died without heirs and was behind on his taxes...so the city took it over. The council's not interested in investing much in the place."

"Without maintenance it won't be worth anything."

"They hope I'll stay around and buy it. If I don't, I suspect they'll give up trying to find a doctor and just tear the place down." She paused, then added with a half smile, "They did fix the roof, though."

Remembering what Ed had said about her wealthy family,

he gave her a curious look. "Maybe you can strike a deal. Your father could finance the work, and if you leave later on, the council would have a building worth selling. They could repay him with interest."

She visibly stiffened at the mention of her father, and her warm expression turned cool. "Nice idea. Assuming *I* had the cash." She pointedly glanced at her watch. "School must be out now. I hope Lily and Charlie are adjusting well here."

He didn't need to be told twice—he'd stepped across some invisible line and this was a blatant hint to leave. "They're doing fine." He headed for the front door of the clinic. Hand on the doorknob, he looked back. "Good to see you, Jolie."

From the haughty tilt to her chin he expected a frosty response. So when she spoke, her words surprised him.

"I...it's hard, coming into a small town as a new student. Acceptance is a difficult thing. If the kids have problems and need to talk...well..." She gave a small gesture with her hands, palms up.

"Thanks."

Her perception surprised him. As a daughter of the richest man in the state, she would have had the best clothes, the right vacations. Even if some of the locals resented her father, prominent social standing surely would have been hers from the cradle.

If Jolie Maxwell needed help, all she had to do was call her father.

GOOD JOB, Maxwell. You've just alienated your only neighbor for three miles.

Another inner voice reminded her that it was probably a very good thing. As neighbors, they would be running into each other a lot, and he was possibly the most attractive man she'd ever met. She didn't need to guess where that would lead. *Nowhere.*

Lost in thought, Jolie wandered to the front of the clinic and idly flipped through the empty appointment book.

The good Lord knew exactly how great Jolie's track record was with the opposite sex. Friendly distance was fine—but romances invariably ended in disappointment. And at the age of thirty-three without a single serious relationship under her belt, she knew nothing was going to change.

Her return to Montana, on the other hand, might help heal a family situation that had been rocky for years. It could happen—Jolie was willing to try. Maybe her sisters, Thea and Cassie, and their younger brother, Bobby, were also willing to try. Maybe even Robert was ready to put differences aside.

A tentative knock sounded at the front door. *A patient?* Jolie was halfway there when a young woman pushed it open a few inches and peered inside.

"Is this—uh—the new doctor's office?"

She looked as though she was ready to turn and flee. "You bet." Jolie gave her an encouraging smile. "Come on in."

"Well, I…" Her voice trailed away. She appeared frightened and unsure, and even a little embarrassed.

"I don't bite, honest."

The girl hesitated a moment before coming in and sitting down at the edge of one of the waiting-room chairs, her head bowed. Her tangled auburn hair fell like a curtain around her face.

Jolie had the sudden, eerie feeling that this delicate girl had spent the past day and night outside. Even with a jacket on, her thin frame emphasized the slight roundness of her belly. Four or five months along, maybe.

Jolie took a chair across from her. "My name's Jolie Maxwell. What's yours?"

The girl's gaze slid away.

"Is there anything you need to talk about?"

The girl's trembling hands were clasped tightly at her knees. "I—I'm worried about my baby."

She couldn't have been more than eighteen, maybe less. No wedding ring. Her baggy painter's pants were torn at the knees and her cheap jacket was faded and worn.

"Where do you live?" Jolie asked gently.

The girl gave her a wary look. "Out on J—" She caught herself. "South of town."

Jolie stared at her face. Bruising on her left cheek was dark red, changing to purple. The abrasion above her right eyebrow looked raw. These were new injuries.

Required by law to report all instances of suspected child abuse, Jolie knew she'd have to contact the authorities if this girl was under eighteen.

"How old are you, honey?"

The girl's gaze darted uneasily toward the door. "I...I've got to go. I shouldn't have come here." She stood abruptly.

"Please, I want to help."

Jolie reached out to touch her arm, to offer comfort and encouragement. The girl jerked back as if she'd been slapped, then bolted across the room.

"Wait—you said you're worried about your baby."

She stopped, one hand on the doorknob.

"Are you afraid there might have been some...injury?"

Her shoulders slumped in defeat. "I don't have any money."

"That's okay."

"I shouldn't have come if I can't pay."

"There are state-aid programs.... Have you applied?"

"No." Her voice was even softer now, tinged with desperation.

"What about the baby's father?"

"I don't need anything from him. Not ever."

No last name, no address—if the girl walked out the door she might never come back, and Jolie wouldn't know how to find her. "Please, don't leave. Think about your baby."

The girl hesitated. Then she fled out the door.

THE GIRL STILL HADN'T returned by Friday. Other patients came in, though. Two ranch hands with burns—an occupational hazard during branding. A crotchety old man with gastroesophageal reflux who'd been wolfing down antacids for months before seeking medical advice. A skateboarder with a broken wrist.

And one snippety woman who stopped by to ask if the rumors were true about the multimillion-dollar malpractice lawsuits filed against Jolie in California. Where, Jolie wondered on a heavy sigh, did these crazy rumors start?

Charlie—trailed by Lily—appeared every day after school. They popped in the front door, and if there weren't any patients in the waiting room, they sat and talked with her. Charlie seemed as hungry for motherly attention as he did for the jar of Tootsie Rolls on her desk.

Now he was hanging over the counter at the receptionist's window, grinning from ear to ear.

"I think you should come for supper," he announced. "Dad said we were gonna grill steak tonight, and then you wouldn't have to eat supper all by yourself."

Behind him, Lily rolled her eyes. "Some invitation. Invite her and then point out that she has no life."

Jolie looked up from the Medicare forms she'd spread out on the desk. "Is this your idea, or does your dad know?"

Matt had been rounding up his kids in front of her clinic

for the past few days, but he hadn't come inside and hadn't said a word to her. Dollars to doughnuts, this was Charlie's idea alone.

He had the grace to look abashed. "Well...we always have lots, and it would be so much fun. Please?"

"I'd love to, but I stay here until eight or nine every evening. I'm sure you'll be eating earlier than that."

Matt appeared at the door of the clinic in time for the last few words. "Earlier than what?"

She'd forgotten how tall he was, Jolie mused. His blue flannel shirt and well-worn jeans emphasized his long, lean legs and powerful build. Most days were still cool enough for jackets, but he was already looking tanned and fit.

Lily slung her backpack over one shoulder. "Charlie just invited her for supper tonight."

Matt took a sharp breath. "Tonight?"

"I was just telling him that I couldn't make it, so don't panic. I appreciate the invitation, though, Charlie."

"She says she's gotta stay here late every night," Charlie said, his voiced laced with disappointment. "I think she should come over and eat with us, instead. Don't you?"

"She's busy, Charlie." Matt glanced down the hallway. "Any news on that door?"

"The council is sending someone over to install a new lock."

With a grunt of disapproval Matt strode to the back door, the kids and Jolie in his wake. "Run your fingernail along this door frame and tell me that any lock will hold if someone hits it hard enough."

"Well, I—"

"Look, I'll find you a good steel door at a contractor's discount. I'll deliver and install it for free." He sounded exasperated. "Deal?"

Jolie mentally tallied her financial status. The portable X-ray machine, EKG cart, defibrillator and monitor, basic lab setup, and the host of other necessary clinic equipment had cost far more than she'd expected. It would take a good long while until her accounts were in the black, and until then she needed to make every dollar count. And anyway, structural improvements on the building weren't her responsibility. "Maybe later..."

"I'll charge it to the council, and see what happens. Consider it returning a favor." He turned his hands palm up. "My kids stop here all the time, and you looked after Charlie's scrapes. Since their mother died, just having a woman to talk to means a lot to them. I owe you."

That explains a lot, Jolie realized. Charlie's hunger for attention, the way he'd been shadowing her. A loss through death, not divorce. Poor kid.

"And we could all talk about it over supper tonight!" Charlie broke in, beaming at them both.

"Another time might be better," Jolie said dryly, reaching out to ruffle his hair. "I'd better invite *your* family someday, if your dad is going to insist on this door."

After they said their goodbyes, Matt and Lily walked out to his truck. Charlie hung back to give her a big wink and a thumbs-up before following them.

Why, she thought, did she have the feeling she'd just been manipulated by a master who was less than five feet tall?

BY SATURDAY Megan's stomach didn't hurt as much. Not the way it had when she'd gone to the clinic. Now she just felt as if she could throw up, but that was only because Dad would be at home. *Waiting for her.* And when he saw her come in the door, it would start all over again.

On Valentine's Day he'd finally noticed the pregnancy she'd concealed with baggy sweatshirts. He'd hit her until she finally gave up and told him the name of the baby's father.

Her dad's anger had changed to eager anticipation when he found out. He'd gone after Bobby's father that night to demand money, but when Robert Maxwell kicked him off the property, Dad had come home and…

Megan shivered, hugging her arms tightly around her waist.

Bobby had never once called her after that night. The Maxwell lawyer had, though. He'd offered payment of expenses and some child support *if* the Wheelers proved Bobby was the father.

The humiliation of it all was overwhelming. But worse— how could she ever stop the richest man in all of Montana if he decided to come after Bobby's baby?

Megan cut across the cow pasture and dropped to her knees on a grassy hill overlooking her family's ranch. Or what was left of it. Most of the land was gone now, auctioned after her dad had gone bankrupt when she was little.

Tumbledown outbuildings straggled haphazardly throughout the overgrown barnyard. Half-hidden in the trees sat the house—paint curling from its siding, the roof a patchwork of shingle colors left over from her dad's odd jobs over the years.

For years the family had scraped by on what was left after he closed down the local bars on Friday and Saturday nights. *No wonder Bobby doesn't want you anymore,* she thought bitterly. *What did you ever have to offer except love?*

And no one knew better than Megan Wheeler how little that meant.

She'd seen her parents' endless fights over money, had seen the light in her mother's eyes die a little more each year. Mom had grabbed Megan and her sister, and fled to

Aunt Leena's house in Big Timber too many times to count, often staying for weeks at a time. The girls' grades had suffered and the school officials had been irate, but the three of them had been safe for a while...until Abe wheedled and cajoled, and made promises he never intended to keep, to lure his wife home.

Megan still prayed that one day Mom would find the strength to stay away for good.

As soon as the baby came, Megan would leave and take any job that was far away from her father and from the Maxwells.

Laying a protective hand over her belly, she closed her eyes. "I promise you, little one, that you'll have a better life than I had," she whispered.

An image of the baby's father slid into her thoughts. Handsome, reckless, daring. She'd loved Bobby since third grade, but that didn't matter. His wealthy family was so far above her own that she'd always known there'd never been a chance.

Lost in thought, she didn't hear her father's approach until he came up behind her.

"Where the hell have you been?" Grabbing her upper arm he hauled her to her feet and started dragging her down the hill. "You and me have a lot to talk about, girly."

She could smell the whiskey on his breath. She tried to pull away but he moved ahead, as relentless and unstoppable as a bull, even when she stumbled and fell to her knees. "Please—don't," she cried out. "My arm—"

When he stopped and turned on her, she fell into him and nearly went down. He grabbed both her arms and shook her as if she weighed nothing at all. Nausea rose in her throat.

"You damn well better not try runnin' off again. We're gonna make Maxwell pay, and pay good for what that no-account son of his did to you." An eerie, self-satisfied gleam filled his eyes. "You and I both know the Maxwells can damn sure afford it."

He turned and started down the hill, one meaty hand clenched tight as a tourniquet around her arm.

She tried to escape into that secret place where she didn't feel the pain, didn't hear his voice any longer. She knew all too well what awaited her in that house.

But now there was far too much at stake. Her *baby*. Gathering up every bit of her strength, she charged forward and rammed into her father's back just as he started down the boulder-strewn trail at the bottom of the hill.

With a bellow of surprise he released her arm and flailed his arms for balance, then pitched forward into the rocks.

He wasn't dead—she could see the rise and fall of his chest—but he wasn't moving.

Caught between terror and guilt, she hesitated only a moment. Nothing ever stopped Abe Wheeler for long. She spared one last glance at the only home she'd ever known.

And then she ran for her life.

CHAPTER FOUR

"SHE HIRED YOU to do this?" Ed gave Matt a dubious look as they lifted the cardboard-encased steel door onto the bed of the pickup. "You gave her a quote and set this up?"

"Not exactly. This is a favor. At cost." Matt eyed the streaks of purple and rose sunset over the mountains to the west. "The lights are always on at her clinic late at night, so I figured I'd just go get this done."

They settled the door on the tailgate of the truck and both pushed it forward. "As if she needs a deal. I told you about her family. She sure as hell doesn't need a handout from us."

"My kids like her. They stop in at her clinic a lot, and she's a neighbor."

A stubborn one. A week ago, she'd politely declined his offer twice, but every time Matt drove by the clinic a feeling of unease crawled down his spine. He resolutely tugged his ball cap lower over his forehead.

Ed shook his head. "Typical—all the money in the world, yet those people always look for a free ride."

"She didn't ask. She doesn't even want me to do it."

"You're doing the damn job anyway?" Ed's expression turned to disbelief.

Matt shrugged. "I get the feeling things aren't as easy for her as you think."

"You wouldn't be doing this if she was twenty years older and weighed another couple hundred pounds."

Silently counting to ten, Matt ignored Ed's leer as he rounded the back of the pickup and slid behind the wheel. "See you tomorrow morning at the Thompson place by seven."

"Yeah, sure. And you can tell me about how far you got with the doc."

Ed and he had been partners for a few weeks now, bidding on projects, working on the kitchen renovation Ed had set up earlier. Things were going pretty well. God willing, there would be enough work to keep them busy. But adjusting to each other was still proving to be a challenge.

As if still caught up in their old sibling rivalries, Ed seemed bent on establishing control, clearly resented being questioned. And sometimes his decisions just weren't sound.

Simple oversights, maybe. Quick decisions made under stress. *That's all it is,* Matt told himself. *Everything will be okay.*

He just hoped it was true.

As HE'D EXPECTED, the lights were still on at the clinic when Matt pulled to a stop in the alley.

Jolie's Blazer rarely bounced up Coyote Creek Road past his place before nine, and sometimes she passed by after midnight.

When he heard her, he always wondered what it was like for a woman to drive home by herself to that desolate, darkened cabin without even a dog there to greet her. Dolly and the old sheep couldn't offer much protection. Lord knew, his wife hadn't even liked driving alone in the city, where there were streetlights and neighbors.

The one time he'd flagged Jolie down and offered to go with her to check for prowlers, she'd given him a breezy smile and continued on her way.

He still sometimes found himself lying awake at night,

listening to the owls and coyotes and whatever else rustled through the underbrush, wondering if she was all right up in that isolated cabin by herself.

To avoid startling her, he walked around to the front of the clinic and rapped lightly on the door before stepping inside. The waiting room was lit by just a small lamp at one end, but light poured from a doorway down the hall.

"Be out in a sec," Jolie called out. "Just have a seat."

Matt eyed the waiting-room chairs, none of which appeared comfortable, then headed for the receptionist's window. "I brought your door."

"You what?" Sounding startled, Jolie stepped out of the lab, clad in old jeans and an oversize sweatshirt, a paintbrush in her hand. A paint-spattered bandanna covered her hair, and a streak of white paint trailed across her right cheekbone. Even without makeup, the fine bone structure of her face gave her a natural beauty that would undoubtedly age with elegance.

"I could use a little help moving it in here, though. Got a minute?"

She swept a glance down the front of her paint-spattered shirt, then met his gaze dead-on. Another woman might have shown embarrassment, but Jolie was clearly made of sterner stuff. She lifted her chin. "I don't think we settled on anything."

"Easy decision. Free labor, material at cost."

Her gaze shifted toward the back door, and the inky darkness beyond its single pane of glass. "Well..."

"My *kids* stop in here. What if some creep let himself in?"

"I—" She hesitated. "You're right. I don't know what to say."

"Just say thanks and help me bring in the darn door."

"Thanks." She gave a weary sigh. "There were more

problems here than I anticipated. I've pushed the council only on the most important ones for now.''

"I'll go have a talk with—"

"I'll deal with them on my own, but thanks.''

The unmistakable thread of steel in her voice startled him. Had she learned to be tough growing up in the shadow of a powerful father? Moving back into the man's territory and remaining independent had to be a challenge.

"Promise,'' she added in a softer voice, "that you and the kids will come for supper sometime soon. That's the least I can do to repay you.'' A smile played at the corners of her lips. "This ought to make Charlie happy. He's been trying to wangle an invitation for quite a while.''

"Deal.'' If her old man was half as stubborn as she was, it was no wonder that he'd built one of the biggest ranching empires in Montana. Feeling absurdly victorious, Matt waved her ahead of him and followed her out to the alley.

Even with her loose clothing, it was hard not to stare. And imagine.

Where the hell was that coming from? Maybe just because it had been so long. He could barely remember his last date, much less any feeling of strong desire for a particular woman. And this one, old money to the bone and with an education that left his in the dust, couldn't be a less likely prospect.

The security light at the back of the clinic now glowed against the remaining sliver of indigo at the horizon. Above, stars twinkled. A lone pickup creeping down the street— probably someone who'd had a few too many at the Lone Wolf—switched on its headlights.

At the truck, Matt released the tailgate and pulled the heavy cardboard box forward. "I'll move it to the edge of the tailgate, and then you can take the other end, okay? Can you manage?''

"I was born on a ranch," she retorted dryly. A dimple flashed in her cheek. "I grew up throwing bales and driving a tractor. Piece of cake."

By the time they'd wrestled the door sideways through the back entrance of the clinic, she didn't seem quite as chipper.

"What did you put in this box, lead weights?" She blew wisps of hair out of her eyes. "Rocks?"

"Steel. Here...let your end down. I can take it from here."

She did as he suggested and stepped back, dusting her hands against her hips. "Now what?"

"I'll get my tools, and have this done tonight."

"What about your kids?"

"This won't take long. Lily's watching Charlie at home, and they're both busy. She has a test tomorrow, and Charlie has a school project due." At Jolie's raised eyebrow, he added, "They're safe. We've got good dead bolts on every door, locks on the windows, and Lily has my cell phone number. She baby-sat a lot in south Chicago. And then there's our watchdog," he added with a grin.

"That little black-and-white powder puff? Weighs maybe a pound?"

"Hey, don't insult him. Samson has a heart bigger than he is. By next fall he'll weigh a good fifty."

"Charlie introduced me when I walked past your place one evening. He says your watch-puppy is afraid of dust bunnies under the bed," Jolie retorted dryly.

"He's forgetting that Sam just needs to grow a little."

Jolie's expression softened, and something akin to sadness flickered through her eyes. "You're lucky. You've got good kids."

"Yeah. Lily isn't too thrilled about being here, but I think she'll come around." Matt retrieved his toolbox from the truck, then cut the strapping tapes securing the box and slit it open.

Jolie leaned a shoulder against the wall and watched as he worked. "What made you decide to come out here?"

"Lily mostly, and Charlie."

"For all the fresh air?"

"To get away from the neighborhood."

"Ah."

"They were both hanging around after school with kids who oughta be in juvenile court. Charlie's baby-sitters never lasted more than a week, and with Lily's after-school activities, she wasn't always available to watch him. Add to that my long hours and I could see we were headed for trouble."

Jolie nodded. "I worked in an area that was pretty tough. It has to be hard, trying to raise kids right with negative influences luring them every day."

Quite a difference from how you were raised, sweetheart. "It wasn't a bad place, a few years ago. Decent houses, safe streets. But not anymore." Matt gathered up the packing materials. "Trash out back?"

Jolie nodded.

As Matt stepped through the door, some of the strapping material slithered through his fingers. She reached for it at the same moment he did, her cool, slender fingers brushing against the sensitive flesh of his inner wrist.

And just that quickly, his heart skipped a beat.

Surprise must have registered on his face, because Jolie gave him a curious look as she tucked the strapping between two pieces of cardboard. "Everything all right?"

With a curt nod, he headed for the trash containers in the alley and dropped the materials inside, then jammed his hands into the pockets of his jeans and looked up at the stars.

Barb had been gone four years last October...and before

that, it had taken her two painful years to die. Sometimes, he couldn't hear her voice in his thoughts anymore, or even conjure up her lovely face, unless he looked at the family portrait on the bureau in his bedroom. The kids hadn't cried in his arms in over a year. Life went on, day by day.

Something about Jolie was far too compelling, calling up emotions and desires he'd never expected to feel again, an unexpected awareness of her that could only place him and the kids at risk of heartbreak once again.

Moving here gave them all a chance for new beginnings, a place to build new memories, but that wouldn't include allowing another woman into his life. His priorities were the kids and the new business. Period.

He would fix Jolie's door. He would be a good neighbor. But he would definitely keep his distance.

SUNDAY AFTERNOON brought balmy mid-April sunshine, brilliant blue skies and a restlessness Jolie hadn't felt in a good long while. Shouldering her purse, she locked the cabin door behind her and stepped out onto the shady porch, breathing in air so pure and sweet she felt like dancing.

In a month the meadow would be awash in a palette of delicate colors—Indian paintbrush, pink gentian and yellow wood sorrel. There would be shy does and fawns at dusk, and perhaps a mother bear and her cubs lumbering past. A sense of peace settled in her chest.

The cabin, with its great room, two bedrooms and big loft, was perfect. She could imagine living here in her old age, sitting out on the wraparound porch to simply watch the mountains change color from dawn to dusk, year after year after year. Why had she waited so long to move home?

Next to the barn, Dolly looked up from a tuft of still-brown grass, her furry banana-shaped ears cocked forward with interest. Checking, no doubt, to see if Jolie carried a handful of soda crackers. The old ewe bleated and bumped against the llama's legs, as if begging Dolly to stay put.

"No crackers left," Jolie called out as she headed for her Blazer. "I'll buy five boxes in town. Promise."

If any of her Los Angeles co-workers had heard her talking to a llama, they'd probably have stared with open-mouthed astonishment, Jolie thought as she drove down the rutted, rocky road toward the highway.

She'd heard them often enough, whispering behind her back about the aloof doctor who didn't socialize, didn't join in the banter at the nurses' stations or ever meet for drinks after work. *Brilliant,* they'd said. *But cold as ice.*

She hadn't been aloof because of arrogance, no matter what anyone thought. Growing up on an isolated ranch, she'd just never become adept at small talk or social banter.

As she passed the lane leading up to Matt's place, she gave a rueful laugh. She'd never been much good at making idle conversation with the opposite sex, either. Especially with the guys who attracted her the most.

Though clearly concerned for her safety and determined to help, Matt had barely talked to her on Friday night once he started installing that new door. If there'd ever been a guy she truly would have liked to know better, it would have been Matt Dawson, but he'd shot out to his truck the moment he finished the job.

You're charming from head to toe, Maxwell. No wonder you're always alone.

Down at the highway she switched on her right-turn signal to head toward the clinic. Then snapped it in the opposite direction and headed in the direction of the main highway.

Maybe she'd never find a man who loved her for herself instead of her earning potential, but she *could* start trying to mend the family bonds that had been broken long ago.

THE THIRTY-MILE TRIP to her family's Walking Stones Ranch confirmed her second reason for coming back to Montana.

The sheer raw beauty of the rugged mountains on three sides, still heavily cloaked in winter white, felt like balm to her soul. Whatever else she did—or didn't—have in her life, this was *home*.

Her breath caught at the sight of a herd of pronghorn speeding across the valley floor to the left, their white rumps flashing as they bounced over clumps of sagebrush. She pulled to the side of the road and watched until they disappeared.

There were often herds of antelope grazing within view of the narrow, twisting roads that led from the ranch to Paradise Corners.

"Aren't they beautiful? So wild and free," Mom had always said. Even after all her years as a Montana rancher's wife, she'd pull over, shade her eyes against the bright sunshine to watch them and lose all sense of time and urgency. *"Life's too busy,"* she'd say with a smile of contentment. *"You've got to slow down and just savor it now and then."*

As a child, Jolie had always been impatient. As an adult, she finally understood. "You were right, Mom," Jolie whispered. "I should have listened to you earlier."

At the massive gates to the ranch, Jolie slowed, pulled the Blazer to a stop and took a deep breath. Walking Stones—a hundred fifty thousand acres of the most beautiful land anywhere on earth, where rich grassland rose to pine forests rimmed on three sides by jagged, snowy peaks.

High in the foothills, overlooking a steep cliff, lay the boulder-strewn clearing that had given the ranch its name. Legend had it that each spring and fall, Indian tribes feasted and performed sacred ceremonies below the cliff, then at dawn the chief and elders would climb up to the clearing.

The massive boulders were always found in new positions that guided the tribe to plentiful game, good shelter, and safety from their enemies.

Excitement fluttered through her as she started down the long lane leading to the heart of the ranch. She'd seen everyone at Thea's wedding on Valentine's Day, but with all the excitement, and her next-day flight back to California, there had been little time to visit.

Maybe Thea or Bobby would be here. Or maybe—stranger things had happened—Dad would be in a better mood this time, and would even take a few minutes for coffee with her.

During the past three weeks she'd been to the family's First Methodist Church twice, but with everyone at the ranch so busy with calving at night, they'd arrived at the last minute and left promptly after Sunday Services. There'd been little time for conversation.

Thea had called once, late at night, but hadn't made it into town, and Jolie had been working too hard at the clinic to get away. *Mom, you're still right after all these years. We should all savor life just a little more.*

At the Y in the ranch road she debated a split second, then took a left toward the barns instead of going up to the house. Beth probably would be bustling around the kitchen, running the household with her usual quiet efficiency. But the likelihood of finding any family members there was just about nil—unless they were exhausted and catching a couple hours of sleep.

As she drove around the last curve, the main calving barn came into full view. Rolling pastureland rose behind the barns to the north and west, framed on the horizon by the Crazy Mountains. A herd of several hundred heavily pregnant Angus cows were grazing in the pasture behind the barn. Two sorrel horses were saddled and tied out front.

Her father strode out of the barn toward the horses, followed by Bobby.

Robert glanced at Jolie's car, gave a brief nod of acknowledgment as she pulled to a stop, then turned away to untie his horse.

Nice to see you too, Dad. It never took more than five minutes in Robert's presence to remember why she'd wanted to move away. After her mother died unexpectedly from an aneurysm during Jolie's senior year, Jolie had tried hard to help out until she'd left for college. But to Robert Maxwell, no one was ever good enough, thorough enough, fast enough.

He'd always tried to control his children just as he controlled his business—with an unyielding, unsympathetic hand—and he'd never understood the simple power of love. Standing in his way was like challenging a Brahma. More than one businessman had failed in town due to Robert's influence, and Jolie suspected that he'd interfered with all his children's lives more than they'd ever know.

"Get the lead out, Bobby," he roared as he swung into the saddle.

Bobby, six feet of pure resentment, angled toward Jolie's car and met her as she stepped out. "Home sweet home," he drawled loud enough for their father to hear. "How's everything?"

"Good. The clinic is mostly done." She reached forward to give him an awkward hug. "Where's Thea?"

"She's up in the northwest pasture, checking heifers."

"I'm living almost a thousand miles closer to home, and still have trouble making connections with everyone," Jolie murmured. "I'm glad I caught you."

From his wind-tossed, jet-black hair to his thickly lashed brown eyes, Bobby had charm to burn and had been spoiled from the start—more so after Mom died, because he'd been just a preschooler at the time.

Now he leaned lazily against the side of Jolie's car, as if he had all day to shoot the breeze—aiming to aggravate Dad, no doubt.

"We all should've come to see your clinic, but you know how it is." He jerked his chin toward their father. "We never, ever get done around here." He spat out the words.

Jolie knew indeed. The ranch always came first with Robert Maxwell.

"Maybe you can come in sometime on your own, to see me?"

Bobby gave her an odd look. "Yeah, right."

"I imagine you have lots of other things to do on your time off." She fought to keep her voice level. "But I'd like that a lot. If you find the time someday."

With surprising agility for a man of fifty-five, Robert leaned over in his saddle and untied the other horse, then rode over to the car and held out its reins to Bobby. "We're fifteen minutes late. Now get on this horse and *ride.*"

Bobby waited a beat before taking the reins, another mild insurrection that registered in Robert's darkening scowl.

"Everything going well?" Shading her eyes against the sun, Jolie managed a smile as she looked up at her father.

Intelligent, stubborn and with a single-minded determination that brooked no opposition, he'd been a stern, implacable ruler of his domain for decades. After her mother's death he'd become even more distant and cold.

"Busy." He tugged the brim of his hat lower over his face and imperceptibly cued his horse into a neat one-hundred-eighty-degree pivot toward the pasture gates at the north side of the barn.

Gathering his reins, Bobby stepped lightly up onto his mare and settled her with a quiet hand on her neck. Anger simmered in his eyes as he watched their father nudge his horse into an easy jog. "I'll come to see you the next time I get a ride into town."

"A *ride?*"

"Judge LeVay ruled on my case a while back. You didn't hear?" He gave a harsh laugh. "Probably not. Communication isn't a Maxwell trait."

Sorrow swept through Jolie as she remembered the car accident last Halloween. Four people—Bobby, two friends and the driver of the other vehicle—had been injured, and Bobby's closest friend, Danny, had been in a coma for a while. All because of Bobby's drinking, his reckless driving. *Such an incredible waste.*

Rising anger warred with concern for her little brother. "How did he rule?"

"I was way over the legal blood-alcohol limit, so Dad's lawyers decided to plead a lesser charge before going to trial. They said a trial would be too risky." Bobby's tone turned sarcastic. "Not that LeVay would've dared put Robert Maxwell's son in prison."

"You only lost your *license?*"

Bobby sliced the air angrily with the side of his hand. "What, you think I should have gone to jail?"

"No, I—"

"Well, don't worry, *sis.* I got three years' probation, a thousand hours of community service, and have no wheels for a year. I'm stuck here under Dad's thumb from morning till night," he snarled. "And Dan's parents are threatening to sue. I would have been *better off* in jail." He spun his horse away and took off at a lope toward the pasture gate.

"Bobby, wait!"

She knew he'd heard her, but he didn't give any sign. Pulling to a sliding stop by the gate, he neatly sidestepped his horse into position and navigated through the gate, opening and shutting it without dismounting.

From the corner of her eye, she saw a flash of color. Cassie, her middle sister, who now worked in Billings, stood in the doorway of the barn, her somber young son, Zak, at her side.

"Hi, there! How's my favorite nephew?" Jolie smiled at Zak, but he gave his usual almost-imperceptible shrug and looked away. She lifted her gaze to Cassie's. "Nice surprise—I didn't see your car when I drove in."

Cassie ignored the greeting. "Still handling our family problems as well as ever," she said coldly. "Why isn't that a surprise?"

With her bright red hair and hazel eyes, Cassie had taken after the Maxwell side of the family, and she had the temper as well. Even after going to college and establishing a successful career with Montana Child Protective Services, her childhood hostilities still surfaced whenever Jolie came home.

"I don't want to take over," Jolie said evenly, trying to mask her hurt. "I couldn't even if I wanted to, because no one ever tells me about what's going on out here. How is Dan doing? And what's this about a lawsuit?"

"The Maxwell lawyers say Danny's family plans to sue for at least five million."

Jolie stared at her sister. "Do we have that kind of insurance?"

"I guess." Cassie shrugged. "You know Dad never shares anything about ranch business with anyone but Thea and Bobby. The whole situation could get nasty."

"And Dan?"

"He had some sort of surgery that helped, but his family's lawyers say he may never walk again." Cassie rested a protective hand on her son's thin shoulders. "I hear he's done with rehab for now, and they've got him back at the family's ranch.''

Which meant either he'd reached the maximum benefit of therapy, or the family's insurance and personal funds had run out. Jolie's heart sank at the thought of what the Aikens were going through. The emotional, physical and spiritual toll could be overwhelming for the family as well as the victim. ''The last I heard, Dan was slowly recovering.''

''No miracles, that's for sure. Still, his speech is better, and he can move his arms well enough to write.'' Cassie shaded her eyes with a hand and watched Bobby ride out into the pasture. ''That's sad enough. But Bobby seems to be more concerned about the lawsuits and his truck than the welfare of the boy who was injured. Our little brother has a long, long way to go.''

Unbidden, an image of Matt came to mind. His firm but loving approach to parenting. His patience with his son. If Bobby had been given a father like Matt, would he have turned out better?

NINETY-SIX POUNDS. Fear washed through Lily as she stepped off the scale on Monday morning before school. A month ago she'd been a hundred-five. Two weeks ago, on the day she'd started school here, she'd been a hundred.

Her knees shaking, she braced her hands on the bathroom sink and stared at the hollows of her cheeks and the violet shadows under her eyes. Most of the other kids in middle school grew a lot at her age. She'd seen those changes in neighborhood friends back home.

Mom got thin before she died.

Lily sank onto the edge of the bathtub and wrapped her arms around her waist. The scared feeling was in her stomach all the time now, making her want to scream and run, or hide under the blankets and not even get out of bed each morning.

Maybe I have cancer, too. But telling Dad how she felt, going to a doctor, might make it all too real. *I don't want to know. I don't want to know.*

Fragments of last night's dreams floated back. The way Mom's beautiful face had turned yellow, her skin felt like tissue paper. The way her shiny dark hair had fallen out in tufts until she'd looked like an old, worn doll at a garage sale.

The cold, numb feeling of standing at the silver casket and seeing her mother's face for the very last time.

"Lily! Are you ready yet? You're going to be late for school!" Dad's impatient voice shattered the silence. "Charlie is already in the car."

"Coming." Lily stood up—too fast, because a wave of dizziness nearly sent her to the floor.

And then she prayed that she wasn't going to die.

CHAPTER FIVE

"IF YOU NEEDED that inlay cutter, why didn't you order it yourself?" With increasing impatience, Ed hunted through an overflowing file-cabinet drawer for a misplaced receipt.

Scraps of paper—and probably the missing receipt—fluttered to the floor around his chair.

Matt silently counted to ten. "Because," he said evenly, "you said you'd ordered it *last* Monday."

"Like hell I did."

The spare room in Ed's basement was dimly lit, the air smelled damply of mildew. A cluttered desk, two four-drawer file cabinets and a bookshelf crammed haphazardly with books and magazines took up most of the space.

Five minutes down here and Matt wanted nothing more than to escape outside to the fresh air.

Every Monday morning they took care of invoices, checked orders and caught up on other business before getting out to the current job site. If they ever got done this morning, they'd head over to the Thompson kitchen-remodeling job in Fairfax.

Matt glanced at the lumberyard calendar on the wall and sighed heavily. They'd promised to finish the kitchen by the twenty-second of April, and today was the twentieth. It just wasn't going to happen unless Ed moved into a higher gear.

Fighting the urge to pursue the argument, Matt settled into a creaky desk chair and thumbed through the open file in his lap—a project for someone named Bailey living on

Aspen Way, the upscale development at the edge of town. He whistled. A remodeling job of this size would keep them busy for a good five weeks, easy.

"Heard from these people?" Matt asked, reaching for his coffee mug at the edge of the desk.

Ed shrugged a burly shoulder.

"The date here says you did this estimate four weeks ago. That would have been the Monday after the kids and I moved to Paradise Corners. I don't think you ever mentioned this one."

"Yeah, well, probably doesn't matter. I think they changed their minds."

"Did you call them to make sure they got the estimate?"

Ed reached for a battered leather planner on his desk and flipped through the pages. Stopped. Then searched again, more slowly this time.

A dull red flush crept up his neck, and Matt wondered what Ed had been doing in the evenings. Anyone could make a mistake. *But if he'd been drinking again...*

"It isn't here in my planner, but I did call."

Matt scanned the figures on the estimate. "Did you figure in the Durock for the kitchen floor?" He tried to hide his annoyance but failed. "Or the cost of the grout?"

"'Course I did," Ed retorted. "It's there."

"Guess I just don't see it. Financial surprises in the middle of a job can sure rile a client."

"You don't need to check up on me, little brother."

Yes I do. "I thought we were *supposed* to be going over future projects," Matt said mildly as he tossed the file on the desk. "Take a look at these figures before you call the owners. Maybe you could fax them an amendment and then call in a day or two." He glanced at his watch for the third time. "What else do you have going?"

"A couple of messages on the machine. Small stuff,

mostly, but it could keep us busy till we start that house in June. A screen porch, a rec room in someone's basement. One call sounded good—the dentist's son is moving back into town and wants to build on the west side of town. Says he's still negotiating on the land, but wants to start construction by late summer if he can find the right contractor.''

"Call him yet?"

"He didn't leave a number. Said he'd get back to us."

"Might not hurt to give Doc Farnsworth a call, ask a few questions.'' Matt stood, grabbed his faded Chicago Cubs jacket and gestured toward the stack of bills they'd just paid. "Do you want me to drop those off at the post office?"

Ed shrugged on his insulated flannel jacket, then picked up his coffee mug and the stack of envelopes. "I'll tell Tina to mail these, then I'll meet you out at the Thompsons'.''

Matt hesitated, then headed up the stairs, a sense of uneasiness curling through his gut. *I should have mailed them myself.*

With two kids to support and a new mortgage, he couldn't afford to let this business fail. But with every passing week he felt less sure Dawson Brothers Construction would succeed.

Deciding to work with his brother might have been one of the bigger mistakes in his life.

MY TWO-WEEK ANNIVERSARY, Jolie thought with a sense of satisfaction. And things are just…great.

Mostly. Monday mornings tended to be her busiest time so far. And there were *three* patients in the waiting room. At this rate, she'd soon be able to hire someone to help in the office.

She studied the new-patient registration form on the clipboard in her hand. "Bill?"

The wiry, sun-cured cowboy hovering by the entryway

glanced up, a startled look in his eye, and appeared ready to bolt. "Ma'am?"

She suppressed a smile. "Want to come back?"

Relief flooded across his weathered face. "I surely can. Mebbe tomorrow?"

The smile escaped despite her best effort as she imagined having to lasso him as he fled out the door. "No. Why don't you come on in so I can take a look at that burn?"

Darting a nervous glance at the other two people in the waiting room, he swallowed hard and then started across the reception area.

A lot of cowboys patched themselves up as they would their cattle; some even sutured their own smaller lacerations with the veterinary supplies every ranch kept on hand due to the vast distances between ranches and towns.

For this one to come into town and seek medical care was either a credit to his intelligence or an indication that his injuries were significant. Given the sheen of perspiration on his craggy face and the glazed appearance of his eyes, he was either in a lot of pain, running a fever or both.

In the exam room he gripped his hat with both hands, slid a look toward her, then eyed the table with true fear. "I ain't taking my clothes off."

"No. Of course not. At least, not your jeans. But I really do need to see that arm." Jolie took a medical history—which didn't take long given that the man hadn't seen a doctor in twenty years—then moved to the door. "I'll be back in a minute. Just take off your jacket and shirt, and hop up on the exam table."

Not giving him time to disagree, she stepped into the hallway, gave him two minutes, then returned.

Hunched over and scrawny—reminding her of a turkey vulture—he didn't meet her eyes. A four-inch-wide white bandage had been wrapped around his arm. It was a horse-leg wrap, she knew from her own ranching experience, but looked clean.

"Do this yourself?"

He gave a nearly imperceptible nod. She could see his respirations were fast and uneven as she began gently unwrapping the wound. "Branding accident, you said?"

Again another nod.

"How did it happen?"

"Had the calf down, but my buddy's horse slacked off on the rope. Ended up with a real wrestling match."

"Out at Walking Stones we had those now and again. Hurts like heck to get in the way, doesn't it? Which outfit are you with?" Keeping up a steady conversation to distract him, she unwrapped the final length of bandaging and gently supported his arm for a visual exam.

A partial-thickness burn, approaching full thickness at the medial edge, roughly twenty-by-fifteen centimeters. Bits of charred flannel were driven deep into the burn. From the looks of it, Bill would likely bear half of the Rocking M's brand for the rest of his life.

The heat and swelling round the perimeter of the wound told her he hadn't been in any hurry to seek help. "When did you say this happened?"

"Couple days."

Giving him an encouraging smile, Jolie collected the equipment she needed and silently started a wish list of personnel she'd like to hire.

An office nurse.

A receptionist.

A lab tech.

She handed him a stainless-steel basin. "Hold this, to catch the water."

Mindful of his pain, she ran a continuous saline flush over

the wound as she carefully debrided it; patiently soaking the scab, working bits of charred cloth free.

Throughout the process Bill remained stone-still, though she heard his respirations accelerate when she touched the more sensitive areas.

"I'd like to dress this with Silvadene and a gauze dressing. Are you allergic to sulfa?"

"No, ma'am."

Recalling his lack of regular medical care, she smiled up at him. "Have you ever *had* sulfa?"

"Works good."

She looked at him, waiting for him to elaborate. Expecting him to say he'd used a topical sulfa-based ointment on wounds.

"We've got the big white sulfa pills in the barn, for calf scours and pneumonias."

"You take...calf antibiotics?"

"Yep. Got long-acting penicillin, too—250cc bottles."

"You *inject* yourself?"

He shrugged.

Jolie sighed. "What protocol—er—how do you know what to take? And when?"

He gave her his first smile since walking in the clinic door. "I figure I'm big as a hunnert-fifty-pound calf, and go from there. I gave myself a good dose yesterday."

Jolie tried to hold in her exasperation. "That didn't necessarily help one bit with your burn," she muttered through clenched teeth. "Even if you have infection, bacteria aren't all sensitive to the same drugs. And if you don't take enough medicine, for long enough, those bacteria can mutate into resistant strains."

He gave her a blank look, but Jolie continuing talking as she dressed the wound with Silvadene cream and applied a gauze dressing. "You need to keep this clean, and redress the wound every day. Any chance you can come back in three days?''

''No, ma'am. We'll be moving cattle up into the higher ranges, then hauling steers to Billings.'' He shrugged into his flannel shirt, then pulled a worn billfold from the hip pocket of his jeans as he slid off the exam table. ''How much do I owe?''

''We can submit this to your insurance. Do you know what your copay is?''

He gave her another blank look.

''What portion you pay out-of-pocket for medical care?'' Belatedly, she remembered that he never *sought* medical care.

''Hell, we don't have no insurance where I work.''

From his worn boots and battered jeans, to his crumpled hat, he was clearly a man who didn't have a lot of cash to spare. She knew ranch hands were often paid subsistence wages, maybe given marginal housing in the bargain.

Jolie quoted an office fee a fraction of what she'd charged in California...and mentally crossed off some of the equipment items on her wish list. Many of her patients would be like Bill, she realized; hardworking, low-income people who barely made ends meet.

But I didn't come home to get rich. With no kids, no mortgage and no responsibilities beyond the clinic, llama and the old blind ewe, Jolie's needs were minimal.

A sense of satisfaction warmed her heart as she sent Bill on his way and turned to the next patients in the waiting room. ''Next?''

A gray-haired woman glanced at the young mom and toddler across the room. ''If you want to go first, it's okay. I won't be but a minute, though.''

The mother looked up from reading *I'll Love You Forever* to her child and shook her head. ''We're fine, Aunt Irene.''

"Did you fill out one of the registration forms?" Jolie asked as she led the woman down the hall to the first exam room.

"Nope. That's not why I'm here. Let's sit in your office."

Once seated in one of the chairs placed in front of Jolie's desk, she thrust out her hand. "Irene Fuller. I came because you need me."

Bemused, Jolie settled down behind her desk. "I do?"

"I see you just had Bill Cuddy in here. How'd that go?"

Jolie cleared her throat. "I'm afraid I can't discuss my other patients, Irene."

"I'll bet he tried everything from bear grease to voodoo before giving up and seeking medical help."

Jolie had to smile at that. "I wouldn't go quite that far."

"And what about the paperwork, and getting him settled for his exam? Did you have to do labs?"

"I'm not sure why—"

"I used to work in this clinic, with the physician's assistants who came out twice a week from Rapid Creek." Irene beamed at her.

"You worked as an RN?" Jolie thought wistfully of the efficient, hardworking RNs who ran the E.R. in Los Angeles. *What I'd give for one of them now.*

"Sure did. When we moved to Billings I went back to school, so the last few years I worked as an X-ray tech in a thirty-bed hospital. Helped in the lab, too—so I went to school again for that. Not that you can do much in a medical clinic's lab anymore without an awful lot of expense for certification."

This was sounding almost too good to be true. "Are you looking for a *job?*"

Irene nodded, and winked. "My husband, Jack, retired, so now we've moved here. I'm not ready for pasture."

There weren't enough patients yet. Jolie's savings

couldn't support the expense of paying salary and benefits for an employee. *Impossible.* "Um...do you have references?"

Irene fished an envelope from the needlepoint bag at her feet. "A résumé and references. You're welcome to call anyone on the list."

Give her your regrets. "Did you include a phone number?"

Don't. Don't. Don't. You can't afford this. But despite the warning bells in her head, Jolie's next words just tumbled out. "Could you come back for an interview? Maybe this Thursday, the twenty-third?"

Irene nodded and offered her hand. She had a good handshake, strong and decisive.

The phone on the desk jangled. "Thanks," Jolie mouthed as she picked up the receiver. "See you then."

As Irene left the office, Jolie heard her sister's voice on the line. "Thea, here. I'm really worried about Dad."

Jolie drew in a sharp breath. "Is he hurt?"

"It's his heart. He's always so out of breath, and he won't slow down. I'm sure he doesn't take his medication."

"Has he had chest pain?"

Thea gave a short laugh. "He'd never admit it unless he was on death's door. Remember what he did after my wedding reception?"

After the guests had gone he'd looked quite gray, with white lines of stress at his mouth. Thea and Jolie had exchanged worried glances, then Jolie had tactfully approached him. He'd fixed her with an angry look, turned on his heel and disappeared into his office.

Robert Maxwell wasn't one to listen to advice. Not from the doctors, who'd ordered cardiac tests that he'd refused last Thanksgiving after his mild heart attack. And especially not from his daughters—even if one was a practicing physician.

"Overall, does he seem worse?"

"He goes from morning till night, and half the nights he's up even when someone else is covering those hours. You know how it is during calving." Thea sighed heavily. "I'm really sorry I missed you when you came out, by the way. Bobby said you were here."

"I should have called you first."

Thea gave a weary laugh. "Unless you'd called my cell phone, you wouldn't have reached me. I'm either on horseback checking cows or in the barn. Rafe says he hasn't seen me more than five minutes in the past three weeks. Except for the time he spends helping out here—and then we're off with different parts of the herd."

"Are you almost done?"

"Almost. The last seventy-two heifers are due in the next twenty days or so. I'm sorry about not coming in to see your clinic. After faxing you that advertisement and encouraging you to move home, none of us have even gotten into town to welcome you."

"I understand." *But no one bothered to tell me about Bobby's court case, and that would have taken just a phone call.* "About Dad..."

"He's probably worn out from the schedule he keeps. But I think it's more than that. He doesn't eat right, yet I think he looks like he'd putting on some weight through the middle. And he isn't wearing his favorite old boots anymore. A few days ago he borrowed a pair of Herman's ropers, and Herman must wear size thirteens. Dad *hates* ropers."

Some inappetence, maybe. Increasing lower-extremity edema. She hadn't seen evidence of fluid retention when she'd seen him briefly at the ranch, but he'd been wearing a bulky coat, chaps, and boots that would have masked any problem. "Can you get him to come to the clinic?"

Thea snorted. "We only managed to get him to the hospital last Thanksgiving because he was unconscious."

"I'll come out to the ranch, if you tell me when I can catch him at home. But it would be better to see him in the clinic."

"You could make the thirty-mile drive for nothing. Until calving is over, it's impossible to say when he'll be here. I'll…do what I can to get him to come into town."

Jolie hesitated, knowing her sister was deeply worried. "It's important, Thea. He needs to take his meds, follow his diet and slow down. Excessive physical stress could weaken his heart even more."

"I know."

Jolie's schedule in Los Angeles had been grueling, and she hadn't been able to get home often, but she'd seen how gruff and dismissive Dad had been with the one child who'd given her heart and soul to Walking Stones Ranch. Thea deserved far better from him. She had to be angry and hurt over the way he favored his wild son above all of his girls.

But even so, Jolie was almost certain she heard a catch in Thea's voice as she said goodbye.

ON SATURDAY EVENING, Jolie made good on her offer to have Matt and the kids over for supper.

After changing the menu three times, her clothes twice, and lighting a dozen candles through the great room and kitchen—just for the scent, certainly not for any sort of romantic mood setting—she was tired, a little anxious and more than a little bemused at her reaction to having them as guests.

But it was all worthwhile, just seeing the children's delighted reaction to her meal.

"This looks great!" Charlie's megawatt smile beamed at Jolie across the table with enough voltage to rival the sun setting over the mountains to the west. "I *love* fried chicken!"

"That's lucky, because my repertoire in the kitchen doesn't extend far beyond chicken and meat loaf," Jolie said dryly. "More mashed potatoes?"

Charlie nodded vigorously, watching with obvious anticipation as Jolie passed the bowl of butter-drenched fluffy potatoes.

Lily gave her brother an exasperated look. "You aren't in a feedlot," she said under her breath, giving him a sharp nudge with her elbow as she handed him the bowl.

"Lily. Charlie." Matt's voice brooked no argument. He lifted his gaze to Jolie's, his warm brown eyes twinkling with the reflection of the candles Jolie had arranged at the center of the table. "We haven't had to use our company manners for some time."

"Dad!" Embarrassment tinged Lily's pale cheeks with pink. "It's Charlie who—"

"Enough." Matt broke in, his voice low and even. "Jolie was kind enough to invite us here, so let's be polite, okay?"

Lily flopped back in her chair, obviously fuming.

"I grew up with two sisters—and a brother, who came along much later. Our meals weren't always such quiet affairs, believe me." Jolie directed her smile at Lily. "You have the most beautiful name. It makes me think of the lovely little lily of the valley flowers, so sweet and delicate. Were you named after someone?"

Charlie snickered. "That goofy lady in *Peter Pan. Tiger Lily.*"

"Was not, brat." Lily glared at him. "You're a slimy—"

"Lily!" Matt's voice nearly shook the rafters. "Enough!"

After a moment of strained silence, Jolie tried again. "How's school coming along? Making new friends?"

Charlie launched into a convoluted story about the boys in his class. A shadow passed across Lily's face, but she sat silently, picking at the meal she'd barely touched. She hadn't smiled once the entire evening, and hadn't been stopping by the clinic after school lately, either. Depression, maybe?

When Charlie finished his tale, Jolie reached out to lay a hand on Lily's arm. "How about you?"

She gave a sharp jerk of her shoulder. "Fine."

"Do you have any special friends yet?"

"Sure."

"Have you invited anyone over to your house after school yet?"

"No." Lily pointedly picked up her glass of water and drank it slowly, down to the last drop, clearly declaring the topic off limits. She reached for the pitcher and poured a second glass.

Matt watched her, his forehead creased. "Your friends are always welcome. If they don't have a ride, we can always pick them up."

"Lily doesn't *have* friends," Charlie announced.

"Mind your own business," Lily snapped, her eyes flashing.

Charlie continued as if he hadn't heard her. "I heard kids say they think she's stuck up."

"Charlie!" Matt gave him a stern look, then turned toward Lily. His voice gentled. "It's hard being a new kid in school. Sometimes kids misinterpret a little shyness—"

"*Please,* just drop it, okay?" Twin flags of crimson marked her cheeks. "Can I be excused?"

Charlie wolfed down his second helping of mashed potatoes, then pushed his plate back. "Can we go see the llama?"

"What do we say, Charlie?"

Charlie ducked his head. "Thanks for supper, Jolie. Can I go see the llama?"

Matt raised an eyebrow.

"Uh…please?" Charlie wiggled in his seat. "Can I please be excused? It's gonna be dark soon."

"Clear your place, then. Lily, do you want to go with him?"

Both kids were out the door at the speed of light, slamming the door behind them.

Matt gave Jolie a rueful look. "I'm sorry. We don't go out much, and I haven't been very successful at teaching them their manners. Without their mom…"

"I'm really sorry about your wife. It must have been so hard." Jolie stood and started gathering dishes from the table, stacking plates and glasses and silverware onto a tray. "For all of you."

Matt rose and followed her into the kitchen, carrying a platter and casserole dish half filled with green beans. "Let me help, here. I can wash."

"No, I'll just toss everything in the dishwasher. It only takes a minute." She waited a beat, then added, "How old were the kids when she died?"

"Charlie was just six, and I don't think he remembers her as clearly as Lily does. Lily was ten and took it harder. Still does, though she would never admit it."

"And you? How are you doing?"

"The first year was the hardest. Do you mind?" He nodded toward the coffeepot and mugs on the kitchen counter. "Please, help yourself."

After pouring them both a cup of coffee, he leaned a hip against the counter and watched her fill the dishwasher.

"It's been four years now. I still miss her, but the pain of it has faded."

"Replaced by acceptance."

He blew on the surface of his coffee, then took a long sip. "Yeah, I guess so."

"Charlie told me his mother passed away, but didn't say how."

"Ovarian cancer. By the time she was diagnosed, it was too late. Now there's some sort of annual blood test to help find it earlier. But then…we just didn't know."

"And that's one tough cancer to beat."

He'd had four years to grieve, and to move on…. *I wonder if he has started dating again? If there has been someone special in his life?* The thoughts came out of nowhere, a sneak attack that caught her unaware.

There really was no point in wondering. She should simply accept that she had a pleasant neighbor to visit with from time to time. Anything more would lead to heartbreak.

Matt moved to the front window of the cabin and looked out toward the mountains, where rays of purple, pink and gold streaked through the peaks and valleys, and radiated like a vast light show above the range.

She found herself watching him as she worked. One hand braced high on the window frame, one hand cradling his cup of coffee, he looked…big. Masculine. With the type of broad-shouldered, lean-hipped athletic build she'd always found so intensely appealing. Capable of defending, building, taking charge.

Shaking off those foolish thoughts, she wiped down the counters and surveyed the kitchen, then poured the rest of the coffee into an insulated carafe. "Dessert? I've got peach pie and ice cream."

He turned away from the window, a smile deepening the laugh lines at the corners of his eyes. He had such beautiful eyes…the warm brown flecked with gold made her think of autumn sunshine.

"Pie?"

Jolie laughed as she bent to retrieve the pie she'd set back in the oven at a low temperature. "It isn't homemade, but it's the best I can do. Bread and piecrusts have forever been my greatest challenge." She cut four slices, left two on the counter for the kids and topped the other two with ice cream. "Let's go outside. These spring evenings are sheer heaven."

Out on the porch Jolie nudged several pillows aside and settled onto the porch swing, lifting her plate to gesture toward the other end of the swing. "Have a chair."

Matt hesitated, then set his coffee on the porch railing and sank onto the seat next to her, his forearms resting on his thighs. After he finished his dessert, he set the plate on the railing and reached for his cup, then draped his other arm over the back of the swing.

"How are things going at your clinic?" he asked.

She laughed. "On Thursday I hired my first employee, but she doesn't start until mid-May. I'm hoping Irene and I don't outnumber the patients."

"You'll do fine."

His voice was low, rich, and when his fingers idly toyed with her hair, a thrill of anticipation skittered down her spine. She fought the urge to lean into his touch.

I could get used to this, she thought. *A beautiful Saturday evening. A handsome guy…kids. A taste of what I hoped for, once upon a time.*

Before reality and disillusionment came along.

"Dolly is the strangest creature," he observed, looking out toward the meadow where the llama was following Charlie toward the barn. "With that long, high neck and that shaggy body, she reminds me of an elongated ostrich."

Jolie laughed. "Don't you dare say that around Fred."

"Fred?"

"Walters. The old fellow who owns this place. He dearly loves Dolly, and I think she dotes on him, too. When he came out to visit she hummed at him the whole time. Even let him pet her face, and she's otherwise pretty shy about being touched there."

Matt had been focused on the kids, the llama, the sunset, but now he turned toward her, and his hand stilled at her nape, sending a shiver of sensation clear to her toes. For one dizzying moment she saw his eyes darken, sensed his deepening awareness of her. *Oh, yeah.*

She suddenly imagined him trailing a fingertip down her cheek, settling that sensual mouth over hers…enfolding her in a deep, passionate embrace as he…

"Dad!" Lily called out from the top railing of the fence near the barn. Her arms were folded over her stomach. "Can we go home?"

"In a while." Matt shifted into the opposite corner of the wide swing. "It's a nice change, spending an evening with another adult."

Remember that, Maxwell. You're just a diversion from the nightly hassle of homework and chores.

Charlie and Dolly disappeared into the barn, trailed by the old ewe.

Matt frowned. "Maybe I should go check on what he's doing. For all I know—"

A squeal of delight erupted from the barn. Dolly burst out of the barn in a disjointed gallop with Charlie on her back, his arms wrapped around her neck.

The llama gave a loud screech.

Took a sharp left.

Charlie flew over her neck and landing with a thud. He groaned, rolled over.

Lily screamed.

"Charlie!" Matt roared, launching off the porch swing.

Jolie stared in disbelief as Dolly stopped and turned back, her nose and tail raised and ears flattened in the classic stance of anger. Her jaws worked furiously as she prepared to launch a volley of partially digested feed at her attacker.

Dolly had apparently rethought the matter by the time Matt arrived. With a snort of disgust, she sauntered out into the meadow, her tail still twitching with irritation.

Matt dropped to his knees next to Charlie. "Are you okay?"

Charlie rolled into a tighter ball.

"Talk to me. Are you hurt?" Matt ran a hand over Charlie's arms and legs. "Say something!"

Charlie's shoulders quivered, then shook as he slowly sat up. But his eyes weren't filled with tears, as Jolie expected. They sparkled with delight.

He burst into laughter. "Wasn't that just the coolest thing? She's so *fast!*"

Matt rocked back on his heels, his face pale. *"Charlie."*

"The coolest! Can we get a llama? Or a horse? Wouldn't that be super? I could ride all the time and—"

"Quiet!" Matt reached forward and grasped Charlie by his upper arms. White lines of tension bracketed his mouth and eyes. "You owe Dr. Maxwell a big apology for endangering Dolly. I don't know, but I'd guess a boy your size shouldn't be on a llama. And you could have broken your neck, falling against a rock or tree stump." His voice caught. "You scared me to *death,* Charlie."

He stared at his son, then folded him into a tight embrace. After a long moment he set Charlie aside and rose to his feet. "So now you are grounded," he said with a finality that brooked no argument. "Possibly forever."

The boy's chin dropped to his chest. "I'm sorry, Jolie. I didn't know Dolly didn't want to be ridden, honest."

Taking in Charlie's misery, Jolie had to stop herself from telling him that it was all okay. He needed to learn his lesson, or the next time he acted impulsively he *could* get hurt. "Apology accepted."

Lily hovered at the edge of the conversation. "Dad, I don't feel so good. I want to go home. *Now.*"

"What's wrong?" Laying the back of her hand at Lily's damp forehead, Jolie regarded her thoughtfully. "Do you feel as if you're coming down with the flu?"

Lily pulled away. "No. I just want to go home. *Please.*"

"Do you hurt anywhere?" Matt asked.

"I just want to go home and lie down. I could go by myself."

"No." Matt gave Jolie an apologetic look over Charlie's head. "Sorry to leave you so soon, but I guess we'd better get going. Thanks for a wonderful supper."

"Thank you," Lily dutifully chimed in.

An arm slung around Lily's shoulders, Matt started down the lane.

Charlie scuffed a toe in the dirt. "It was great," he mumbled. "Thanks." He gave his dad and Lily a quick glance, then lowered his voice. "I didn't mean to hurt Dolly, or anything."

Jolie suppressed a smile. "I'm sure she's okay. A little angry, but okay. She'll get over it."

He kicked at another clump of dirt. "There's something else."

"Charlie, come on!" Matt waited at the edge of the clearing, where the lane disappeared into the pines.

"It's Lily."

"Lily?"

"Something's wrong, and I don't know what to do."

Jolie rested a hand on his shoulder. "Is it something at school? The other kids?"

"No…" He fidgeted from one foot to the other. "Not that."

"Troubles between her and someone else?"

"No. I shouldn't have said anything. I gotta go."

"Can you talk to your dad—"

Shaking his head, Charlie spun away and raced down the slope to where Matt and Lily were waiting, leaving Jolie to stare after him.

What could bother Charlie that much—and why couldn't he tell his father?

JOLIE SHIVERED under the covers. She'd turned down the thermostat to fifty-five after Matt and the kids left, preferring the cozy warmth of her down comforters and the fireplace to the furnace, but now the fire had burned down and even her triple layer of lofty bedding didn't keep out the cold.

Somewhere in the mist between sleep and awareness, she imagined what it might be like to snuggle up to someone warm…like Matt Dawson, for instance. The thought made her sigh.

With a yawn, she sat up, pulled one of the blankets around her shoulders and toed around on the floor for her slippers, then shuffled toward the living room.

She'd just reached for the thermostat dial when she heard the sound.

A cry, soft as a kitten's, just outside the cabin door. *It could be a crazed killer, luring you outside,* an inner voice whispered. *A strangler on the loose. Some lunatic survivalist come down from the mountains.*

Her path illuminated only by the last embers flickering in the fireplace, she slipped across the room, thankful she'd pulled all the curtains before going to bed. *I need a dog. A really, really big dog.*

At the kitchen counter she scooped up her cell phone. Then she edged toward the coat closet by the door, where her Ruger 10–22 rifle was hidden on the top shelf.

Moving slowly, silently, she eased open the closet door. Lifted down the weapon. Retrieved the clip from its hiding place in a shoe box on the shelf and slid in ten rounds. In less than thirty seconds she was loaded and ready.

And thankful her dad had insisted that every one of his children learn to use a rifle by the age of eight.

The sound outside was a little louder now, still indistinct. Broken. Like someone trying hard not to sob.

Someone faking a woman's cry?

Or had she just seen far too many scary movies?

She called 911 and reported a prowler. Then slipped the phone into her pocket. Rafe might be off duty, out at Walking Stones helping Thea. How long would it take him to come? Twenty minutes? An hour?

A faint knock sounded through the heavy wood. "D-Dr. M-Maxwell? Please—can you help me? I'm s-so cold."

Common sense warred with an overpowering need to help. She reached out. Hesitated. Then flipped on the porch light.

And found someone staring at her through the glass.

CHAPTER SIX

JOLIE SET the rifle aside and flung the door open. She resisted the urge to rush forward and hug the girl standing outside, for fear she might turn and run. "You came to see me at the clinic, didn't you? How did you get clear up here?"

"Walked," she mumbled.

The two-mile lane leading down to the highway was rocky, rutted, with turns and twists that were hard to negotiate during the day. And in the darkness, in this isolated area, fear of wolves, coyotes and bears would likely have terrified her. "Come in. You must be freezing out here!"

The girl rose stiffly, her head bowed, and slipped past Jolie into the welcoming warmth of the cabin. She stopped just past the welcome mat as if she didn't dare go farther. "Th-thanks."

Jolie lifted the girl's chin gently, searching her face for new bruises. None, thank God. But there were dark circles under her eyes. She appeared gaunt, her parched lips hinting at dehydration. "Are you okay? Do you hurt anywhere?"

"I'm fine," she mumbled, pulling back and dropping her gaze to the floor. Her tangled auburn hair fell like a curtain at the sides of her face.

"What about the baby? Any twinges? Aches? Any bleeding?"

"No." She seemed to fold in on herself, as if trying to make herself disappear.

"Come on over here—by the fireplace. Curl up with those blankets on the couch while I get the fire going."

The girl hesitated, then headed tentatively toward the couch, though there were no obvious signs of pain in her gait.

After locking the door, Jolie turned up the thermostat and rebuilt the fire, and in minutes the room was bathed in warmth and flickering amber light.

She settled into the overstuffed chair to one side of the couch. "Comfortable?"

The girl nodded.

"I don't believe I even know your name," Jolie said gently.

Her voice was barely a whisper. "Megan."

"Is there someone we should call, just to let them know that you're all right?"

Her head shook emphatically, even as a shudder jerked through her. A sob?

"You need a place to stay for a while?"

"Please," she whispered. "I—I'm just s-so cold. I'll clean. Or cook. Or anything you say."

"No child should be outside at night. Of course you can stay." Too many unanswered questions, too many possibilities. A runaway? Victim of abuse? Was her family frantically searching for her this very minute?

But pressing her too hard for information right now might make her flee back out into the night. "I'll make us some cocoa, and then we'll get you settled. Okay?"

Megan pulled the blankets tighter around her shoulders and gave a weary nod.

In the kitchen, Jolie pulled a box of cocoa-mix packets and a bag of mini-marshmallows out of the cupboard, then filled a glass two-cup measure with water and put it in the microwave to heat.

The girl was pregnant and alone, Jolie mused as she prepared the cocoa and set it on a tray. *Maybe Megan was afraid to tell her family…or maybe they'd booted her out of the house.*

When she returned to the great room, Jolie set the tray down on the coffee table that stood between the couch and fireplace. "Here you go, honey. A little cocoa will warm you up and help you relax."

Megan didn't move. The blankets over her rose gently and fell with the deep respirations of sleep. Firelight flickered over her delicate features, accenting the dark circles under her eyes and the bruise—faded now to yellow—that Jolie had first seen at the clinic.

"What happened to you, Megan?" Jolie whispered as she tucked the blankets snugly over the girl's thin shoulders.

The cell phone vibrated against Jolie's hip. She moved to her bedroom and shut the door before answering the call.

"Jolie? Are you all right?" Rafe's deep voice was laced with concern. "You didn't leave much of a message."

"I've got…a girl here. She appeared at my door at midnight. Apparently walked clear up to my cabin alone."

Rafe gave a low whistle. "Is she okay?"

"She walked in the door, seems coherent. An old, good-size bruise on her face, wary of even giving me her last name. A runaway, maybe? Trouble at home? I don't know…she seems awfully scared." Jolie cleared her throat. "And she's pregnant."

"I'm already on my way. I'll be there within fifteen minutes. Can you keep her from leaving?"

Jolie gave a quiet chuckle. "She's not going anywhere fast—the poor thing looks exhausted. Right now she's asleep on my couch."

"I can take her to the sheriff's office down in Big Timber."

"No...please. I think she's better off here, really. At least for tonight."

"We'll talk when I get there."

His truck pulled up to a stop in front of the cabin minutes later. Jolie met him at the door and ushered him in, a finger at her lips. "She's still asleep."

At six foot four he towered over her and probably intimidated most suspects with just a level stare, but Thea's husband also had an infinitely gentle side that showed in his eyes as he looked down at Megan.

"I should have guessed," he whispered. "This poor kid has had it rough."

"You know her?"

"She's Megan Wheeler."

Jolie looked blankly up at him.

Surprise flared in his eyes. "You don't know?"

"She didn't tell me anything, just begged for help, and fell asleep on my couch."

"I told Thea she should say something to you," he muttered under his breath. He hitched a shoulder, cleared his throat. His gaze shifted to the leaping flames in the fireplace. "Megan's father is a drunk. She and her sister, Lisa, were taken into foster care at least twice before I came to town, and I heard that their mother had packed up the girls and fled to a relative's house a few times."

"That's *terrible.*" Memories of past abuse cases flashed through Jolie's mind. She'd provided written statements, had testified in court, but all too often children ended up in the same bad situation as before, where home was a dangerous place to be. Their external wounds might heal, but emotional scars lasted forever.

"I made damn sure Abe knew what would happen to him if he laid a hand on his kids again, but he's been really hitting the bottle lately. She probably came to you because you're family.''

"Family?"

"This is Bobby's ex-girlfriend." Rafe's voice turned cold. "Your brother has been a busy guy over the past six months, in more ways than one."

MONDAY MORNING PASSED slowly. Two patients dropped in. A few people phoned to ask about clinic hours. All Jolie could think about was Bobby's pregnant girlfriend, and the fact that she appeared to be on the run. Why hadn't anyone in the family taken her in? Given her shelter? Protected her?

And why hadn't anyone even bothered to tell Jolie about her?

At noon Jolie flipped over the sign Closed Until One O'clock and raced for her Blazer.

On Sunday Megan had slept most of the day and had offered little conversation when awake. This morning she'd stirred briefly while Jolie got ready for work, but had fallen back into a deep sleep. Jolie had left her a note on the coffee table begging her to stay at least until Jolie returned.

Please be there, Megan, Jolie muttered as she negotiated the tight turns and steep elevations of Coyote Creek Road, and finally crossed over the cattle guard marking the start of the pasture surrounding the cabin. *You shouldn't be on your own.*

The cabin came into view after the lane curved around a stand of pine. Megan—thank God—sat on the top step of the porch, with Dolly hovering close by.

Jolie parked and climbed out of the Jeep, holding a brown paper sack aloft as she ascended the stairs. "Lunch, courtesy of Grizzly's Diner."

The girl had taken a shower and had changed into the emerald-green sweats Jolie had laid out for her. With her long auburn hair tied back in a gleaming ponytail and her face freshly scrubbed, she looked too young to be out of high school.

She gave Jolie a tentative smile. "I—hope it's okay that I'm still here. Really, I don't want to be any bother, and I'll understand completely if you want me to go." As if she'd just convinced herself that it was better to leave, she rose to her feet.

"Sit! I wanted you to stay. That's why I left that note. Besides, I brought all of this and can't begin to eat it myself. I'm *glad* you're here. Honest." Jolie settled on the top step and reached into the bag. "Ham and swiss, or would you rather have a turkey, pastrami and tomato deli?"

Megan shuddered as she sat down again. "Uh…whatever you don't want."

"Come on, I can tell at least *one* of those choices didn't sound good!"

"Um, if I could maybe have the ham and swiss…"

Well, she definitely wasn't the assertive type. Jolie had thought about Rafe's words on Saturday night, sorting through the possibilities, trying to find a reason for the fact that Megan seemed to have no ongoing contact with Bobby or the rest of the family.

Dollars to doughnuts, this girl had never pushed anyone for a nickel, much less tried to finagle her way into the Maxwell family.

Jolie swallowed a bite of her sandwich, barely tasting the fresh sourdough bread or pungent pastrami. "You asked if you could stay here, and work for me."

Megan's chin dropped to her chest. "If I could."

"How old are you?"

"Eighteen. I graduated last spring, same as…" Her voice halted.

"Bobby?" Jolie asked gently.

Megan's head bowed lower.

"Can you tell me what's going on? I can't help you if I don't know how best to do it."

Silence lengthened while Megan focused on snagging little shreds of bread from her sandwich, as if the process were the most thought-consuming task in the world.

"Megan?"

"I—I loved him. Like, forever and ever." She took a deep, wavering breath. "I n-never did it with anyone before and I thought…he said he'd be careful. I didn't think anything would happen, and then…"

"You got pregnant."

The girl nodded. "I didn't even have a chance to tell him, with everything that happened last fall."

Jolie nodded, remembering the poacher who'd killed deer up in the higher ranges last fall, and how Bobby had run off after his car accident. For a while, some had thought Bobby was the poacher. Rafe, Thea and Bobby had caught the guy, but all three of them had been in danger.

"And when you did tell him…"

Megan laid her sandwich on the folded sack and wrapped her arms tightly around herself. "I didn't." Her voice came almost too softly to hear. "My dad did."

Anger flared to life in Jolie's chest, but she steadied her voice before speaking. "What happened?"

"Y-you don't know? My dad went to Robert Maxwell on the day of Thea's wedding and demanded money. *Money!* Like I was just a bill to pay off." The humiliation in the girl's voice was palpable.

Jolie stared at her. In all the rush and excitement of that day, she'd never known that this was going on. "And Bobby?"

"Dad said Mr. Maxwell called Bobby right into the room, and yelled at him." Megan's voice grew almost too soft to hear. "B-Bobby said he didn't care about me. He said he never h-had, and if I got pregnant it had to be with someone else. But I n-never…I never…"

Megan was sobbing silently now. Jolie scooted closer to wrap an arm around her shoulders, and drew her close.

Dad had spoiled Bobby terribly as a child, all of them had. They'd protected and coddled and loved him, perhaps far too much.

Now Bobby drank too much and ran wild. When had he become so callous, so self-centered? And *stupid?* DNA tests would prove everything needed to award child support later on.

Jolie pressed on, needing to know the truth. "Your dad…is he still angry about this?"

"I—I can't go back there. He…I…"

"You don't ever have to—you're eighteen and can decide where you want to live. What about your mom?"

"She…isn't home. She goes to my aunt Leena's with my sister a lot, to get away, but neither of them would dare stand up against Dad over this."

"Where have you been?"

Megan lowered her gaze. "I left almost two weeks ago," she said in a small voice. "I—I stayed with some friends, then with my second cousin…just moved around."

Poor thing. "If you'd like, I can contact the authorities. We can make sure that your father—"

"No!" She stiffened. "*Please,* no."

"Okay, okay," Jolie soothed, giving her an extra squeeze. "I won't."

Megan gave her a wary look. "Promise?"

"Promise." Jolie thought fast, seeking safer ground. There would be another time to delve into her past, to try to set things right. "Do you have a job?"

"I…I did."

"What happened?"

"Some days, Dad wouldn't let me go to...if there was work at home. Then a couple of times he came to the drugstore and he was...was..." She sniffled, rubbed at her nose angrily. "They said they couldn't have him coming around like that. Before that, I worked at the post office. They decided they just didn't need the extra help. But I know they let me go 'cause of Dad."

The daughter of a drunk. Homeless and pregnant at eighteen, in a small community where someone should have interceded on her behalf. Well, *someone* in the Maxwell family was going to take care of this girl and her unborn child.

If Bobby wasn't man enough to take responsibility, then Jolie would take over. *I may never have a family of my own, but this niece—or nephew—is going to have the best of everything,* she vowed silently.

And the next time she saw Bobby, he was going to learn some truths about himself—and about life—that weren't going to be pretty.

BY LATE THURSDAY afternoon Jolie had diagnosed a strep throat and two ear infections, completed several well-child exams and had rearranged the lab three times.

Not exactly a busy week...but things were slowly picking up. The phone rang five or six times a day. A few of them were silent hang-ups—kids, probably—but most were people asking about her services or wanting to make appointments.

Pacing to the front door, she stared out at the late-April sunshine and wished she was on horseback this very moment, riding up to Hidden Lake high above the ranch.

There'd still be snow, no spring flowers yet. But closing her eyes she could imagine the sharp, clean scent of mountain air and feel the easy cadence of a good saddle horse beneath her.

"Hey Jolie, are you okay?"

Startled, Jolie looked down into the upturned face of Charlie Dawson. With green poster-paint streaked across one cheek, spaghetti sauce on his T-shirt and a tear in the knee of his jeans, he looked as though he'd had a very full day at school.

"I'm just daydreaming." She grinned at him, holding the door open. "Maybe someday your dad will let you and Lily come to the ranch with me. We could put you two up on horses."

"Cool!" He worried at his lower lip for a moment, then plopped his backpack on the closest waiting-room chair and unzipped the front pocket. After fishing around inside, he withdrew a crumpled wad of dollar bills. "I need you to do something."

Taken aback, she shook her head. "You don't need to give me money for anything."

He looked over his shoulder through the front doorway. His sister was still coming down the sidewalk at a snail's pace, her face pale. "It's Lily. She…she made me promise not to tell, but something is wrong. I think she needs a doctor."

"Your dad needs to know, so he can take care of her. I can't treat her without his permission."

"But she won't *tell*. And she said if I did, she would tell Dad about the time I—" He broke off, a bright red flush creeping up his neck and cheeks. "Anyway, I heard her cry last night, and she's *really* crabby. I think she's scared."

His sad eyes held compassion born of old grief and loss no young boy should experience. Perhaps he feared losing his sister, too. "Maybe I can talk to Lily, and find out what's going on. Okay?"

At the sound of Lily's footsteps at the door, he nodded and surveyed the empty waiting room. "Maybe if I leave, she'll talk to you better," he said, with wisdom beyond his years. "Can I sit in your office? I can study my spelling words."

Jolie nodded, heard his footsteps retreat down the hall. Perhaps this was all in Charlie's imagination...but maybe not. She stood casually in front of the receptionist's window, one elbow propped on the high counter. "Hi there," she called out as Lily stepped inside.

"Hi." Lily glanced around. "Where's the brat? I saw him come in here."

With her dark blond hair pulled back into a severe ponytail, she *did* look...gaunt. "He's in my office. Did you have a good day at school?"

Lily shrugged and slumped into a chair, then pulled out the liter water bottle she always carried and took a long drink.

"You look a little pale. Have you been feeling all right?"

Averting her eyes, she hitched a shoulder. "Fine. Uh...can I use your bathroom?"

"Sure enough—it's still down the hall where it always—" Jolie caught herself. *Why hadn't she picked up on these signs sooner?* Weight loss...thirst...frequent trips to the bathroom... "Wait a minute, Lily. Do you know where your dad is right now?"

Lily halted halfway across the room. "Uh...he's building something, I guess. He always carries his phone."

"Do you know his number by heart? I'd like to ask him a question or two."

Giving her an odd look, Lily rattled off the number.

"Thanks." Jolie jotted it down in the phone book, then lifted the receiver after Lily disappeared into the bathroom. After five rings the call kicked into his voice mailbox.

"This is Jolie. Call me when you can—here at the clinic until seven or so, or at my place after that. I know you'll be swinging by to get the kids, but I'd like to talk privately."

"*About what?*"

Jolie turned sharply, to find Lily right behind her, her eyes narrowed.

"Are you calling about *me?*"

"What makes you think that?" Jolie smiled at her. "I just have some questions to ask him."

"You looked at me, said I looked sick—"

"Pale, Lily."

"You asked if I felt okay and then right away wanted his number." Lily's defiant tone faded. "Do you think I look bad?"

"Oh, honey. Of course not." Jolie curved an arm around her shoulders and led her to the chairs in the corner of the waiting room. "No one is here. Let's sit and talk a bit, okay?"

Lily balked. Then sank into a chair and stared at the toes of her Nikes.

"Is there anything worrying you?"

"No."

"Um…is anything wrong at school, with the other kids?"

"No."

"With your teachers?"

Lily shook her head.

"Charlie? Your dad?"

"No."

Jolie hesitated, not wanting to pry too deeply. "Sometimes things don't seem so bad if we can just talk about them with someone."

Lily tipped her head against the back of the chair. Her eyes welled with tears.

"Can you tell me about it?"

"I've lost a lot of weight. A *lot*. I feel crummy most of the time, and tired. And that was how my mom felt, too."

"Oh, Lily. Your mom had cancer. But you haven't been diagnosed with anything."

"It's too scary to even think about it." A sob rose in Lily's throat. "My mom suffered a lot, and then she died. And I think that's happening to me."

CHAPTER SEVEN

MATT PULLED UP to the clinic at four-fifteen on Thursday. Waited in the truck for a few minutes, hoping the kids would see him and come running out. No such luck.

This really had to stop. The kids invariably preferred walking to Jolie's clinic and hanging around there during the thirty or forty minutes between the end of school and the time he could pick them up.

They need a mom, an inner voice nagged at him.

Jolie always seemed happy to see them, but once her practice grew, she'd have little time to spare. Maybe she already resented the imposition of her daily visitors and was too polite to say so.

Feeling a little embarrassed, Matt stepped out of the truck and went into the clinic. Bow-decorated pots of flowering plants, each with a gift card, filled the end tables, windowsills, the receptionist's window.

He'd been framing the new gift shop up in the foothills all day. Standing in the midst of all this frippery in his flannel shirt, dusty jeans and steel-toed boots, he felt as out of place as a steer in a dress shop. "Lily! Charlie!"

Two heads appeared at the far-right door down the hallway, past the exam rooms and lab. A spare room, if Matt remembered correctly.

"Hey, Dad!" Charlie said. "This is sooo cool. *Animal Planet* has a show on ve-veminous snakes. Did you know we could have some of those at *our* place?"

"Venomous," Lily corrected Charlie sharply. "They have ve-*nom.*" She gave Matt a nervous glance, then disappeared.

That was strange. "Time to go, kids. We've bothered Dr. Maxwell long enough."

Jolie stepped out of the lab door and shooed Charlie into the room with Lily, then crooked a finger at Matt. "Do you have a minute? We can go into my office."

Today she had her hair up in that same classy knot, and wore trim black slacks with an emerald-green shirt under her white lab coat. Professional. Understated. And those clothes probably cost more than one of his mortgage payments.

He'd practically kissed her on the porch swing last Saturday night, and even now, just following her down the hall, he wanted to run his fingertips over the impossibly soft skin at her nape. Reach for the gold clip in her hair and see that mane of strawberry-blond hair tumble free. Which was exactly the *last* thing he should think of doing.

Once inside her office, she shut the door behind them, waved him toward a chair and sat down behind her desk.

This looked like a serious discussion, and again he felt uncomfortable, realizing the kids had probably been an inconvenience. "Look, I'm sorry about the kids hanging around here after school. I'll make sure they stay at school from now on."

She looked startled. "Why? It's no problem having them stop by. They're always welcome if they prefer to wait for you here instead of at the schoolyard."

"I don't want you to think I'm expecting you to watch my kids."

"Good grief, I don't feel that way at all. I won't always have time to talk to them, but they're great kids." Was that a wistful look in her eyes? "It's nice seeing them."

She'd put up a half-dozen framed certificates and diplomas on the wall behind her desk. Matt shifted in his seat, acutely aware of the college degree he'd never been able to complete, the career goals he'd never achieved. Barb's illness…the avalanche of debt…two young kids to raise…he'd done all right. But if things had been different…

"…so I needed to talk with you privately," Jolie said. "Don't you agree?"

"What?"

A flicker of concern crossed her face. "I know it's not my business, but with both Charlie and Lily upset, I just let them talk."

Already focused on the failings in his life, Matt felt a wave of defensiveness wash through him. What had they been upset about? His failings as a father? Lack of attention? Caring? "My kids came to *you?*"

"I've seen you with your kids. You're a great father." She paused, considering. "But with some things it can be a little easier to talk to a woman, or just to someone outside the family. A doctor, for instance."

Matt felt an icy fist clamp over his stomach as a thousand memories flooded back…the first news of Barb's cancer. All of the other times when there had been cautious hope, followed by bad news.

It looks early. We're afraid it's farther than we thought. We think we see a shadow on the MRI. With luck, the chemo will help. I'm sorry, but we've found mets to the brain and lung.

Feeling a warm hand on his arm, he opened his eyes to see that Jolie had quietly moved from behind her desk, and now leaned against its front edge. Her eyes were clouded with concern. "We're not talking cancer, here."

The word *cancer* drove a stake of ice into his chest.

She must have seen the horror in his eyes, because she

added quickly, "No, not at all. Though after your wife's illness, I imagine that was your first thought."

He numbly stared back at her, but the deepening compassion in her eyes made him look away.

"Look, if you ever need to talk to anyone…about your wife, I'm a good listener. Sometimes people try to bury their feelings and never really deal with what they've gone through."

Matt recoiled inwardly at the thought. He'd handled Barb's illness and death okay. He didn't need consolation from a stranger who could never understand how devastating it had been. Not even if she was a damn doctor. "Just tell me about Lily and Charlie."

"Charlie told me Lily had been crying a lot, said he was worried about her."

"Why didn't he come to me?" He tried to suppress the edge in his voice, and failed.

"Lily made him promise not to tell."

"I'll go talk to her, then."

"Lily's been…um…afraid that she might be dying, like her mother did."

Real panic rushed through him. "Dear God. Is something seriously wrong?"

Before he realized what he'd done, he was on his feet, looming over Jolie with his hands braced on the desk at either side of her. His chair crashed backward to the floor.

"No. At least, not what you're thinking." Jolie pressed her hands gently against his chest. "She's been scared, true, but she certainly doesn't have cancer."

He searched Jolie's face for signs that she was holding something back. Softening the truth. "She's…okay?"

"She's been worried because she just hasn't felt well, and she's lost weight—six or seven pounds in the last month—

without trying. For someone starting at a hundred and five, that's a fair amount.''

She didn't say anything to me. His usual feelings of inadequacy as a single parent didn't come close to what he felt now, and now those feelings somehow transformed into unaccountable anger. ''So why the hell did she come to you?''

''I brought it up, after hearing about Charlie's concerns.''

''And?''

''I hadn't picked up on it until today, but she's been really thirsty, and she makes a lot of trips to the rest room. When she went in the second time this afternoon, I had her give me a small sample of urine so I could do a quick UA—a urinalysis.''

''You did lab work on my daughter without talking to me?''

''It wasn't an invasive procedure—just a urine sample and dipstick. I tried calling you first, but didn't get an answer,'' she said stiffly. ''Given her symptoms I thought it important to try a quick screen. I won't charge you.''

Matt felt his blood run cold. *Lab tests. Screens. News no one ever wants to hear.* ''I didn't mean it that way.'' He righted the fallen chair and sank into it. ''Did you find anything?''

He fixed his gaze on Jolie's, felt every cell in his body freeze. The wall clock ticked away three, four, five seconds—each taking a lifetime to pass.

''I think she may have diabetes. Probably type 1, given the signs and symptoms I see so far. She's young, definitely not overweight. There are significant ketones in her urine. Frankly, if she does have diabetes we're lucky that we're finding it now. I've seen kids who weren't brought into the hospital and diagnosed until they were on the verge of a diabetic coma.''

Visions of every diabetic complication he'd ever heard of swamped Matt's thoughts. Blindness. Kidney damage. Amputations. "My God."

"Look, I know this is overwhelming, but we need to diagnose this definitively. Maybe…it's something else. But if she is diabetic and isn't being properly managed, she could collapse sometime when she doesn't have medical help nearby."

Collapse. Coma. Diabetes. The words spun through his mind in dizzying progression. "What do we do? What's next?"

"I don't want to send her home without knowing more. I'd like to do a quick finger prick and check her blood sugar right now. It's very easy—I've got a Glucometer here in the office."

Matt rubbed a hand over his face. "Whatever she needs."

He followed when Jolie straightened and walked down the hall to the lab, picked up a calculator-size object that must have been the Glucometer, then called Lily into the second exam room.

"This is just a little prick," Jolie said, her voice quiet and soothing. "We want to see how much sugar you have in your blood. Okay?"

Lily, her face pale and eyes wide, held out a trembling hand. She flinched as Jolie took a quick sample from the tip of her finger. Then her shoulders relaxed. "That wasn't so bad."

"I'll bet your last mosquito bite was worse," Jolie teased. She held up the meter.

"Three hundred thirty, Lily. See the digital readout?"

She didn't have to say what that meant. Matt could see it in her eyes.

"This is well above normal. I suspect type 1 diabetes, but we don't base a final diagnosis on just one reading. She should be tested further.'' Jolie smiled and rested a hand on Lily's shoulder. ''Don't worry, you wouldn't believe how easy all of this is these days. There are new ways to test that aren't done on your sensitive fingertips—some are coming out that won't be invasive at all.''

''But the insulin?'' Lily's lower lip trembled.

''Easy. Very portable, with pens that you can carry in your purse, and you'll learn really fast. But we're getting a little ahead of ourselves here. I'd like to admit you to a pediatric unit in either Billings or Bozeman.'' Jolie looked up at Matt. *''This afternoon.''*

Lily's eyes widened. ''A hospital?''

''Don't worry. They can do further testing, and get you started on insulin if need be. It may take a bit of regulation to get it just right, so they can monitor that closely. They also have diabetes educators who can start teaching you what you need to know.''

''Will you follow her care at the hospital?'' His own words sounded hollow, distant, as if spoken by someone else.

Jolie shook her head. ''I haven't applied for hospital privileges. Both towns are too far away for me to provide daily coverage in-patient. Bozeman is closer for you—would you want to go there?''

''Who would we see?''

''I have an old friend—Dr. Gwen Thompson—who's a pediatrician in Billings. I'll give her a call to find out who she recommends. Then I'll do a referral, and that doctor will manage Lily in the hospital. Afterwards, I can manage her care locally.''

''But…there's still a chance she's fine. That she doesn't have diabetes? We could come tomorrow and you could test her again.''

"No," Jolie said bluntly. "With a blood sugar over three hundred, it's in her best interest to go today."

Matt looked away. Outside, the sun was shining. He could hear the rattle and squeak of an old truck lumbering up Main Street. Faint strains of some country-western tune probably coming from the jukebox at the Lone Wolf Bar next door. Ordinary sounds, an ordinary day.

For everyone else in Paradise Corners.

JOLIE TWIRLED a pencil between her fingers. Tapped it on the blotter of the receptionist's desk. Debated about closing up and heading for home.

Jolie had called Gwen for recommendations, found the doctor she felt best suited for Lily's case and made the referral. Matt had dropped Charlie at Ed's house, then left for Bozeman with Lily. Thank God for that. A child with Lily's ketone and blood sugar-levels could decompensate quickly, and end up needing inpatient care including IV fluids and insulin.

She glanced at the clock. Most clinics closed at five o'clock, and staying longer was a waste of time, given the number of walk-ins she'd had. *In a few months you'll be too busy to even catch your breath,* she reminded herself.

The door of the clinic opened, and a woman in a Resistol and a denim jacket stepped inside. "Hello," Jolie called out.

"Hi."

Jolie did a double take at the familiar, husky voice. *"Thea?"*

"And Dad, I hope." Thea looked over her shoulder. "We came in to talk to Dillon over at the feed mill about some delivery problems, and Dad's been irritable every step of the way since we left. He says he's got to get home for a conference call with some cattle buyers from South America, but I think he smells a trap."

"So you aren't here just for a tour?"

"That, too." Thea's smile turned apologetic. "I really am sorry we haven't been here until now."

"Believe me, I remember what calving season was like. Think we can get him to agree to an exam?"

"I've been praying on it all week." Thea held the door open for Robert, who stopped just inside the door.

At over six feet, with a powerful build and a commanding presence, he seemed to dwarf everything else in the room.

Taking off his hat, he used it to gesture around the waiting area. "Looks good."

"Hi, Dad. Would you like to see the rest?" Jolie came around the reception desk and tipped her head toward the hallway. "Won't take but a minute."

"We need to get back."

Thea dangled the truck keys in the air. "I'm driving. I'd like to take a minute to see what she's done with the place."

"Get on with it," Robert growled. "Then we leave."

Dear old Dad. Jolie had sworn she would never marry someone with a gruff, controlling personality like his. Though maybe, she thought with mild amusement, she'd gone a bit overboard in the caution department. Her college roommates had often teased her about her propensity for dating guys they termed spineless twits.

She led the way down the hall, pointing out the new paint, the refinished cabinets, the new countertop in the lab. "My neighbor put in a new back door. The council wasn't too concerned, but he thought there was a risk of break-ins. Rafe said so too, when I first moved in."

Thea leaned against the wall, a thoughtful look on her face. "Your neighbor, huh? I don't suppose he's single and available..."

"I'm definitely not looking for a guy, Thea. That's one of many areas where I've had little success."

Thea grinned. "Then why do I see just a hint of a blush?"

"The lighting," Jolie lied. She shot a quick glance at her father, who stood in the hallway, clearly ready to leave. Thea was right—he did appear short of breath, even after the short walk from the truck and several minutes of rest. His color didn't look good at all.

"As long as you're here, why don't you let me listen to your heart, Dad?"

He impatiently checked his watch. "I don't have time."

Knowing he wouldn't stand still for casual conversation, she got right to the point. "You were diagnosed with CHF—congestive heart failure—last Thanksgiving, but refused definitive tests. Without good medical care, you're going to get worse."

"I work hard eighteen hours a day. Most guys half my age can't do that."

"You're too busy to take care of yourself?"

"Too busy to fool around with a bunch of doctors running up my bill. Thea, it's time to go."

"I'm not just a doctor. I'm your *daughter,* and—"

"Althea! *Now.*" Turning on his heel, Robert stalked down the hall and disappeared out the front door.

"I guess this didn't go too well," Jolie said, sighing in defeat.

"If this was a comic strip, he'd have smoke pouring out of his ears by now." Thea slammed her hands on her hips with obvious frustration. "I don't guess I'll be able to lure him here again, anytime soon. Remember that crazy schipperke dog Mom had years ago? Nice enough in the house, but she was a terrible runner. If she got loose, she'd be on the lam for days and no one could catch her."

"And if one of our friends did catch her, she never let that person touch her again. She never fell for the same trick twice."

"Dad won't either."

"We'll figure out something." Thea's worried expression relaxed, and Jolie smiled at her, suddenly aware of how wonderful it was to be with her sister again, to be with someone with whom she'd shared a thousand experiences while growing up. *This is what I've been missing all along.*

"I guess I'd better get out there, or he's going to hot-wire that truck—or maybe he'll just *order* it to start."

"Keep trying with him, and I will too." Jolie shook her head slowly, knowing that nothing would help unless Robert chose to accept the truth. "There's a sense of powerlessness associated with chronic illnesses that's hard to accept, especially for a man like Dad. Refusing to deal with his CHF could be fatal."

"No, it won't be," Thea said flatly. "Whether he likes it or not, I'm going to make sure he lives a long time."

MEGAN HAD SUPPER waiting when Jolie pulled up to the cabin an hour later. The aromas of garlic, beef and sour cream wafted through the door as she stepped inside. Rising above it was the even more enticing scent of still-warm cookies.

"I hope you don't mind," Megan said in a rush, her hands gripping the back of a kitchen chair. "I thought you might be tired, and I was here anyway. I found a box of hamburger stroganoff mix, and there was some ground beef in the fridge. Is that okay? I could start something else—"

Jolie crossed the kitchen and gave her a quick hug. "It smells wonderful. Thank you."

The dark circles under Megan's eyes had faded, but the nervous darting of her gaze revealed her fearfulness. "I...I didn't mean to be snooping in your kitchen, or anything. Honest."

"Oh, Megan. I'm *happy* you made supper." Jolie moved to the stove and lifted the lid of a pan. "Vegetables, too!"

"And there are cookies. I made chocolate chip. Is that okay?"

"My favorite. How did you guess?"

A tentative smile tipped the corners of Megan's mouth. "The five bags of chocolate chips in your cupboard."

OVER SUPPER Jolie weighed the options, considered how best to discuss them without spooking Megan into running. As she finished a last forkful of the casserole, she measured her words carefully. "We need to talk about your future."

Megan froze. "You want me to leave?"

"Of course not." Jolie moved her plate to one side. "I'm new to practice in Montana, and don't yet know about the local agencies. I called my sister Cassie because she works with the child services system."

"Welfare?"

Jolie shook her head. "If Bobby is responsible for—"

Chair legs screeched against the wooden floor as Megan jumped up and wrapped her arms tightly around her waist. "You don't believe me, either."

This wasn't going to be as easy as Jolie had hoped. "That's not it. I believe you. But if we're going to get the courts to grant you support, we have to have proof. Please, just sit down. Let's talk about your choices."

Her eyes bright with tears, Megan wavered, then finally sank back onto the front edge of her chair.

"Honey, I know your dad made it hard for you to even *find* a job in this town, let alone keep one. So you need to be thinking about how you can provide for this child. Unless you are considering other options…"

"*Abortion?*" Megan's voice filled with horror.

"No, it's a bit late for that." Thankful Megan hadn't

chosen to terminate her pregnancy, Jolie resisted the sudden impulse to give her a hug. "Have you thought about adoption?"

"N-no. I couldn't *ever* give up my baby."

"Then we need to look into how you're going to cover medical care and financial support."

Megan's expression changed to desperation. "I'm not going to the Maxwells for money. Never. Not after what Bobby said."

"This is his financial responsibility, too. When paternity is proven—" Catching the glimmer of anger in Megan's eyes, Jolie talked faster, and wished she'd had time to discuss the matter with Thea at the clinic. "Even if we know the truth already, DNA proof will *force* him to provide child support."

Megan's lower lip trembled. "Does that mean he could sue for custody?"

Dangerous ground, here. "That doesn't seem very likely."

"Dad said Robert Maxwell might pay him a lot to get his hands on my baby." A tear spilled down Megan's cheek.

"That's illegal."

"And terrible. Now my Dad hates me 'cause I w-wouldn't cooperate. He'd figured this would be his meal ticket for life." She stood and started edging toward the door.

"Please, stay. I can help you. We can talk about what you want to do with your life. School, a job, whatever. I'll provide prenatal care at no cost."

Megan's chin lifted in defiance. "I can't accept charity."

"Then work at the clinic, if you want to. Maybe we could even check out the classes at the community college in Rapid Creek. You could commute and still have a job and a place to stay." Jolie raised her hands in supplication.

"Give your baby a chance, Megan. You need good medical care. A chance to make something of yourself."

Megan stopped at the door, her head bowed. "I could work for you? Really?"

The glimmer of hope—and fear—in her voice nearly broke Jolie's heart. "Absolutely. We can talk about it right now. But first let's grab some of those cookies, okay? I've been craving chocolate chips for a week."

DAD ROLLED his truck window down. "Remember what you learned at the hospital, Lily."

Like I could forget. She'd gone to the hospital in Bozeman Thursday afternoon, and hadn't gotten out until Sunday evening. Her head still reeled from all she'd had to learn, and do…and accept, for the rest of her life. *Diabetes sucks.*

She swung her backpack over a shoulder and trudged up the sidewalk to the school.

Several groups of boys loitered near the front entrance. A cluster of girls—the most popular girls—sat to one side of the broad front steps, laughing loudly together.

Walking past them into school every day felt like passing through a gauntlet, and she felt almost invisible to the other kids who hung around the school before the bells rang.

Dad's words echoed in her thoughts. *"Sometimes kids misinterpret a little shyness…"* Was it her fault maybe?

Swallowing hard, she nodded a greeting to Sara Forman, one of the kids from fifth-hour math, who reached the front door at the same moment she did. Sara's dad owned the hardware store in town, and Lily had seen her working there after school. "Uh…get that math assignment done for today?"

Sara's eyes flared wide with surprise, then her mouth wobbled into a tentative smile. "Um…yeah. I think so."

Lily scrambled for something else to say, but Sara beat her to it.

"Was that your dad who dropped you off?"

"Yeah."

"I got to help him once at the store. Even when I mixed up his change, he was really nice."

"I guess."

"You wouldn't believe how rude some people are." Sara rolled her eyes. "Hey did you get those last three problems in our assignment? I was sick the day we went over that stuff."

Sara might be one of the most popular kids, but she was a whole lot nicer than the rest of them. Trying not to seem pathetically eager, Lily murmured, "Maybe I could help."

"Super. Can I have your number?"

"Yeah." Lily dropped her backpack to the ground, fished out a piece of paper, jotted down her phone number and handed it over.

Sara stuffed it in a front pocket of her own backpack. "We've lived here forever, so we're in the phone book." The earsplitting five-minute warning bell rang above their heads. "Gotta run—my locker's on the third floor."

In a flash, she disappeared into the crowd streaming down the hall. Lily fell in step with the others. To her right, one of the girls, Gina—Lily couldn't remember her last name— who hung around with Sara gave her a curious look, then offered a smile.

After all this time in Paradise Corners, Lily felt a glimpse of hope. Maybe she would make some new friends. She opened her mouth to speak.

And ran straight into the tall, rock-solid, most gorgeous guy in the whole school—Clint Heath, the oblivious object of her first real crush. His voice was deeper than any of the other boys' in eighth grade, and he looked like he ought to be in the movies, with that wavy chestnut hair and those green eyes. He was even taller than his older brother, Jerry, who sometimes picked him up after school in a really cool red Mustang. Not that Lily paid much attention.

Embarrassment burned through her like wildfire as she stumbled backward, then fell into him again when a crowd of students moved past and pushed her forward. "Oh!"

His large, strong hands reached out, grabbed her shoulders and pulled her next to the wall. "Hey, take it easy, Blondie."

"I—I..." The words caught in her throat as she stared up at him, praying she didn't look totally stupid.

He sauntered away and left her staring after him, still tongue-tied and dazzled.

Lily gave herself a mental shake and headed for her own homeroom at a run, barely hearing the final bell as she slipped through the door. *Clint Heath!* She shivered with awe as his voice echoed through her thoughts. *"Hey, take it easy, Blondie."*

Nothing—not Dad, not homework, not even her stupid diabetes—could ruin what had just become one of the best days of her entire life.

CHAPTER EIGHT

MATT STOPPED BY the clinic Monday morning to give Jolie the folder of medical records he'd brought from Bozeman the day before. He found her at the front desk.

"They said they were mailing these, but I insisted on copies so you'd have the information right away. Just in case."

She rose and took the folder, then leaned against the wall and flipped through the records inside. "Has anyone in your family had diabetes?"

"No...but several of my wife's relatives did."

"I'm sure you learned a lot at the hospital about the insulin, the testing, her diet, what to do when she is ill?"

"Yeah." And he was still was trying to absorb it all.

Her eyes filled with sympathy. "There's a certain element of anger and grieving that occurs whenever someone learns that they have something like this."

For the parent, too. He could already feel the worry seeping into his bones as he imagined the battles ahead. With their erratic schedule, they'd mostly grabbed breakfast on the run, and supper more often than not was pizza. Easy casseroles. Steaks thrown on the grill.

He'd never had to think in terms of insulin and carbohydrate exchanges. The whole concept scared him. Carefully planned meals, carefully scheduled times—what if he made mistakes? Caused Lily harm?

"Compliance is especially hard for teenagers who want

to be just like everyone else,'' Jolie continued. ''She may have a hard time adjusting. But it's *imperative* that she take care of herself.''

How well he knew. Matt moved to a window and stared out. ''I wish it was me instead of her,'' he muttered.

''You'll be able to help her a great deal, Matt. She's lucky to have a dad like you.''

''But I can't change her diagnosis, and I can't make it easier for her. She'll still face those needles every day.''

''But you can be positive, and supportive. It's a new challenge for all of you, but she'll adjust.'' Jolie stood and joined him at the window. ''I've seen kids do wonderfully well. Once they understand their disease, and learn how to manage things like sports and diet, they do better than a lot of adults. Kids half Lily's age do their own testing and insulin—with supervision, of course.''

Little comfort. ''The doctor at the hospital said we should follow up with you in a week, and that you'll take things from there.''

''No problem at all. Would you like to set up a time now?'' She gave the appointment book on the desk a rueful glance. ''Not that finding a slot will be too difficult. Sometimes I wonder…''

''I'd bet this place will be packed before you know it.''

''Maybe not. I keep hearing the oddest rumors. That I've lost my license. That I'm facing a whole host of malpractice lawsuits. One even had me making a fortune in California by performing abortions in a garage for bargain rates,'' she confessed with a hint of a smile.

''Surely most people don't believe that garbage.''

''One can hope, but rumors are hard to fight. What could I do, go on the local news and read the list, denying each one?'' She gave a short laugh. ''With my luck, the national tabloids would pick it all up as fact. *Killer Doc Strikes Montana Town.*''

"You'd definitely put Paradise Corners on the map.'' He looked down into Jolie's upturned face. Early-morning sunlight streaming through the windows lit the highlights of her strawberry-blond hair, turned her eyes more green than blue.

She seemed to sway toward him, and he thought about how it would feel to kiss her, here and now. To hold her close and breathe in the scent of her.

Only now she was more unapproachable than ever. No matter what he wanted for himself, what mattered was his daughter. No personal issues could be allowed to affect her care.

If by some chance he and Jolie were to become...close...what would happen if the relationship ended? Bitterness, anger? Which would make the endless appointments and consultations ahead uncomfortable for everyone concerned.

Wanting to stay longer, knowing he should leave, he shifted uncomfortably in his chair. "Guess I'd better make tracks. We're behind on the gift-shop project because I've been staying in Bozeman with Lily.''

He gave her a curt nod, spun on his heel and headed for the door without looking back.

MEGAN HESITATED at the door of Benson's Drugstore, wanting to buy a magazine, then walked past. There was no chance she could go in without the clerks whispering about her. No one could have forgotten that last humiliating day she'd worked behind the soda fountain, when her dad had lurched into the store dead drunk and bellowed her name over and over.

Memories were long in this town. Old scandals were rehashed forever, made darker and more dramatic with time.

If she stayed in Paradise, twenty or thirty years from now the same gossip would still follow her out of a room.

She's one of those low-class Wheelers, you know. Abe's girl. Got herself pregnant by a Maxwell, probably figured she'd get to live in that big house at Walking Stones Ranch. Goes to show the Wheelers don't have the brains our good Lord gave a hen.

With a shudder, Megan walked a little faster past the drugstore. If Agnes Benson noticed her pregnancy…

Coming into town this morning had been a welcome change, but now that she was here, there just wasn't much to do until Jolie took her back to the cabin at noon. Time could pass slowly in a town the size of Paradise Corners.

Megan wandered farther down Main Street, past the post office, to the street leading to the high school. Looking down the block to its two-story brick facade made her think about Bobby, and the fun of being in school with Racey Taylor, her best friend.

Her heart heavy, she glanced at her watch and then headed toward the school. The students inside were all busy in class, still having fun with their friends, as carefree and optimistic as she'd once been.

With a sigh she sat on the massive front steps of the school and turned her face up toward the weak sunshine.

Maybe by the first week in July her baby would be here. The thought was scary, and overwhelming…and even a little bit exciting. What would it be like, having—

The sound—a very familiar sound—of an old Chevy truck coming up the street made her heart skip a beat.

She was on her feet in a split second, wondering why she'd ever left Main Street. Why she couldn't have just sat at the clinic and waited.

There were blinds on most of the school windows, so someone inside might not see her. Still, there were houses all around the school, and across the street a lady with a rake was in her front yard cleaning out the dried refuse of last year's flower garden.

Megan rose and started down the steps toward her.

Abe Wheeler pulled the truck to a rattling stop at the curb, right in Megan's path. Leaning across the seat of the truck, he cranked down the window. "Get over here. *Now.*"

I'm eighteen. I don't have to do what he says. She started to skirt the truck, giving it a wide berth.

The door squealed open on rusty hinges. As he climbed out, his narrowed eyes glittered beneath the shade of his beat-up old western hat. "I said, *come here.*"

The lady across the street shaded her eyes with a hand. "You need any help?" she called out to Megan.

Abe spun on his heel to glare at her. "This here is my daughter, and she's gotten herself into a hell of a lot of trouble."

Recognition flared in the woman's eyes when she got a good look at him, followed by a healthy dose of caution. She lowered her eyes, set aside her rake and headed for her house.

Abe watched her disappear into the house, then he turned to Megan with a satisfied smirk. "Respect."

Megan could think of a few other words that fit a little better. *Dislike. Disgust. Anger.* She kept walking, avoiding his eyes.

"You messed up big time, getting pregnant by some spoiled rich boy who don't even give you the time of day," he spat, starting after her. "You and me are dirt to that family. How does that make you feel?"

His words hit all too close to home. A sob rose in Megan's throat as she broke into a run.

But Abe caught up to her in a few strides, grabbed her arm, and spun her around. "That family is gonna pay for what that boy done.'' His voice lowered to a growl as he jerked her close. ''And you, Missy, sure as hell owe me an apology.''

She warily raised her gaze to his face, then drew in a sharp breath as she focused on a wide scab that snaked across his forehead and disappeared under the brim of his hat.

''Yeah—that was your doing, all right. But maybe it wasn't enough. Maybe you were hoping I'd die when you shoved me into those rocks.''

''Let me go!'' She pulled away, taking advantage of the split-second when his grip loosened.

He frowned as she started backing away. ''Where have you been?''

Remembering the scene he'd caused at the drugstore, Megan knew specifics were a dangerous thing. ''I've been…a lot of places. With friends.''

''You get in my truck, hear? Who's gonna keep a roof over your head? Give that baby a place to live?'' He wheedled. ''We'll sure as hell make them Maxwells treat us right.''

At the sound of another truck coming up the street, he stopped and looked over his shoulder. A black Ford crew-cab pickup cruised slowly up Aspen Street, and pulled to a stop behind Abe's truck. The man who stepped out was huge, more important-looking for his height than the uniform he wore. Rafe Rafferty, Megan remembered after a moment's thought.

''Any trouble here?'' he called out, tipping his Stetson back with a forefinger as he sauntered toward them.

The woman who'd been working out in her yard now stood watching from her front window, her arms folded. *Thanks,* Megan mouthed silently, hoping she understood.

''Guess you have all sorts of protectors in this town,''

her dad muttered in a voice so low that only Megan could hear. "But I'm not finished with you."

"I'm not going home!"

"That deputy may have married into the Maxwell family, but he sure as hell can't stop me from talking to my daughter." Abe turned toward Rafferty. "My daughter got herself in trouble and ran off," he said loudly. "She needs to come home so I can take care of her."

Megan edged away, shaking her head. Her father's words sent a shaft of ice right down her spine. *Don't listen to him. Please.*

Apparently Rafferty didn't, for he barely spared Abe a glance. "Do you need a ride somewhere, Megan?"

Relief flooded through her. "*Yes.* Thanks." Megan edged around her dad and started for the deputy's pickup.

Abe made no motion to interfere, but the back of her neck tingled as she climbed into the front seat, and she knew her dad was watching.

Maybe it wasn't such a good idea to stay with Jolie after all. All Megan would bring her new friend was trouble.

Rafe settled behind the wheel and gave her a comforting smile. "Where to, ma'am?"

To the end of the world, if you've got the time.

JOLIE STAYED at the clinic for the rest of the day after Rafe stopped by with Megan and offered to take her to Jolie's cabin.

Unaccountably restless, Jolie paced the hallway. Sat down to study Lily's hospital reports. Then she started once again on the billing statements she'd been working on the day before.

Irene would be starting Monday after next, she realized with a sigh of relief. The woman seemed to be a competent, take-charge sort of gal, and could help with the bookwork and a variety of office duties until the practice grew busier. She could help teach Megan basic reception skills as well, if the girl was truly serious about wanting to work.

As Jolie stepped out of the clinic at five o'clock and locked the door behind her, the phone rang. She went back inside and hurried across the waiting area, catching it on the fourth ring. "Paradise Corners Medical Clinic, Dr. Maxwell speaking."

"We need an appointment." The woman's voice was brittle as ice.

Jolie grabbed the appointment book and a pencil. "The name?"

"My son, Danny. Danny Aiken."

Bobby's friend. The one who'd been seriously hurt in the accident last fall. Jolie's heart twisted. "Oh yes, I remember the name, though I don't believe we've met."

The following silence vibrated with hostility.

"Hello? Mrs. Aiken?"

"Do you have anything tomorrow afternoon?"

Not a problem—the schedule was blank. "Three o'clock?"

"Fine."

"Is he having any problems?"

"He's going to have problems all his life," the woman snapped. "Up until recently he was at a rehab facility in Billings, but now I guess we'll have to see you." She hung up.

The shelves behind the desk were filled with yellowed folders. Records going back for decades, many for people who'd probably long since died or moved away.

Jolie rounded the desk and ran a finger along the tabs. Twelve charts for various Abrahams…five Ackerlys…six Adamses…on the second shelf down she found three Aiken charts. *Bingo.*

Pulling Dan's, she took it down the hallway to her desk so she'd be sure to read it before he came in, then headed out the front door once again.

"Hey, Jolie!" a familiar voice called out as she finished locking the door.

She turned, and found an old Toyota parked at the curb. Her sister Cassie stood at the open door, her bright red hair aflame in the spring sunshine. Cassie's seven-year-old son, Zak, sat in the front with his head bowed, and didn't so much as look up at Jolie's approach.

Cassie laced her fingers and rested them along the top edge of her car door. "I was heading out to the ranch, and thought I'd...um...just swing by and see if you were here. I'm afraid I wasn't very sociable when we last met."

The words were right, but Cassie's tone was distant as ever, reminding Jolie just how far they had to go before they could be close. If that were even possible, given all that lay between them.

They'd always been polar opposites—Jolie the older sister, the quiet peacemaker, admittedly a little too authoritative at times. Cassie, three years younger, the rebel, who resented Jolie's interference. The difficult time after their mother's death had only made things worse. Jolie's departure for college had probably been a relief to all concerned.

"Do you want a tour of the clinic? Believe me, it doesn't take much time."

Cassie shook her head. "Another time. We've got to get out to the ranch." Her expression turned pensive as she ducked down to look in at her son. "Can't you say hi to your aunt Jolie?"

He darted a quick glance up, then riveted his attention on the coiled lariat in his hands.

Jolie headed for Zak's side of the car and drummed her fingers lightly on the windshield to draw his attention.

As if he hadn't heard, Zak continued to run his fingers along the stiff rope.

"His grandpa gave it to him," Cassie explained as she straightened. "He practically sleeps with it."

Jolie leaned down to admire it through the open window. "That's a good one. Better than I had when I was your age. I'll bet you're already better with your rope than I ever was with mine."

Zak twitched a shoulder—already emulating the silent, modest response of the ranch hands whenever a compliment came their way.

"Maybe you can show me someday, buddy." She stepped away from the window and raised an eyebrow, and Cassie shook her head.

Little progress, then. Zak had been terribly withdrawn since Cassie's divorce almost a year ago. Jeff Warren had walked away from the marriage without looking back, and certainly hadn't shown any compassion for or interest in his young son.

Jolie could think of more than a few things she'd like to say to that man if she ever ran into him.

"So how are things going?" Cassie asked. "With your clinic, I mean."

"Fair."

"Busy?"

Jolie gave her a rueful smile. "I've somehow acquired two employees, and I think we'll outnumber the patients for some time to come."

"There isn't another doctor anywhere close. You'd think the community would be lined up outside your door."

"Funny thing—I thought that, too." Jolie hesitated. "It might have been easier if I'd come in as Jane Doe instead of a Maxwell."

Pursing her lips, Cassie nodded. "The name does have a certain...element of recognition around here."

"I met Megan Wheeler."

Cassie didn't even blink, much less give away what was apparently common knowledge in the Maxwell family. "Nice girl."

They don't even feel I'm a part of the family anymore. "I *know* about her now."

Cassie's eyes flared wider, then she gave a meaningful glance toward Zak and lowered her voice. "Thea and I found out about her pregnancy when Bobby ran off for a while last fall. She made us absolutely *promise* not to tell anyone...not even Bobby, because she wanted to tell him herself. Since you were living way out in California, Thea and I figured we'd keep that promise. At least, until later on."

You couldn't even tell your own sister? Bobby is my brother, too. Jolie tried to ignore the hurt that curled around her heart. "She's staying at my place now because she doesn't dare stay at home. Her...father."

Cassie's mouth fell open. "I didn't know. Megan told me she was fine there."

"The bruise on her cheek tells a different story. We need to talk."

"I'll call you." Cassie glanced at her watch. "Zak and I are staying overnight out at the ranch, but I could come to town after I drop him off. Maybe at six?"

"Okay. Megan will be there, but we can take a walk up to Silver Falls and talk along the way."

Cassie nodded, her expression grim.

After watching her drive away, Jolie headed for her own vehicle, her stomach fluttering. She and Cassie had just had an adult conversation—the first one in years! Down the road, perhaps there could be more. Maybe Bobby had given them all a chance for new beginnings.

And with all of them pulling together, perhaps his child would have a chance at happiness that none of them had been able to achieve.

CHAPTER NINE

CASSIE DIDN'T ARRIVE at Jolie's cabin until almost seven o'clock. She got out of the car and stared at Dolly and the old ewe, her mouth open. "I'll bet Zak would love them," she said, shaking her head in amazement. "He *loves* anything on four legs."

Jolie stepped off the porch to meet her. "He's welcome anytime. Did you happen to see Megan on your way up here?"

"Nope." Cassie slammed her car door and pocketed her keys.

Jolie frowned. "Rafe brought her back at noon. She should be here." She turned on her heel and headed back up the porch steps. "I'm going to check her room again."

Megan had arrived just over a week ago with a duffel bag and the clothes she wore. Jolie had glanced in the room earlier, but now she took a closer look.

Her heart sank as she quickly opened the closet and dresser drawers. Nothing. Not even a note. Why hadn't she checked sooner? In the kitchen she searched for a note, but again found nothing.

Out in the yard Cassie leaned against the hood of her Toyota, watching the llama graze. "Find her?" she called out, looking up at Jolie's approach.

"She's gone—with all her things. But why? She and I had talked, and agreed she could stay. She was even going to work at the clinic a little because she didn't want to accept what she thought would be charity."

Cassie gave her a knowing look. "I suppose you had everything figured out for her, too?"

A recurring theme with Cassie. Memories flooded back of her youngest sister's wild escapades. Jolie had never possessed the experience or the authority to make a difference, and Cassie had resented every effort to corral her.

Jolie took a steadying breath. "I was trying to *help* Megan. The girl is pregnant with Bobby's baby, comes from an abusive home situation and had no one else to take her in. I didn't even know about Bobby and Megan until this week. It hurt, Cassie, that none of you shared a family matter like this with me."

"We were afraid that if we pushed her too hard, she might just take off."

"Thanksgiving was a very long time ago."

"We kept our promise to her." Cassie lifted her hands palm up. "And anyway, you were here just overnight at Christmas, and only a weekend for the wedding. What could you have done?"

"Probably nothing," Jolie admitted. "Apparently, she didn't get to tell Bobby herself. Abe showed up right after Thea's wedding and confronted Dad—demanded support, damages, the whole nine yards."

"Maybe that's why our dad looked so stressed after the reception." Cassie gave a bitter laugh. "It's so typical of Dad to keep something like this under wraps."

"He probably figured he'd let the lawyers deal with it."

"I've only been back once since the wedding. I figured everything had been handled by now. Is Megan getting financial support?"

"Support? Bobby denied the baby was his."

"*What?*"

"Now Megan wants absolutely nothing to do with him. Without proof, the Maxwell lawyers aren't going to step in."

"But legally—"

"She says she'll run away rather than allow DNA testing," Jolie said flatly. "Even now, maybe she's hitching a ride to who-knows-where."

Cassie's forehead creased. "Why would she run now, if she had a place to stay?"

"Rafe said she had a confrontation with her father in town." A shiver crawled down Jolie's spine. "What if Abe came after her while I was still at the clinic?"

She reached through the open window of the Blazer and withdrew the cell phone she'd left on the seat, then punched in the phone number of the sheriff's office, drumming her fingernails on the roof of the vehicle as she waited. *Three rings. Four.*

Rafe picked up on the fifth ring, and Jolie rapidly related her concerns about Megan's disappearance.

He gave a low whistle. "I dropped her off after lunch, and waited until she locked the doors of your cabin before I left. She didn't seem too worried about her dad bothering her again."

Because she'd decided to leave town, or because she'd decided to give in and go home? Neither option was good.

"Last night Megan seemed happy with the idea of staying at my place. Surely she would have talked to me before deciding to leave."

Rafe didn't miss a beat. "I'll take a run out to her dad's place."

"Thanks. I'll scout around for her, too. Do you know of any friends she might go to?"

"Racey Taylor...Kim Rawlins...Jerry Heath, they're the only ones I can remember." He paused. "They were all

Bobby's friends too, though I haven't seen them running together since the accident. They used to all raise hell on Saturday nights.''

Jolie gave him her cell phone number. ''Let me know if you hear anything, okay? I'm really worried about her.'' After she hung up, she looked up to see Cassie studying her. ''What?''

''When I was a kid, I figured you just had a big thing about control.'' She gave a self-deprecating laugh. ''I guess now I'm finally seeing things from an adult perspective. Maybe you really did care.''

''I never wanted to be in control, but after Mom died, Dad could go a month without saying a word to us. Beth tried hard, but she just wasn't Mom…and she had quite a time with you. I tried to help, but I just wasn't Mom, either.''

''Thea was out working with the livestock, and you had your nose in a book when you weren't trying to be dictator. I…I guess I was the lost soul.''

''Try *the rebel*,'' Jolie said dryly.

''That, too.'' Though she was now thirty, the cocky grin Cassie flashed made her seem sixteen once again. ''The last thing I could handle was Dad's brand of iron-handed patriarchal parenting. I think half the crazy things I did were just to spite him.''

''I remember.'' Jolie could still hear the heated arguments that had waged between their father and his wild middle daughter. Cassie had come in late more nights than not, defying him at every turn.

Cassie tapped a forefinger against her lips, lost in thought. ''About Megan…I'll help any way I can. There are lots of resources we can check into for financial assistance, child care, legal counsel…whatever she needs.''

"That'll be great. She ought to receive support from the Maxwells, though, not welfare."

Cassie gave Jolie a snappy military salute—one softened by a faint smile instead of the sneer that had marked her teenage years. "If you find her, I'll do my best."

Again, Jolie felt a shift in their rocky relationship, a hint of possibilities. "I'm going to drive down the highway and see if I can find her, just in case she's trying to hitchhike. You're welcome to come with me—or you could make yourself at home in the cabin."

Cassie glanced at her watch. "I'd better get back to the ranch. I hate to leave Zak alone out there for very long— he seems to like being with his grandpa, but you know how busy Dad is."

Ignoring her disappointment, Jolie matched her sister's breezy tone. "Zak probably helps slow him down a little. Thanks for coming up here. Maybe we can get together again sometime soon?"

"Umm...sure. Sometime soon."

But probably not.

Jolie sighed as she watched Cassie's car speed down the lane, then disappear around the first bend.

Regaining what they'd all lost was proving much harder than she'd imagined.

A DRIVE UP AND DOWN the highway, five miles in either direction—five miles north, and five miles south of Paradise Corners—revealed no sign of Megan Wheeler.

Rafe called, and said he'd checked out the Wheeler place, but found only Abe Wheeler and Megan's younger sister, Lisa. He'd also found her friend Racey outside the grocery store and had questioned her, to no avail.

You can't help someone who refuses to be helped, Jolie

reminded herself as she headed for home. Her heart ached at the thought.

Coyote Creek Road twisted and turned past rocky out-croppings and dense stands of pine. A mile up from the highway a narrow lane turned off to the south, wound be-tween several massive boulders, then headed up to Matt's place. Only the tip of his chimney showed through the trees.

Maybe Matt had seen Megan. Not likely, but Jolie turned up his lane anyway, telling herself that she was looking for Megan, not hoping to run into Matt again.

She'd seen Matt's place years ago, remembered it mainly for its rustic stone exterior and spectacular view of a deep valley and the Crazy Mountains beyond. It was as impres-sive as she'd remembered, with gray stone walls and steep, half-log-trimmed entryway and eaves.

A wealthy family had built the house as a mountain re-treat many decades ago, then fallen on hard times in the 1960s. Since then it had passed through a number of hands...perhaps because the steep approach made access difficult. Perhaps because the cityfolk who purchased it found the isolation less appealing than they'd first thought.

Now, years of short-term owners and subsequent neglect were showing in the missing shakes on the roof and the tumbledown split-rail fence surrounding the yard.

Charlie bounded out of the house, a black-and-white puppy at his heels, and ran up the stone walk to Jolie's car as she pulled to a stop. "Hi! You came to see us!" He grinned from ear to ear. "It sure was fun coming to your house for supper. You have the coolest llama ever."

"Is anyone else at home?" Jolie lifted a hand to shade her eyes and scanned the area, wondering if she might catch sight of Megan.

"Lily's inside." He rolled his eyes. "She's been *really* crabby. Dad's home, too—but he's in the shop out behind the house.'' Charlie cupped his hands at his mouth and raised his voice to an ear-splitting level. "Da-ad! We got company!"

She might have just quietly left for home, but no one could have missed Charlie's voice. It echoed from the cliffs above the house, sending a flock of birds flapping and squawking up into the air.

"Thanks, Charlie," Jolie said dryly. "Maybe you could point me in the right direction so I can meet your dad partway."

He nodded, and turned up a path that led around to the back of the house. The puppy cocked his head at her and, finally deciding she was a stranger, gave a timid *woof* before racing after Charlie.

A stone building matching the house stood a few hundred feet away, at the edge of the clearing. Matt stepped outside as Charlie and Jolie approached. He stared at Jolie, clearly surprised, then his mouth curved into a welcoming smile.

Jolie tousled Charlie's hair. "Do you suppose I could talk to your dad alone for a minute?"

His face fell. "Uh...sure." He snapped his fingers and turned toward the house. "C'mon, Samson."

Jolie stopped, watched Matt approach. And almost forgot to breathe.

He really had the most arresting face. Lean, chiseled. With laugh crinkles at the corners of his eyes and dimples that slashed deep when he smiled.

"Nice surprise," he said, raising an eyebrow. "Anything wrong?"

Warmth eased through her, welcome as sunshine on the last days of Indian summer. She'd been right to stop here. Matt Dawson would be a man to count on, no matter what the situation. She'd found herself thinking about him far too much over the last few weeks...

"Jolie?"

"Um…right. I've been looking for a young girl who was staying with me. Have you seen her? Dark auburn hair, about five foot four, eighteen."

Matt frowned. "You think she's lost up in the hills?"

"No…at least, I don't think so. She's from this area and had some trouble at home. She landed at my place, but now her duffel bag is gone. I'm afraid she's taken off again, and I hate to think of her on the road at night, alone…"

"Did you call the sheriff?"

Jolie nodded. "He's looking for her, too. She must have come down our road. I was hoping that maybe she'd stopped here, or that you'd at least seen her."

"Neither one." He reached out and laid a comforting hand on her shoulder. "I'll help you look, though. Lily can stay here and watch Charlie."

That hand on her shoulder might have been meant to be comforting, but his touch sent sensations shimmering through her nerves, made her want to step closer. Except that the most important thing right now was to find Megan and make sure she was safe.

"Any chance she'd head across country instead of taking the road? Someone raised in the area would know all the shortcuts. I've seen a bloodhound in the deputy sheriff's car. If she doesn't turn up, maybe he'd be able to tell us something."

"Jed?" Jolie tried but failed to suppress a laugh. "That dog is a big sweetheart, but he must have the worst nose in all of bloodhound history. Of course, he did come through when Rafe and Thea had tracked the poacher last February. But usually he can't find a dog biscuit if it slides out of sight."

"Would she risk hitchhiking?"

Jolie shuddered. "I hope not."

His forehead creased with concern, Matt glanced up at the house. "It's almost seven o'clock, and it'll be dark before long. I'll tell the kids I'll be gone a while, and then I'll go with you."

She waited while he went in, and through the open windows heard him warn Lily and Charlie to lock the doors tight and stay inside. He stood on the porch until they both heard the deadbolt slide home from the inside.

"Let's go," he said, tipping his head toward his truck. "I'll drive, you can keep an eye out for her."

He opened the truck door for her. Took her arm to help her climb in. "I could get used to this," she murmured as she fastened her seatbelt.

"Search posses?" he grinned at her as he slid behind the wheel and slammed his door shut.

No, spending time with you. "Uh...yes."

"Should we head out to the main highway or cruise through Paradise first?"

"Let's start in town—that won't take long at all."

It didn't. With an area of no more than twelve square blocks, except for the roads that meandered up into the hills, the town was quiet at this time on a Monday evening.

After cruising up and down each street, Matt pulled up in front of the Lone Wolf Bar at the south end of town, then hooked an arm over the back of the seat. "Where should we go next?"

"I don't know. I'd just like to know that she's—" Her cellular phone rang. "Hold on."

Rafe's voice came through loud enough that even Matt would be able to hear. "I found her."

"Is she okay?" Jolie gripped the phone tighter.

"She'd gone down to the highway and was planning on hitching a ride, but she was having second thoughts by the time I found her. A few truck drivers honked at her—scared her half to death. I talked her into coming back to your place, if you still want her to.''

''Absolutely!''

Muffled voices came through the receiver as Rafe apparently asked Megan some questions, then he returned. ''I'm taking her out to her dad's place so she can pick up a few things. We'll be up your way in about an hour.''

Matt cocked an eyebrow after Jolie ended the conversation. ''Problems?''

''No. *Good* news. Rafe is bringing her back in about an hour.''

She expected Matt to turn the truck around and head through town toward Coyote Creek Road, but he just sat there, pensively studying her, as if debating the wisdom of his next move. ''You have some time before she arrives. I can call Lily and make sure everything is under control at home... Want to stop for a drink? Coffee?''

This was no request for a date, no promise of anything more. Just a simple, friendly gesture. But Jolie's heart lifted anyway—even as her brain started sending urgent, conflicting signals. ''Thanks. Coffee would be great.''

He threw the truck into gear and made a U-turn in the street. Grizzly's was just a block away, across from Jolie's clinic, but the town's bachelors tended to congregate for a late supper every night after the family crowd had left, and all the parking spaces in front were filled. He drove past, then turned up the alley behind Jolie's clinic and parked there. They climbed out.

As they reached the curb, a heavily loaded old lumber truck creaked past them on Main. Matt casually draped his arm around Jolie's waist as they waited for it to pass. *Just a normal protective gesture,* she told herself. *Just an instinctive male thing.*

But when she glanced up at him he wasn't watching the

truck go by. His eyes were on her, as warm and inviting as melted chocolate, that irresistible dimple deeply creasing his cheek—as if he was enjoying this moment more than he'd expected.

"Um—I think we can cross," she murmured, suddenly feeling a little out of her depth.

He didn't step away from her until he opened the door at Grizzly's, where he ushered her in with the grace of a man escorting a date to a fine restaurant.

For a moment, she allowed herself to imagine that this *was* a date. That they were dining at a good restaurant, then looking forward to a late night of dancing and...

Mona Rangel, the middle-aged owner and manager, led them to a table in the corner. She handed them both menus, but her smile was directed at Matt alone.

No surprise there. She'd been Bobby's sixth-grade schoolteacher. Jolie remembered him crowing about the fact that she'd lost her job when she refused to pass him out of sixth grade. Jolie had always felt the woman had deserved a medal and a raise for standing her ground, despite Robert Maxwell's influence on certain members of the school board.

"Hi, Mona. I love your place," Jolie said. Stunning Robert Bateman wildlife prints adorned the varnished log walls, and the open beams overhead gave an airy, spacious feel to the small building. A pewter vase of fresh flowers brightened every table. "The atmosphere is perfect."

"Thanks." Mona responded politely. She lifted the pot in her hand. "Coffee?"

"Please."

"Matt?"

"Black, thanks. Any of your blackberry pie left?"

Mona gave him another smile. "I've had a piece held back all day, just in case you showed up."

In a flash she'd poured steaming cups of coffee, and had set a thick slice of blackberry pie in front of him.

He clearly savored each bite. "Is there any sort of pie you *don't* like?" Jolie teased, watching the dessert disappear.

"Nope."

"And this is how you stay in such good shape?" she marveled, shaking her head.

His eyes twinkled. "I'm working on it."

She cocked her head as if giving it great thought. *Actually, there's nothing to work on—you're perfect.*

He forked up the last bite. "The kids and I have been talking about hiking the hills past your cabin. Like to come along?"

His intent gaze settled on hers as if her answer truly mattered, and the thought sent a curl of pleasure right through her. "Sure—why not?"

She'd lost count of how many times she'd told herself that it would be best to stay just friends with Matt Dawson. Now she'd lost track of the reasons.

Sitting across from her, lean and tanned and fit, he radiated a level of sensual promise she'd never expected. Never *wanted* to find. Not in her neighbor, not in the father of one of her patients.

Lifting an eyebrow, he laughed. "You appear to be getting cold feet already, and we haven't even set foot on a trail. I promise, we'll make it easy on you."

Her bone-deep Maxwell competitive drive kick-started into high, leaving all thought of sex, sin and Matthew Dawson in the dust. "Easy on *me!* Before moving back here, I jogged several miles a day—" She caught the glint in his eye and sputtered to a laughing halt. "I'll do my best to keep up with you and your kids, Dawson."

"We wouldn't want you to get hurt trying."

Her coffee cup raised partway, she stilled and looked at him, suddenly aware of something much deeper sparking between them. Mutual interest taken to the next level without conscious thought. There was no denying the undercurrent of anticipation as they stared at each other in silence.

"More coffee?" Mona had soundlessly materialized at their table.

Jolie stared blankly at her for a moment. "Uh—yes. Please."

But it wasn't a good idea to stay longer. Distance would be much, much better. After a few sips, she glanced at her watch. "We'd better get back," she said a little too quickly. "Your kids will worry, and Megan will be arriving soon."

"Yeah." Matt gave her a wry smile as he tossed a five and a dollar bill on the table and rose. "I understand."

He took her elbow as they threaded their way through the tables, but released her arm when they stepped outside and headed for his pickup. And though he opened and shut her door, he was careful not to touch her again.

CHAPTER TEN

ON TUESDAY MORNING, Jolie pulled up to the rear of the clinic and dropped her head briefly to the steering wheel. *Okay, Maxwell. You tried to help Thea with Cassie, and you failed miserably on all counts. How are you going to deal best with Megan?*

Megan had come back after her abrupt departure Monday evening somber, with tear streaks down her face, and had gone to bed early after saying little.

She'd been asleep when Jolie left for the clinic this morning, but even knowing the girl would probably sleep much of the day didn't calm Jolie's concern about leaving her alone. Tonight, she'd talk to her and—

Knuckles rapped against her windshield.

Startled, Jolie jerked away and twisted in her seat, instinctively hitting the door locks with her left hand. It took another second to focus on the stranger looming outside her door.

"Bobby! You scared me half to death." She swung the door open, one hand over her racing heart. "What are you doing here?"

"Stopping to say hi." From the twinkle in his eye, she suspected he'd snuck up on her car to scare her. Before his accident, Bobby had taken great delight in teasing his sisters. His actions were not always appreciated.

She glanced around, but there was no trademark blue truck from the ranch in sight. "How did you get here?"

Taking a deep breath, she tried to soften her sharp tone. "I didn't think you were supposed to be driving."

"I'm not." His expression turned mulish. "Though I think that's a real crock. I said I wasn't gonna drink and drive anymore. So what do they want? If they took away the license of every guy—"

"I get the picture." The fourteen-year span between them had never seemed wider. Bobby might be nineteen, but he had a lot of growing up to do. "You're in town just to see me?"

That brought out his first real smile since she'd moved back to Montana. "Yeah. Well, I've got an hour until I gotta meet a guy out at the fairgrounds for my community service. But I had Herman drop me here so I could see your place." He ducked his head boyishly. "You being my favorite sister and all."

His first real smile as well as a bit *too* much of his infamous charm. "I'm honored," she said dryly. "Would you like a tour?"

He nodded, but didn't seem particularly interested as she led him through the back door and showed him the layout of the exam rooms, office and waiting area.

"So, what do you think?"

His smile wasn't as broad as it had been outside. "Uh. Great."

After unlocking the front door, she shooed him down to her office. "Sit."

He sat, reluctantly, looking as if he was ready to bolt.

"Now, why did you *really* stop by?" She settled into the chair next to his, in front of her desk.

He jerked a shoulder. "To see your place?"

"Wrong answer. What's up?" For just a moment his teenage bravado slipped, and she saw a hint of confusion and fear sweep across his face. "Is Dad being hard on you?"

"That sure as hell wouldn't be new," he said bitterly. "I've tried. Honest, I've tried so damn hard after everything that happened last fall. But me and Thea could kill ourselves over that ranch, and nothing would ever be good enough for him."

Jolie reached out and laid a hand on his knee, quietly encouraging him to continue.

"If I never saw another cow again, it would be too soon." He shrugged. "And now I'm stuck, without wheels, and—" He fell abruptly silent.

"And?"

Not meeting her eyes, Bobby launched himself out of his chair. His fight-or-flight reactions were apparently well tuned—he was definitely fleeing now. "I've gotta go, or old man Bishop out at the county fairgrounds is gonna be pissed."

She followed him to the back door. "Is this your first day of your community service?"

"Yep, and then there'll just be nine hundred ninety-one hours of hell to go." He stopped at the door, his hand on the knob. He didn't turn around. "I...heard Megan Wheeler is staying with you."

Jolie edged forward to partly block his exit, hoping he wouldn't leave. "That's right. She's a friend of yours, isn't she?"

All of the fire seemed to drain out of him as he leaned his forehead against the door. "Yeah, I guess."

You *guess?* Jolie bit back the first scathing comment that came to her mind. "I understand that her father confronted Dad at Thea's wedding."

Bobby closed his eyes. "Yeah."

"Want to talk about it?"

"No...yes...I don't know."

"You know she's pregnant. Her father says the baby is yours."

A scowl darkened Bobby's face.

Jolie stared at him. "You think she's causing trouble for *you*?"

He didn't answer.

"Bobby, I've got a young girl at my cabin right now who is scared, hurt and angry. She's facing a tough situation with a lot of courage, and you don't want to *talk* about it? Does she deserve this?"

When he didn't answer, she continued. "You know what kind of man Abe Wheeler is. He *forced* her to reveal the name of the baby's father."

Bobby's head bowed.

"Now she's refusing to confirm it, even though she needs and deserves financial support during her pregnancy, because you hurt her so badly when you told Dad the baby isn't yours."

Bobby gave a harsh laugh. "Dad—"

"*Your* dad may be full of fire and brimstone, but he sure doesn't lay a hand on you. She's had to leave home because hers *does*. Abe's determined to make her cooperate so he can try to go after Maxwell money. Think about what that means."

Muscling Jolie aside, Bobby tried to jerk the door open. She stopped it with her foot.

"I don't know anything anymore," he said miserably.

"I'll help you with details. Megan is now homeless, thanks to you. She wants to leave Montana for good, which means you might never see your child. *Ever.* If she disappears, we can't hope for DNA testing, and the Maxwell lawyers won't arrange any financial support without proof.

Your child could grow up in poverty, for all you know. Do you care?''

He took a sharp breath. ''I just had a few drinks. Now my best friend might never walk again, and his family lawyers are like vultures, circling over the kill. My girlfriend got pregnant—'' He swallowed hard. ''How was I to know that this would all happen?''

Surprising both of them with her burst of strength, Jolie grabbed Bobby's arm and swung him around. ''So things are really tough for Bobby Maxwell, right?''

''I can see you don't care, either.'' He glared at her, his chest heaving.

She glared right back. ''You're wrong. I do care. So you come back and talk to me when you're ready to grow up, Bobby. The family coddled you from the day you were born. That's not your fault.'' She lowered her voice and emphasized each word. ''But now it's your choice whether you act like a man and take responsibility, or just whine and sulk about how tough your life is.''

Stepping out of his way, she let him leave.

He marched down the alley, heading toward the fairgrounds with his head high and shoulders rigid.

All pride and no sense, Jolie thought sadly. *Maybe not even a heart.* How much more harm would he cause before he finally decided to grow up?

MIDDLE SCHOOL IS A BUMMER, Lily thought glumly, doodling pictures of princesses and gossamer-winged fairies down the side of her notebook. The lunch menu looked yucky. There were still three and a half days until the weekend. It was way too warm in here, and she was too tired to even listen anymore.

Worse, the math teacher was boring and...

Silence fell. The kind of expectant, tense silence before

something really awful is about to happen to someone—when everyone holds their breath and is glad it's not *them*.

She froze, looked up toward the front of the room. And found the teacher staring straight at her. *Oh, no. Did she ask me a question?*

"Lily. Are you okay? Do you need to go to the nurse's office?" Mrs. Porter's forehead creased with concern. "Do you need some help?"

She knows. Dad must have brought that doctor's letter to the school, or talked to her teachers already! Horror washed through Lily. *Don't say any more. Please, no more!*

The entire class swiveled in their seats to look at her with open curiosity. The kind reserved for major accidents on the highway and truly horrible social disasters.

"No...no, I'm fine. *Really.*" But with embarrassment clogging her throat, she choked on the words.

Mrs. Porter started threading her way through the casually arranged tables, heading straight for Lily's.

Clint Heath sat at the next table, like always. He hadn't said much of anything to her since the day she'd bumped into him in the school hallway, but now he looked from the teacher, to the other kids, then to the mortification that must have shown on Lily's face.

He stood up abruptly and moved to Lily's desk, took her arm and hauled her to her feet. "I'll take her out into the hall, Miz Porter," he announced. "It's hot in here."

Stunned, Lily blindly followed him out the door. *Clint Heath had come to her rescue!*

From behind them, the teacher called out, "Thank you, Clint. Go straight to the nurse's office. I'll call her to say you're on the way."

Out in the hallway, Clint shut the door then made a fist and drew it sharply downward in a gesture of satisfaction. "Yesss! We're outta there!"

Back in the classroom a buzz of excited whispers rose until Mrs. Porter's voice sharply ordered silence.

He peered at her more closely. "Hey, are you okay?"

"I...I'm fine."

Except she did feel crummy...sort of queasy, with a headache starting to pound at her temples. It was hot, even out here in the hallway. She lifted a wrist to wipe at the cold perspiration on her forehead. "Thanks for helping me out of class."

He shrugged. "You're a friend of Sara's, right? She's my second cousin. Anyway, I hate math."

"Maybe I should go back in."

"Mrs. Porter is the most boring teacher in the whole school. You sure won't miss much."

Great. Now he probably thinks I'm boring, too, for even thinking about going back. She tried to think of something cool to say, but her thoughts grew fuzzy at the edges, as if wrapped in cotton wool. *I want to go home to Chicago. I want everything to be like it was last week, before I ever heard about blood sugar and insulin and syringes...*

Way down the hall, past the principal's office, a curly gray head of hair popped out into the hallway.

Clint sighed. "There's the nurse. Come on." He eyed Jolie uncertainly. "Should I tell her to come down here?"

"No." Lily started down the hallway, but her feet didn't seem to be moving in the right direction and the seams of the gleaming waxed floor started to waver, like the flowing tail of a horse...

OUT AT THE GIFT-SHOP building site Matt startled when his cell phone rang. Within seconds of answering the call, he was in his truck and heading back to Paradise Corners.

The diabetes educator at the hospital had explained hypoglycemia and insulin and emergency care. He'd known these situations might occur. But nothing had prepared him for actually *hearing* his child was in trouble.

What if Lily had been alone at the house? Off on a field trip? Oh, God—what if it happened at night sometime, and he didn't even know?

At the school, his steel-toed boots echoed like cannon fire as he strode down the hall to the nurse's office. Faces peered out of classrooms as he passed. A group of kids quietly heading into the school library turned to stare at him, then collapsed into excited whispers.

"He looks like he's out to *get* someone—like Arnold Schwarzenegger—"

"Terminator!"

"Shh!" A woman materialized at the door of the school library, spared him a swift glare, then herded her charges into the library.

In the nurse's office, he found Lily sitting on the edge of a cot, doubled over, her arms wrapped at her waist. A woman hovered over her with a half pint carton of juice in her hand.

"I'm Matt Dawson. Is my daughter okay?"

The gray-haired woman extended her free hand. "I'm Reva Baxter, the nurse for all three schools here in Paradise Corners."

Lily bent lower over her arms and moaned. Pulling up a chair, Matt sat down beside her and curved an arm around her shoulders. "How is she?"

"This has been a traumatic experience," Reva murmured. "Her first insulin reaction, from what she's been telling me. Her blood sugar was down to fifty. I gave her a half cup of orange juice, and fifteen minutes later it was up to sixty-five, so I gave her a half cup more." She's up to a hundred ten now." She tipped her head toward the paper lying on her desk. "I followed the doctor's instruction sheet that you left in the main office this morning."

His mind spinning, Matt gave her a distracted nod. "Maybe I should take her to the doctor right now. We have an appointment on Friday, but I don't want to wait that long."

A sob shook Lily's thin shoulders. "I don't want to go there. I don't want any of this. It isn't fair!"

Reva gave her a comforting pat on the shoulder. "No one asks for diabetes, but millions of people have it and do just fine. It just takes a while to get this all regulated. Even if you do everything exactly right, your insulin needs can vary during adolescence."

Sniffling, Lily leaned against Matt. The nurse grabbed a box of tissues and held it out to her, but Lily averted her eyes. "I hate all of this!"

"*Lily.*" Matt said quietly. "She's just trying to help. We all are."

Snagging a few tissues from the box, Lily took a deep, shaky breath. "Thanks," she mumbled.

"You two get going," the nurse said. "I'll call ahead and let Dr. Maxwell know you're coming over."

Reva gave Lily a quick hug, and suddenly everything—the motherly hugs and pats she hadn't had for years, her fear and embarrassment and futile anger—all crashed in on her.

Giving way to her overwhelming emotions, not caring if she was still in the nurse's office with a stranger looking on, Lily turned into her father's arms and burst into tears.

AT THE SOUND of the front clinic door opening, Jolie set aside Lily's chart and rose from her desk to greet her next patient.

Lily and Matt had stopped in before noon, Lily's face

streaked with tears and Matt's expression grim. Though she knew better, Lily had skipped breakfast, and now she'd experienced the result of taking insulin without eating properly. In time, she'd learn to carefully manage her diabetes, and should experience few difficulties.

Dan Aiken's problems were a whole different story.

The teenager in the wheelchair gave her a tentative smile when Jolie appeared in the waiting room of the clinic, but his mother's face was hard, impassive.

"So you're Dan Aiken. Nice to meet you." Jolie walked across the room and extended her hand.

He managed to lift his partway, then dropped it in his lap. "H-howdy, ma'am."

She knew he was nineteen, but instead of muscular and fit, he had the pale, almost porcelain appearance of someone who hadn't been outside in a very long time. With the silver-blond hair and those soft blue eyes, he could have passed for an angel, though she'd bet her favorite stethoscope that he wouldn't want to hear that. Even in his current state, there was a glint of challenge in his eyes.

Dan's old clinic charts were cursory at best. After the illegible scrawl of Doc Grimes ended, there were random entries by a series of physician's assistants—a tetanus shot, a few sutures, a bout of bronchitis in 1997.

"Want to come on back?" Jolie asked.

Following her, Mrs. Aiken pushed his wheelchair into the first exam room.

"What can I do for you today?"

His mother reached into a denim bag suspended between the handles of his wheelchair and withdrew a thick folder. "These are photocopies of Dan's hospital records," she said coldly. "Surgical reports...discharge information...everything."

Jolie accepted the folder and leaned against the exam table. "I'll glance through these now and then study them later."

"Go ahead." Probably in her late forties, Mrs. Aiken's weathered skin bore the dry, deep wrinkles of someone who'd worked hard outside all her life, and the bitter expression of someone who neither found nor expected much joy in her life. "Like I told you, the doctors at the hospital said we had to establish contact with—" she faltered over the words as if they tasted bitter "—a doctor close to home, now that Dan's out of the hospital."

Dan's mouth tightened. As clearly as if he'd spoken aloud, Jolie heard him say, *Don't treat me like I'm not even here, dammit.*

For a vital young man at the cusp of independence and adulthood, it must have been hell losing all control to countless doctors and nurses...and his mother.

"Are you comfortable?" Jolie asked him, pausing over the first document.

"I—I'm—" He seemed to search for the word.

"He's fine right now," Mrs. Aiken snapped, hovering at his wheelchair as if ready to protect him from assault. "His improvement has been amazing, but he still has a way to go."

"I see." Jolie scanned the discharge summary, her heart turning over at all the boy had been through. *Oh, Bobby. Do you even realize what you did to your friend?*

Comatose for weeks, Dan had suffered a temporal blow when thrown from the back of Bobby's pickup truck, resulting in language and swallowing difficulties. Tube feedings had given way to pureed foods by December; he'd advanced to soft foods by March. His speech had improved markedly, but he still had residual speech defects and was being followed by a speech pathologist in Billings. No wonder his mother had spoken for him.

Jolie tried to hide her dismay at the rest of the discharge summary.

The boy had also suffered a traumatic cervical spine injury—a teardrop fracture with cord involvement resulting in quadriplegia. After three months of extensive physical therapy he'd finally been discharged from the program because his progress had slowed markedly.

From his mother's obvious concern, Jolie guessed the woman would have preferred ongoing efforts. But insurance and personal financial limitations were sometimes cruel realities to families still living with hope.

Emotion clogged Jolie's throat. Tears burned beneath her eyelids. This beautiful boy had nearly died, and might never walk again, because Bobby had chosen to drink and drive. *Distance,* she told herself harshly. *This is a patient. This is your job.*

After a few moments, when she could again control her voice, Jolie looked up and found Mrs. Aiken's hard eyes staring at her. "What about rehab? Will therapists do home visits?"

"None of them travel this far from the city," she said stiffly. "We have an exercise program to follow every day, and we'll be driving to Billings twice a month." A glaze of unshed tears glittered in her eyes. "When he starts showing real improvement, we'll find a way to get him back into rehab."

Now wasn't the time to delve further into the case, with Dan sitting between them. But that angry, stubborn tilt to his mother's head, and his discharge from the rehab hospital, told a different story: a family warned not to expect much improvement, a mother determined to prove the experts wrong.

Mrs. Aiken had taken on an immense task just to have her son at home.

"I know this must be very, very hard for Dan and your family," Jolie said slowly. "It doesn't change anything, but I want you to know that my entire family regrets beyond measure that accident last Halloween."

"Do you?" Mrs. Aiken said bitterly. "*Do you?* It's bad enough that your family's lawyers kept your brother out of jail. He nearly *killed* my son, and the charges were reduced to a slap on the wrist. Now they're going to fight us tooth and nail to make sure Dan has as little support as possible."

And if I could change that, I would. "The insurance companies will handle most of that."

"A lifetime of support? Therapy? It could never be enough."

Jolie gave Mrs. Aiken a sympathetic smile. "I promise to give Dan the best possible care."

"Daniel has had two bouts of pneumonia since the accident. If I had car trouble way out in the middle of nowhere, with him already ill…" Mrs. Aiken's voice caught. She swallowed hard. "We need a local doctor. Otherwise we'd never, ever come to a Maxwell."

Mrs. Aiken stepped away from Dan's wheelchair. Lowered her voice. "Now I'm just praying that all the rumors about you aren't true."

CHAPTER ELEVEN

"DO NOT HARASS the sheep. Do not get on the llama, trespass in Jolie's barn or wander through her house. Is that clear?" Matt propped his hands on his hips and gave Charlie a stern look. "We'll be here for just a few minutes."

Charlie gave him a guileless grin in return, slid down the porch banister, then raced toward the edge of the clearing where Lost Coyote Creek tumbled through a maze of boulders.

Lily, who'd plopped into a wooden Adirondack chair at the far end of the deck, looked up from her book and scowled. "I don't want to go on any hikes. Saturdays are supposed to be fun, not work. And I don't think I should have to watch that beast of a brother again this century."

"Lily." Matt's voice was low, laden with warning.

"*Sor-or-ry.*" She dragged the apology out into three long syllables. "But *you* try to keep track of him. Did he tell you what happened in the hardware store after school yesterday? Or about what he did in your shop just before we came up here today?"

Matt sighed. "Tell me."

"I promised not to."

"*Lily.*"

Her mouth curved into a mutinous pout.

"Is the shop likely to go up in flames?" His expression darkened. "Do we owe the hardware store any breakage fees? Is there any other destruction I need to know about?"

"No..." she slumped farther down in her chair, then capitulated after a moment's thought. "He knocked over a whole revolving rack of garden seeds in the store, but I think we got everything in order again." She shuddered. "There must have been five hundred of those stupid little packets. Do you know how much *alike* the green-vegetable packets are? That tall, skinny guy watched us like a hawk and complained the whole time."

Matt growled words that Jolie didn't catch.

"Oh, and in your shop? Charlie just tipped over a few buckets of nails. He shoveled them up—most of 'em, anyway."

"There were different *kinds* of nails in each of those buckets. Sorted."

She buried her head in her book. "Not anymore."

Matt shifted his gaze to the creek, where Charlie's whoops and hollers were punctuated with splashing. His shoulders sagged.

"The kid needs a *cage,*" Lily muttered under her breath. "But does anyone listen?"

"Well," Jolie said brightly. "Should we go on that hike?"

"Not me."

Matt shifted his gaze to his daughter. "You can stay here and read, if it's okay with Jolie."

"Of course it is." Jolie glanced at her watch. "Have you two met Megan Wheeler? She's been staying with me for the past two weeks. She ought to be waking up pretty soon."

Lily eyed the cabin doubtfully. "Maybe I should just go home."

"Please don't. Megan might really enjoy some company. She's a few years older than you, but you'll probably like each other. She can tell you all sorts of things about Paradise Corners, and the people around here.''

"Well…" Lily sighed dramatically. ''I guess.''

Minutes later, Jolie and Matt were headed up a path. Charlie bounded ahead with a short, child-size fishing pole protruding from his backpack and binoculars swinging from his neck.

''Any wildlife within a mile is no doubt fleeing for the next county by now,'' Matt said as he stepped over a fallen aspen trunk. He raised his voice. "Charlie! Stay within sight or we go home.''

The little boy was waiting around the next bend for them, kicking at pinecones strewn across the trail. ''Jeez, Dad. You old guys are so slow!''

''Thanks, kid.'' Jolie stepped forward and tousled his hair. "Tell me how old thirty-three is when *you* get there.''

Matt shifted the weight of his own backpack, then folded his arms over his chest. ''You were a Cub Scout in Chicago, son. Tell me what you learned about hiking safety.''

Charlie kicked another pinecone and watched it arc into a rock-strewn ravine. ''Have a map, and a compass, and a first-aid kit…and a *really* good knife.''

''I'm thinking more in terms of behavior.''

''Hike with a buddy.''

''And?''

''Don't run?''

''And?''

Charlie rolled his eyes. ''Stay together?''

''Good enough. There could be bears up here, or coyotes…even wolves, I hear. Or other hazards you wouldn't expect. Slow down, okay?''

Charlie gave a grudging nod, then slowly headed up the narrow trail. Within a few strides he'd escalated into a fast jog punctuated by slam-dunk leaps at overhanging pine branches.

"Getting tired?" A corner of Matt's mouth lifted as he looked down at Jolie. "Of hiking, or my son?"

"Not at all." Jolie took a deep breath, savoring the crisp mountain air. "I wish we'd done this sooner."

"You're a patient woman."

"Charlie's a great kid. Full of energy, true, but he has a big heart. You've done a great job with him."

After a few strides, Matt shook his head slowly. "Sometimes I'm not at all sure." As they rounded the next curve, he held out an arm and stopped. "Look at that, will you?"

A few feet ahead, Charlie stood staring out across a steep valley. A half-dozen elk grazed on the opposite slope, while several fawns bucked and played amongst them.

"They're probably very new," Jolie whispered. "They're usually born in May or June."

"Wow! They are so cool!" Charlie exclaimed. "I wish we could get closer."

"They'd be off and running. They aren't nearly as curious about you as you are about them." Jolie gestured farther up the path. "If I remember right, there may be a pond up ahead. You might see something else interesting up there, if you're really quiet."

Charlie gave her a double thumbs-ups and moved quietly up the trail.

"I hope this isn't going to be anything with fangs or claws," Matt said under his breath.

"Hopefully, just furry and cute."

He glanced over his shoulder. *"Hopefully?"*

"I came up here a few times on horseback when I was a kid, and we never saw any sign of bears."

The path rose and wound past several boulders tall as Matt's head, then stretched across a small meadow. At the far side lay a crystal-clear pond, fed by a stream tumbling down the side of the mountain.

A shrill whistle split the air.

Charlie breathed a sound of awe as he stepped off the path and sank onto a boulder to watch several marmots playing a game of tag near the pond. The size of large cats, they sported brown fur with buff around the neck and belly, and were completely oblivious to the interlopers along the path.

Jolie slid her pack from her shoulders and unzipped the top. She tossed Charlie a plastic bag filled with day-old bread and fresh vegetables for the marmots. "They aren't used to people, so be really quiet when you scatter this on the rocks, then come back here," she said. "You can eat your lunch while they eat theirs."

Under his father's watchful eye, Charlie picked his way slowly down the trail and quietly spread the food along the edge of the pond. The marmots sent up a chorus of warning whistles and disappeared in a flash as he spread out the booty.

Charlie tiptoed back to fetch his own lunch from Matt's pack, then settled down on a flat rock to watch.

Five minutes passed before a furry brown head peeked up from between the rocks. In another five, several marmots were squealing and wrestling over ownership of the treats.

Clearly entranced, Charlie's shaking shoulders were the only sign of his silent laughter.

Jolie pulled a thin blanket out of her backpack and spread it out on a grassy patch by the trail. She sat down on one side and, rummaging deeper into the pack, pulled out a box of crackers, a small jar of peanut butter and a Ziploc bag of seedless grapes. "Want something to eat?"

Matt's eyes twinkled as he hunkered down over his own pack and withdrew an identical menu—except his peanut butter was extra crunchy. "I guess we think alike."

In the bright sunlight his hair gleamed like ebony. A little too long, a bit tousled. He had the kind of hair that made her want to reach up and comb it back with her hands, just to feel the silky strands slip through her fingers.

With those broad shoulders and muscular arms, she could imagine him as a rugged trapper, explorer or scout ranging through this mountain a hundred years earlier. Her imagination soared...

"Hey, Dad!" Charlie's voice echoed through the rocks above them. "Can I fish in this pond?"

Matt lifted an eyebrow at Jolie.

"Sure, just stay out of the water," Jolie called out. "It's probably not more than forty-five degrees. Need any help?"

"'Course not!" Charlie bent over his backpack and withdrew his small rod, assembled it, then industriously began untangling the line. In a few minutes he was heading for the edge of the pond.

"He's been on some Scout outings," Matt said, a smile lifting one corner of his mouth. "Caught a few sunfish and now figures he's ready for the big time. This morning he told me he was bringing Secret Weapon Bait."

From what Jolie could see, he was baiting his hook with hot-dog cubes, so dealing with the cleaning of fish would probably not be a problem.

"Do you guys do much camping?" she asked. "Backpacking?"

Matt settled more comfortably on the blanket next to her, with the food between them, though his watchful gaze didn't stray from his son. "As a kid in northern Wisconsin and Minnesota. Never out here, though. And once I grew up..." His expression grew somber. "There really wasn't much chance anymore."

"Tell me about what happened," Jolie asked quietly, surprising herself. "With your wife."

She'd always kept a certain reserve with patients, careful not to edge out of a comfortable professional distance. She'd done the same with friends. Never allowed herself to get too close to anyone.

But now she found herself wanting to know everything about this man sitting next to her—what he did in his spare time, what his entire life had been like up to this point.

As if she had a right. Suddenly uncomfortable, she felt a faint flush of warmth creep into her cheeks.

He'd leaned back on one elbow, still watching his son. Without shifting his gaze, he answered. "Not much to tell, really."

"I'm sorry—I didn't mean to pry."

He didn't speak for several moments, then he cleared his throat. "I was going to college. Had big plans for a bachelor's degree in commercial art, and a job somewhere in New York or Chicago. Advertising, maybe."

"How far along did you get?"

"I met Barbara on campus. Bright, funny, pretty—I couldn't get enough of her. We were both only twenty, and I was in the last term of my sophomore year. We eloped during spring break."

Jolie expected to see regret in his eyes, but found only sorrow.

"Neither of us had a clue about life, or the responsibilities of being married and having a family. She got pregnant with Lily almost right away."

"So you dropped out of school?"

"There was no other way. Her family was appalled, my dad was angry. Neither one wanted much to do with us after that."

"You didn't go back to night school later?"

"I tried a few times, but I was supporting the family, making enough time for the kids after work—then trying to race off to night classes. Study time was a little hard to come by.''

''And your wife?''

''Barb couldn't work much. She'd started to feel ill before Charlie was born, and the doctors couldn't figure out why.''

So his hopes and dreams for a career were lost long before he lost his wife, and Jolie didn't need to ask why he hadn't gone back to school later.

She slathered peanut butter on a couple of crackers and tore a cluster of grapes from the stem. ''I'm sorry.''

''Don't be. I don't regret any of my decisions—I had a wife I loved, she gave me kids I couldn't love more. What would I ever want to change?''

''Nothing at all.'' Drawing her legs up, Jolie wrapped her arms around them and rested her chin on her knees.

He'd had more hardship, more struggle in his life than she'd ever had, maybe hadn't achieved all the goals he'd held dear, but he'd had far more joy, too. She might have received her coveted M.D., but who had achieved more—and who was happier?

''You seem awfully quiet,'' Matt said after a while.

''Just thinking.'' Thoughts of her single-minded pursuit of a degree had hopscotched into other topics. Her practice. The patients.

And what Daniel Aiken's mother had said on Monday. Her words had hovered over Jolie like a dark cloud ever since. *Now I'm praying that all the rumors about you aren't true.*

The rumors again. Spread by whom? Would they account for the nearly empty waiting room day after day? The several phone calls to the clinic each day, when the caller said nothing and just hung up?

And how did one fight something so vague?

Matt pitched a pebble into a puddle of water held by a

depression in the rocks. "I wanted to tell you—while we were alone—how much I appreciate your support and patience with Lily. With all of us."

Jolie tilted her head to look over at him. "She's done well. I've seen her every day this week, and I think she's really got the hang of taking her insulin and doing her Accu-checks. Her blood sugars are excellent at this point."

"She still doesn't want people to know about her diabetes."

"Apparently she has a bit of a crush on the boy who took her to the nurse's office. That insulin reaction at school scared and embarrassed her."

Matt's eyes narrowed at the word *boy*.

"It would be better if she just let people know, instead of being secretive. People tend to imagine the worst."

"*Boy?*"

"He's only fourteen—I doubt he's much of a Don Juan."

"Have *you* ever been a fourteen-year-old boy?" Matt ran a finger around the neck of his polo shirt. "He's probably already thinking about ways to—"

Jolie elbowed Matt in the ribs. Playfully—as she might have teased her sisters years ago. He was as solid as the rock behind them. "I really, really don't think he's going to elope with her just yet." She raised an eyebrow and tipped down her sunglasses with one finger. "Have you had The Talk with her?"

"Sure." He cleared his throat. "Well, sort of."

Jolie chuckled. "I'll bet you did. Look, I know it's tough being a guy raising a teenage daughter. If you ever think she needs to talk to a woman, I'm available."

Giving a vague nod, Matt shifted his weight. And suddenly he was closer than he'd ever been...his long legs stretched out next to hers from hip to ankle.

He smelled of after-shave, sunshine and soap; a clean and

all-too-compelling combination that made her wonder what it might be like to kiss him. To be held in his arms in front of a campfire.

Or even along this sunlit trail, in broad daylight.

The hitch in Matt's breath told her that he was probably wondering the same thing. And Charlie's rapt attention on his fishing line hadn't changed.

"Jolie…" His voice was deeper than before. Rough. "I figure this probably isn't a good idea."

He lifted a hand and trailed his fingers through her hair. "But I've wondered. For so long."

Those gentle fingers traced the line of her cheekbone. The curve of her jaw. "And I don't think I can wait any longer to find out," he added softly.

Without volition, Jolie found herself turning into his hand, and looking up into those autumn eyes of his. Only they were much darker now, the amber highlights subdued, and something inside her responded to the intensity of his gaze as surely as if he had argued his case before the bar.

Matt's gaze slid one last time toward Charlie, then his lashes drifted downward. Warmth and tension and urgency spread through her as his mouth settled over hers. His fingers threaded through her hair and brought her closer, harder into his kiss. *Heaven.*

The universe narrowed to the heat of his mouth. The exquisitely gentle touch of his strong hands. The subdued, masculine scent of his after-shave.

"Oh, *yuck,* Dad!"

Ice water couldn't have had a more chilling effect than opening her eyes and looking into Charlie's horrified expression. Breathless, she pulled out of Matt's arms and moved away.

"*Charlie.*" Matt's voice was low, lethal. "I don't think this is open for your comments, do you?"

"But—"

"*No.*"

Charlie looked back and forth between Jolie and Matt, his mouth set in a stubborn line. "I want to go home."

"We waited for you to watch the marmots and fish, and now we're going to head up the trail a little farther," Matt said evenly.

"I'm *tired.*"

"Just another half mile or so."

"I want…"

Charlie's voice trailed off, and Jolie saw the pain and sadness in his eyes. "You want your own mom to be with your dad."

Turning away, he didn't answer.

Matt stood, and looked down at her. And she saw that same pain reflected in his own eyes. "I'm sorry," he said simply. "This shouldn't have happened. It isn't fair to the kids to give them expectations, and it isn't fair to you. I'll make sure it doesn't happen again."

ON MONDAY MORNING Megan was fully dressed—her hair combed neatly into a high ponytail—before Jolie's alarm even rang. Her expression of eager anticipation touched Jolie's heart. For two weeks the girl had been eating and sleeping well, helping out around the cabin for something to do.

From the sparkle in her eyes, to the rich sheen of her dark auburn hair, she was an entirely different person from the nervous waif who'd appeared at Jolie's door after midnight.

"I've been going a bit stir-crazy," Megan admitted as they walked into Jolie's clinic an hour later. "I'm really glad you're giving me a chance to work here. There's a lot to learn, but I can't wait—"

She gasped, stepped backward into the waiting area and bumped into Jolie, who was still pocketing her keys.

"What the—" Jolie moved around her. Stopped.

Shards of glass glinted along the floor of the hallway. Far too much for a single window.

But it was the object lying in the center of the broken glass that held her horrified gaze. *What on earth was it?*

Taking care to block Megan's view, Jolie reached into her bag and withdrew her cell phone. "Take this. Go out to the sidewalk and call the deputy sheriff. *Now.*"

"But—"

"Now! And *stay* out there."

Megan spun away and raced out the front door, leaving it wide open.

Jolie held her breath and listened intently, every cell of her body on alert. There was no sound of anyone in the clinic. Silence, save for the chatter of birds outside.

She'd bet there wasn't anyone here, but she wasn't foolish enough to bet her life.

She quietly fished her keys out of her pocket, fingering them until she had one key protruding between her clenched fingers.

And then she backed through the waiting room and out the front door.

CHAPTER TWELVE

RAFE ARRIVED without lights and sirens, thank goodness.

Passersby had slowed at seeing Jolie and Megan on the sidewalk staring at the clinic, and the crowd was beginning to spill into the street. When Irene arrived at nine o'clock, she might as well have issued invitations. Everyone, it seemed, knew Irene.

"Don't say anything," Jolie hissed, giving her a nudge.

Irene nodded, her gray curls bouncing emphatically. But her dramatic air was enough. Her hands clasped at her throat, her eyes wide—anyone might have thought there'd been a triple murder, at least.

And the rumors started to fly.

"What was it? Gunshots?"

"I heard it was a thief—came right in that back door and scared 'em both!"

"Nah—must have been drug addicts trying to find needles."

"Drugs? Here? Holy cow!"

Jolie tried her best to calm everyone. "Look, folks, we only have a broken window. Vandals, nothing more. Megan and I are just waiting out here so we don't tamper with anything the deputy sheriff needs to check. There's nothing to see here."

Several of the storekeepers—Wayne, from the hardware, Agnes from the drugstore—exchanged looks. And stayed right where they were as Rafe sauntered up the sidewalk.

"The doc is right," he drawled, his casual stride conveying boredom. "Might just have been a bird that hit the glass." He stopped next to Jolie and lowered his voice. "I'll make sure the building is secure, then you come on in. Just make sure you don't touch anything. Best if we have a little less excitement around here."

He disappeared through the front door.

A hush fell over the gathering as the minutes ticked by. Three...four...five...

Two of the men in the crowd walked around the clinic and reported that *two* windows had been broken. That information more than doubled Jolie's concern. One broken window could be young kids playing a prank, or maybe challenging one another to a dare. Two indicated a stronger intent. But by whom? She considered the possibilities.

There was strong feeling against her family in the community, certainly. Many people had been angry at finding a Maxwell had taken over the medical practice. Someone had started rumors against her. There were the ongoing hang-up calls.

And now and then, during late evenings at the clinic, she'd had a prickly sensation at the back of her neck. The sensation of something not being quite right. Of being watched. Which was ridiculous, given the closed blinds and that fact that everything—*everything*—was in its right place.

But maybe that premonition hadn't been so ridiculous after all.

Megan hopped from one foot to the other, casting nervous glances between the clinic and Jolie. "Is he okay in there?" she whispered. "There could be some crazy person hiding in there, and—"

"No, Megan," Jolie soothed, wishing she felt as confident as she sounded. "He's just checking for evidence before we go in."

Edging closer, Megan lowered her voice to a whisper. "What did you *see* in there? I saw broken glass, but what was that *thing* lying in the hallway?"

It had been a naked, red-haired doll, with crimson slashes painted across its chest, arms and legs, spelling the word, DEAD. Jolie managed a bland smile. "Probably just something thrown at the window to break it, that's all."

Rafe appeared at the door of the clinic, and instantly a hush fell over the people gathered outside. If she didn't feel so shaken, Jolie might have thought it amusing.

"It's nothing at all, folks," he called out. "Just some broken glass. Dr. Maxwell was wise to call me, just in case."

He motioned Jolie toward the clinic, and both Irene and Megan followed close at her heels. "I'd like to talk to you privately," he murmured as they stepped inside. "Perhaps your staff can wait at the receptionist's desk?"

In her office, he settled one hip against her desk and crossed his arms. "Someone went to a bit of trouble, here, but theft doesn't appear to be the motive. Your cabinets in the lab were still locked, the TV and VCR in the back room are still there. None of the file drawers were open." His gaze flicked to the camera on the bookshelves by her desk. "It's hard to believe that anyone missed that."

She hadn't started filling the shelves yet, but her old single-lens-reflex Minolta sat in plain view, next to the bulging camera bag holding a couple of telephoto lenses.

"Have you had any other problems?"

"Nothing, really…some phone calls where no one answers, but that doesn't mean much. I used to get some heavy-breather calls in California. Changed my number twice, but the calls kept coming. Never had a face-to-face encounter with the guy, though."

"Anything on the caller ID?"

"I'm not that lucky. Just pay-phone numbers."

"Tell me about anyone who might have a grudge against you, Jolie."

She gave him a rueful smile. "Half the town?"

"I'm serious."

"So am I. My first day cleaning up this place, some people stopped by and let me know they weren't happy to see a Maxwell take over. Since then I've heard other people say the same thing, and there are lots of crazy rumors about me." She gave a short laugh. "I don't know what anyone could say if they were being honest. I have no social life, have never been sued and have never done a truly controversial thing in my life."

Rafe lifted the sealed bag on her desk. "Well, someone either has a macabre sense of humor, or is sending you a damn grisly message. And he—or she—came through one of those windows to do it."

An uncontrollable shudder passed through Jolie as she stared at the red-haired doll in the bag. The crimson slashes painted across its trunk and extremities looked entirely too real.

"I'll ask around," Rafe said. He slipped the bag into a larger paper sack. "If I can lift any latent prints, I'll send them to be checked against the prints on file for locals with a record. If nothing turns up, the latents will be sent on to the State Latent Examiner in Missoula."

Jolie nodded. "Thanks."

"Prints might not help, you understand. This was probably the work of local troublemakers who won't have prints in the computer system."

"Please let me know what you find out, okay? And say hi to Thea for me. Has she said anything about how Dad is doing?"

Rafe regarded her with troubled eyes. "I think his heart

problems are worse, but if we say one word, he stalks out of the room. Thea says he got off his horse yesterday, bent over and just gasped for breath. He practically bit her head off when she wanted to bring him to your clinic again.''

Pride and determination might have made their dad a success, but were also probably going to kill him. ''If he gets worse, tell Thea to ignore his protests and call for an ambulance.''

''She will.'' Rafe reached forward and gave Jolie an awkward one-armed hug, then stepped away. ''Don't worry about this too much. I'll ask questions around town, and I'll start cruising up the alley several times a day. Gossip about the surveillance will probably discourage any locals from making another move.''

''Thanks, Rafe.''

''People notice any strange cars or new faces that linger. If anyone sees anything else unusual around here, I'll hear about it.''

It was true—word traveled fast, and secrets were impossible to keep in Paradise Corners. As she watched Rafe walk out to his patrol car, Jolie wondered which would be worse: a stranger—anonymous and unpredictable—looking for drugs, or someone she knew wanting to scare her.

Jolie closed her eyes, but the image of that doll with DEAD written across its chest stayed with her.

AS EXPECTED, the latent prints Rafe lifted from the doll matched nothing in the local file. Jolie had met with Rafe, considering and dismissing every possible suspect she could think of.

None of them seemed like logical choices. Dan Aiken's family needed Jolie's services. Megan's dad surely wouldn't threaten the only Maxwell to take his daughter's side.

Bobby's friends were wild, but would they go so far as to leave a macabre, bloodied doll?

After the incident, Matt had answered his cell phone and arrived within the hour to replace the shattered windows, then started calling Jolie several times a day to check on her. Rafe cruised past the clinic day and night.

By Friday morning, it all was getting a little old.

"It's your friend, honey." Irene's mouth curved into a big smile. "Worrying about you again."

"I'll take it in my office." Jolie spoke through clenched teeth. "Look," she said when she picked up the phone. "There are three of us here all the time. We're fine. *Believe* me. And I promise to look into security systems as soon as I can afford a good one."

"Good." Matt's voice was laced with amusement. Through the receiver she heard the steady pounding of nails and the whining of a saw. "But I called this time because I need to talk to you before Lily's appointment this afternoon. Her evening glucose readings have been in the three hundreds again."

Jolie sank into her chair and rubbed her eyes. She had scheduled Lily for an appointment this afternoon, and then planned to phase her into less frequent visits. "Things aren't going so well?"

"She becomes defensive whenever I try to talk to her. She says, 'Everything is fine. Just leave me alone!' and walks away. Suddenly, the numbers in her record book for yesterday are all in the normal range. I figured maybe she started writing down what I *hope* to see, but when I asked her, she was furious."

Jolie could well imagine the self-righteous anger of a young teenager at being questioned. Especially if her dad was right. "Is she eating properly?"

"We're doing okay at breakfast and supper. I check what

she packs for lunch—she won't take the hot lunch at school anymore because she doesn't want the kids to notice that she's given fruit instead of desserts.'' Matt gave a deep sigh. ''What she does otherwise, I just don't know. She says she's careful, but why would her blood sugar be so high?''

''We might need to make further adjustments to her insulin. She could be eating the wrong things, or she could be one who is simply hard to regulate. Eventually we might want to look into using an insulin pump.''

''This is…overwhelming. Millions of people may be diabetic, but that doesn't make it any easier for me and Lily. If she doesn't take care of herself…''

Obviously, controlling Lily's diabetes was proving to be a battleground between father and daughter. Jolie wished she was standing next to him right now, and could lay a comforting hand over his. ''We'll get this under control.''

She heard only the sounds of building construction in the background for a minute. ''I was just wondering,'' he said after a long pause. ''That is—the kids and I were wondering if you'd like to stop by for supper tonight. Maybe six-thirty?''

Jolie glanced at the photocopy of today's schedule that Irene—bless her—placed on Jolie's desk every morning. Six appointments today. A record, though getting away in time for supper would be no problem. ''And Megan, too?''

''Of course. Lily would enjoy seeing her again.'' His voice lowered. ''I…we've missed you this past week.''

A sudden memory of their kiss along the trail sent a flood of warmth through her. Possibly for the thousandth time in the past six days. ''Thanks. We'll be there.''

''I have to make a run to Billings this afternoon, so this will be something easy, just steaks on the grill.''

Closing her eyes, Jolie imagined the wonderful aromas and taste. ''Heavenly.''

For the rest of the morning, she tried to convince herself that it was the *steak* that sounded heavenly. And not just the company of the man who occupied her thoughts far too much.

LILY SAT on the top step of the middle-school entrance and lifted her face to the warm sun.

Charlie played baseball with the other boys at the playground after school these days, and there really wasn't any point in walking downtown alone for the hour until Dad came. *Boring.* And then—lucky her—when Dad showed up, she had yet another appointment at Jolie's clinic, where she'd be grilled once again about her diabetes.

With a sigh, she dug a new paperback novel out of the backpack at her side and started reading.

Until a shadow fell over the pages, she didn't realize anyone had approached.

"Hi."

Clint gave her a shy grin, and just like that she felt her heart do a somersault. "Hi."

He'd barely spoken to her in school, but she'd watched him from afar and imagined what it might be like to date someone who was so ultimately, impossibly cool. She wouldn't ever find out, though, because she could never think of a single thing to say when he walked by.

"Want to walk to the drugstore with us? I hear they got black cherry supreme in today."

A few of his buddies loitered at the curb. Sara and Gina, too. A thrill of excitement rushed through her at the thought of being included in the crowd.

Clint might have a wild reputation around town, but if he'd asked her to help grease a car or mow a fifty-acre yard, she would have followed him anyway. *And black cherry supreme ice cream?*

Jolie's words of warning buzzed in her ears, but Lily ignored them all. A treat now sure couldn't matter much, not when Dad was so strict at home. And the drugstore was just a block away. There was plenty of time.

Sparing a quick glance at her watch, she smiled up at him. "I...um...I've just got to be back here when my dad comes."

"No sweat."

Clint fell in step with her as they headed for the store, and just like that, her knees went weak and her throat turned dry. *What did girls say to guys like him?* She'd seen other girls laugh and flirt, and attract guys like crazy—how did they do it?

One of the boys walking ahead of them reached over and gave Sara's ponytail a tug. "Hey, brainiac—no fair you getting a hundred on that history test. What did you do, study?"

"What's that, a new concept?" She rolled her eyes and smiled at him, softening her reply. "You could try it sometime, just for kicks."

He moved closer and their heads bent in a conversation Lily couldn't hear. Sara made talking to a boy look *easy*.

The group split up inside the drugstore, the boys moving to a rack of magazines to flip through the latest issue of *Car and Driver,* while Gina and Sara wandered over to the cosmetics counter.

Lily hesitated, feeling stupid and uncertain—should she follow Clint, or the girls? There were so many things she didn't know. Didn't have anyone to ask. Not really, 'cause what would her dad know about all of this?

A shudder swept down her spine. The last thing she wanted to do was to get him started again about boys, and— yuck—a discussion on *sex.*

The major embarrassment of her first period had been

awful enough, when she'd needed to buy her supplies. As soon as she'd started baby-sitting, she'd taken care of that on her own, never wanting to put those packages in the grocery shopping cart in front of him. If Mom had lived...

With a sigh, Lily started toward the cosmetics counter.

And saw Gina slip a tube of lipstick into her pocket.

Lily stopped. Swallowed hard. She'd bought one of those with her own money a week before—a soft, hardly-there baby pink, though she hadn't told her dad because he still thought she was too young. It had cost almost seven dollars.

"Hey, Lily," Gina said softly. "You got a problem, or something?"

She stepped closer, brushed roughly against Lily and kept walking toward the soda fountain.

Speechless, Lily stared at her. Gina had just shoplifted, and looked as innocent as a lamb. Hadn't anyone else seen her?

But there wasn't a clerk in sight, and the boys were now shelving the magazines and heading for the soda fountain, too.

"Come on," Clint called out.

Gina turned around, her gaze hard. "You look a little weird. Maybe you should go home."

"Stay," Sara urged. "Your dad won't be picking you up for a while yet."

Had Sara taken something, too? Uneasiness prickled through Lily, but leaving might brand her as a loser, and maybe they wouldn't ask her to join them anymore. "I...I'm fine," she managed to say.

At the old-fashioned soda fountain at the back of the store the group settled boy-girl-boy-girl on the red stools lined up along the counter, with Clint and Lily at the far end.

This is almost like a date. Lily gave Clint a shy smile. "Thanks for asking me to come along."

He didn't answer, just slid her a quick wink and a grin, but her heart fell right down to her shoes. And suddenly it didn't matter what Gina had done, because this was turning out to be a fabulous, wonderful day.

The girl behind the counter went down the line, taking orders, her pencil poised over an order pad.

"Hot-fudge sundae—extra nuts and whipped cream."

"Triple-chocolate marshmallow, on a waffle cone."

Gina dug into her backpack to check her money and then murmured, "Chocolate malt, large. What about you, Sara?"

"Hmm...my usual, I guess."

"Hot-fudge sundae, with chocolate-chip ice cream. And a Coke." The girl behind the counter smiled as she wrote the familiar order on her pad. "You order that every time, Sara."

Clint ordered a double-scoop sundae of the black cherry supreme, with fudge topping. "The same for Lily, and I'll buy hers, too." He grinned at Lily, then added, "If that's okay?"

He was buying *hers?* Suddenly feeling as though she'd just been crowned homecoming queen, prom queen—no, queen of the whole *world,* Lily shut away Jolie's warnings, her dad's worries, and everything she'd read in those stupid books about diabetes.

It was hard enough being a new girl in school and not having close friends anymore. Being *different,* even if none of the kids knew about her diabetes, made it all worse, but now she had a chance to be part of a group. To be accepted.

How could she possibly refuse?

"PERSONAL CALL for you, Doctor. Line two."

Jolie closed the file she'd been studying. The afternoon had been quiet—two patients after lunch, then a lull of over an hour.

For about the hundredth time she thought about how different this was from her crowded clinic in Los Angeles and the crush of patients that usually overflowed well into the evening. She'd rarely left until after eight.

Consider this a mental-health break, she told herself dryly. *Heaven knows you've needed one for a long time.*

"Rafe here. I've got a bit of a problem."

Laid-back as Rafe was, that could be anything from a gunshot wound to an accident out on the highway. Or maybe he'd found a clue about the person who'd broken into the clinic. "Yes?"

"I've got a young lady here at my office, along with some of her friends. I called her dad's cell phone and didn't get an answer. Lily told me to call her aunt Nina, and Nina said Matt and Ed had made an emergency run to Billings for supplies. They might be home late."

And this involved the deputy? Mystified, Jolie murmured, "Lily and Charlie can come here, if they need a place to stay until he gets back. I have a four-thirty appointment with her in any case, if she wants to walk over."

Rafe cleared his throat. "Actually, it's more complicated than that. I'm not letting any of these kids go until a parent comes, and then each one is receiving a good lecture. Agnes Benson caught them shoplifting at the drugstore."

"Lily?" Stunned, Jolie closed her eyes. Of all the kids she knew, surely Lily wouldn't have done something so stupid.

"Two of the girls took cosmetics. One of the boys slid a magazine inside his jacket. Agnes said she's been noticing stock disappearing for some time, and had become suspicious of the after-school crowd. She's had her clerks watching."

"I can't believe Lily would do that."

Rafe gave a short laugh. "The kids all denied it, of course. But they did have the merchandise."

"What do you want me to do?"

"Lily tells me you're a good friend of her dad's."

"We're neighbors."

"She says that he calls you if he's running late, because she and Charlie often hang around your clinic after school. You've helped him out a time or two."

"That's right."

"If he calls, let him know that he needs to come to my office to get his daughter. I hope he gets back in good time...I've made reservations at a dinner theater for Thea and I over in Bozeman, and I hope to leave the office on time."

"Calving must be slowing down a little. Are you going out to celebrate?"

Rafe cleared his throat. "Well, not exactly..."

Jolie could hear the tinge of embarrassment in his voice.

"It's our...uh...three-month anniversary."

Despite her best effort, a chuckle escaped. "You old romantic." From the pause that followed, she guessed that the deputy sheriff of Paradise Corners didn't want it widely known. "My sister is a lucky woman."

"No. I'm the one who's lucky." Rafe's voice grew husky. "And there just hasn't been much time to let her know."

Hearing the emotion in his voice, Jolie guessed that he'd already shown it in many ways, in many small acts of affection and caring. And Jolie felt the empty place in her own heart expand. What would it be like, sharing life with someone who loved you that much?

"Let me come and get Lily. It's almost four-thirty, and this way you might be able to finish up on time and get going. I'll see that Matt brings her back in."

"I shouldn't do that."

"Look, you certainly know Lily will be safe in my custody. As I said, she's scheduled for an appointment with me now, anyway. And I can swear that Matt will take this very, very seriously. Please—I want Thea to have a wonderful night out with you."

The last plea did it. As soon as he capitulated, Jolie headed for the front door of the clinic. The sheriff's office was in the basement of the courthouse, just two blocks up Main. An easy walk...one that would give her time to talk to Lily on the way back.

At the front desk, Irene was seated at the computer with Megan beside her, learning to do invoices. Both heads looked up in surprise at her rapid approach.

"Irene, I've got to leave for a few minutes. If Matt Dawson calls, tell him to call again in an hour, okay? I need to talk to him."

LILY SAT on the bench in the sheriff's office. The other kids had already gone, picked up by parents who'd shown up right away. Dad hadn't answered his cell phone, and she had no idea where he was.

She felt so cold. So alone. So sick with dread. The deputy had said that the old witch at the drugstore might press charges. What would happen then? Reform school? Her name and picture in the newspaper? *Jail?*

No one had believed that she'd bought that lipstick in her purse. Without the receipt, she couldn't prove it, and she couldn't remember which clerk had sold it to her the week before. Even if she could, how would a clerk remember one small item that many customers ago?

Feeling a little woozy, she dug into her backpack for a package of saltine crackers and started nibbling them, though even the thought of eating made her stomach churn.

Dad is going to kill me, she thought miserably. *He'll yell for a week straight, and then he's going to kill me.*

Clint's mom had seemed more irritated at the deputy than she had at her son, and Gina's mom had looked almost bored during the lecture Rafe gave them. Those kids were lucky.

Dad wouldn't be bored. He wouldn't be irritated at the deputy. He'd be enraged at her apparent dishonesty, and probably never, ever forgive her. And he'd never, ever let her hang out with the kids she'd just been with after school.

Her life in ruins, Lily leaned her head against the wall and wished she'd never heard of Montana.

CHAPTER THIRTEEN

"SHE WAS *WHERE*?"

Jolie calmly faced Matt from across her desk, as if this issue was of no more concern than a misplaced set of keys. "At the sheriff's office. After I picked her up, we went to get Charlie at baseball practice. Then we all came back here. Lily had an appointment scheduled with me, so we went ahead with that. I hope you don't mind. She had a lot of ice cream at the drugstore so her blood sugar was high, but we talked at length about that. If you have any questions—"

Matt waved a hand impatiently. "I want to hear more about the sheriff's office. She was *arrested?*"

Lily and Matt were seated in the chairs facing Jolie's desk. Lily slid another few inches lower in hers, her gaze glued to the floor.

"No charges have been filed yet. She joined some school friends, and they all went to the drugstore. The owner, Agnes Benson, claims three of them shoplifted merchandise. She claims she's had problems with some local teenagers after school for some time, but hadn't been able to catch anyone until today."

"Lily," he said gently, "tell me your side of this."

"I didn't *do* anything." She spoke almost too softly to hear. *"Honest."*

"But you had some of the shoplifted items in your backpack?"

"No—yes. I didn't steal anything!" Lily gave him a

stricken look. "Last week I bought lipstick there. The same kind the other girl took, and it was in my pack." She lowered her eyes once again. "I know you said I couldn't wear makeup yet, but it's a really light shade, and I don't put much on, and—"

"Okay, okay." Rage flared deep in his gut at the old bat who'd accused his daughter. And at the fact that once again he hadn't been around to help her when she'd needed him most. For the first time in his life he could imagine the physical release of putting a fist through a wall.

Looking back at Jolie, he didn't even try to temper the anger in his voice. "The deputy sheriff didn't believe her? Did *you?*"

"This was never an issue of me believing in her," Jolie returned, her voice deadly calm. "I wasn't present when the situation occurred, though just for the record, I do believe her side of the story. But she doesn't have the receipt, and none of the clerks remember her buying that lipstick. That's no surprise—I've seen some of the high-school kids who work there, and some wouldn't remember what they did this morning, much less a small item they sold last week."

Matt turned to face Lily. "Do you have that receipt at home, honey?"

"No. I…I threw it away." She shifted uncomfortably. "I didn't want you to know what I bought."

Had he seemed like that much of an ogre to her?

Guilt lanced through him as he faced yet another way in which he'd failed his daughter. "Honey, it's no big deal if you have that lipstick. Maybe I haven't understood just how fast you're growing up. If your mom had been here, she would have…" His train of thought faded away as Lily faced him, her eyes filled with tears.

"I'm sorry, Dad. Honest."

Unable to force words past the sudden lump in his throat, he rose and opened his arms to her.

She moved to him in a rush of tears, her shoulders shaking with her sobs. "The...the deputy sheriff says the drugstore lady might press charges," she sniffled against his chest.

"I'll talk to him. And I'll talk to that woman." He glanced at his watch, then at Jolie. "The deputy will still be in his office, right?"

She shook her head. "Your partner's wife said you guys might be late, and you weren't answering your cell phone. One reason I offered to get Lily was that Rafe had to leave for Bozeman, and none of us knew for sure when you'd get back into town."

"We drove Ed's truck and had his phone, but I didn't think to grab mine. I never expected to be back so late and miss her appointment with you." Matt released Lily, feeling frustrated, anxious and more than a little irritated at himself. "You could have called Ed's number, though."

Jolie's expression turned cool. "We didn't have it. Ed's wife didn't answer the phone when Rafe called her back to check. Everything was under control at any rate. Lily is here, Rafe can talk to you tomorrow."

A bad end to one hell of a day.

Ed hadn't ordered nearly enough stain to complete the oak trim at the gift shop, and the closest place carrying that brand of stain was in Billings. The owners of the gift shop had been adamant about stocking their new store Monday, as scheduled.

Just another in an ongoing series of small mistakes, oversights that cost them time and money. Now his daughter had been falsely accused and hauled to the sheriff's office, and the situation couldn't be resolved until tomorrow.

Matt swore under his breath. For the next fourteen or

fifteen hours, until that office opened in the morning, he and Lily would have to live with the tension of that uncertainty.

"It's still only five o'clock," he snapped. "If you'd have left Lily there, the deputy would have been available."

Jolie took a sharp breath. "I'll be sure not to interfere with your business again, Dawson. I was only trying to help Lily. Can you imagine how she felt sitting there—not knowing when you'd arrive?"

Only too well, and the thought made him feel sick.

Jolie rose and headed for the door of her office. "I'm going up to the front desk. It's late, and I need to talk to Irene before she leaves. Let me know if there's anything else I can do."

She'd turned as imperious and cold as royalty, Matt thought.

"Come on, Lily," he said. "Let's go home."

JOLIE HEARD the back door close quietly before she even got to the front desk. The sound felt like a door shutting in her heart. She'd overstepped her bounds maybe, but only because she cared.

Exactly how it had been in the old days, when she'd tried to mother her younger siblings. She hadn't done well enough, and all she'd ever gotten in return was resentment. Even now, returning to her hometown after fourteen years, those same undercurrents were still there.

"And you thought you'd be able to come back and make one happy family," she muttered. "As if *that* will ever happen."

Dealing with her family was hard enough. She didn't need the extra heartache of growing too attached to Matt and his kids.

"Did you say something?" Irene turned off the computer and monitor, then swiveled to face her.

"No. Nothing at all. How is everything going?"

Irene reached out to give Megan a grandmotherly pat on the face. "This here is the sweetest girl. And sharp? She catches on really fast. We're lucky to have her."

Megan blushed. "I did some word processing in high school, but never took any business classes. Irene's showing me all of the office stuff."

"Takes to it like a pup playing fetch. When this place is busy enough for me to be a full-time nurse, she'll be more than ready to take care of the office duties."

If she stays in Paradise Corners that long, Jolie thought.

"I want to thank you so much for this—this chance," Megan said. "It means a lot to me."

"I'll be needing the help, and we want to see that baby come into the world with the best possible care, right?" Jolie gave Megan a quick hug. "Afterward, you'll have a job with me as long as you want one. We could even work out something so you could go on to school."

The light in Megan's eyes died. "I can't afford that."

"Yes, you can. You'd qualify easily for financial aid, and you could do anything in the world you wanted to, if your grades are good enough."

"I had a 3.4 overall grade point in high school," she said shyly.

Despite little or no support at home, Jolie guessed. "You sure sound like a winner to me. If you want, we can start researching schools and majors you'd be interested in. If you plan to raise this baby alone, you're going to want a good career."

"That's a darn good plan, Megan," Irene said. "Education is the best investment you could ever make, and no one can ever take it away from you." Irene surveyed the desk, then settled the shoulder strap of her purse into position as she headed out the front door. "Are we all set to go?"

Jolie gave Megan a weary smile. "I think we're both ready for supper and a nice fire in the fireplace, but I have a few things left to do."

"Then come with me, Megan," Irene offered. "I'll take you to Jolie's place before I head home."

They'd only been gone a few minutes when the phone rang.

"Dad's having trouble breathing again. We're in Rafe's cruiser, and Dad's in the back seat." Thea's voice caught. "We're just pulling into town."

"I'll be ready." Jolie thought fast. The closest hospital was in Bozeman, a hundred miles away. If he'd had a heart attack or exacerbation of his congestive heart failure, she could stabilize him and arrange for transfer via helicopter...*if* he'd agree.

As she cradled the receiver, she mentally ran through a list of differential diagnoses. Myocardial infarction. Ischemia. Pulmonary edema. Pulmonary embolism. Bronchospasm. Common words in her profession—but all sounded almost frightening as she thought about her own father coming though the clinic doors at any minute.

Praying that she wouldn't need them, she pulled out the intubation kit. The code kit. Then pulled the cardiac monitor and portable chest X-ray machine into the second exam room.

And thanked God she'd invested in the kind of equipment and supplies an isolated clinic might need. Every second could mean life or death, even with a helicopter on the way.

She'd just gathered her IV supplies, when she heard Rafe's cruiser pulling to a squealing halt.

Rafe and Thea were already unbuckling Dad's seat belt when she got there. She took a quick pulse, then knelt down to press her thumb against the swollen flesh at his ankles. He was at 2+ edema, easily.

"Let him sit at the edge of the car seat. I'll run after a gurney."

"No." Robert's rasping, breathless voice was almost inaudible, but still as implacable as ever.

"Dad," Thea begged. "We're trying to help you."

"I...don't...need any...help. And I'm not...getting in any damn bed on wheels." He wheezed harder, the flesh at his mouth turning a pale blue.

"A wheel*chair,* then," Jolie snapped. If she didn't bully him, he would never get out of the car. "There's no sense in anyone getting hurt trying to haul you inside. Thea works harder than any man on that ranch. What would happen if you injured her back?"

For perhaps the first time in his life Robert didn't utter a sharp retort. Winded, he sagged against the seat and struggled for air.

"Guess you two didn't make it very far out of town tonight," Jolie said softly, touching Rafe's shoulder as she headed toward the clinic.

"A good thing, too," he muttered. "We were right where we needed to be."

In seconds, Jolie returned with the wheelchair. Robert glared at her. "If you don't cooperate, Dad, I'm sending for a helicopter to take you to a hospital in Bozeman."

He swore, but didn't argue when Thea held the wheelchair steady, and Rafe helped Jolie transfer him into it. A good six feet of solid muscle, he had to weigh over two hundred twenty, Jolie guessed as she wheeled him into the first exam room.

Under the bright lights, against the white walls of the exam room, his color looked even worse. "You need to get on the exam table, Dad. I'll elevate your head so you can breathe easier, and start you on some oxygen."

He balked at first, then grudgingly rose, with Jolie and

Rafe supporting him at either side. His passive resistance added considerably to the effort.

As soon as they got him on the table, she clipped a pulse oximeter onto his forefinger. *Low, at eighty-seven percent. No surprise there.*

She positioned a mask over his face, started the oxygen, and hooked him up to the cardiac monitor. After taking his vitals and starting an EKG, she questioned him while beginning her exam. *No chest pain, but he'd been increasingly short of breath over the last few days. He felt worse tonight.*

"This looks pretty normal," she announced as she studied the EKG tracing. "Not consistent with what I'd see with a heart attack, but those changes don't always show up right away."

"Thank God he's okay so far," Thea whispered. She and Rafe hovered near the table, Rafe's arm draped protectively around her shoulders. "What now?"

"I need you two to step out while I do a chest X ray. That will show us if his heart is enlarged, or if he has a lot of edema there."

After she'd taken the X ray, she invited Thea and Rafe back into the room, then left to run the film through the developer.

When she returned, she moved close to Robert's head. "Next I'm drawing some blood, Dad. I'll have to send it by courier to a lab, so we won't know those results for a while. Then I'm starting an IV so I can give you a bolus of Lasix. You'll feel a lot better with some of this fluid out of you."

She'd been talking while she drew blood and he seemed unaware of the stick, but he winced as she started the IV— on the first try, thank goodness. "What meds are you taking now, Dad?"

Still breathing heavily, he closed his eyes.

Jolie looked up into Thea's pale face. "Do you know?"

Her sister didn't react for a moment, then seemed to shake herself into action. She reached into the pocket of her jacket. "I found these in his cabinet. I grabbed every prescription bottle in there."

Jolie scanned the bottles. *Imdur. Lasix. Atenolol. Lisinopril.* "Did he have any bottles of baby aspirin on the shelf?"

"I—I don't know for sure. Maybe. I wasn't looking for over-the-counter stuff."

"Probably not," Jolie sighed. "And I'll bet he was told to take one a day. He hasn't been taking these other meds regularly at all. They were filled three months ago and the bottles are all half-full." She turned back to Robert. "Why aren't you taking your medication? You know better than this, for heaven's sake."

"I—" He wheezed again, then his breathing seemed to ease. "Couldn't. Too busy...calving."

"Taking a few pills doesn't take much time, Dad," Thea retorted. "If you need help, I can start counting them out for you every day."

"I suspect he quit the diuretic because he didn't like the frequent urination. Am I right, Dad?"

He grunted an unintelligible response, a dull red flush creeping up his neck.

"But that's why you *need* it—to keep your fluids from building up. Without it, you end up like this."

Thea moved closer and rested a hand on his shoulder. "Do we need to get him to a hospital?"

Robert cursed. Coughed again. "Not...going. Don't even try."

"He never agreed to an echocardiogram or an angiogram, did he?" Jolie said flatly.

Thea grimaced. "You recommended tests last Thanksgiving, but he refused. After his heart attack the doctors wanted the same tests, but he checked out against medical advice and never went back for any follow-up."

"I was hoping he had, and that I just hadn't heard about it." Giving an exasperated sigh, Jolie squeezed an inch of nitro-paste onto a paper ribbon and taped it to his chest. "This will help the IV Lasix move out your excess fluid."

He didn't open his eyes, but she continued talking to him anyway. "I *know* you can hear me. The X ray shows an enlarged heart. You've already had one heart attack. I'm doing what I can in this setting, but a *smart* man would go to a hospital for definitive tests."

His silence and the sharp jerk of his shoulder gave her the answer she didn't want to hear—that he was still planning to be as stubborn as ever.

She softened her voice. "I know what it's like for you, Dad, when you try to sleep at night. The sheer panic when you can't breathe while you're lying down. The total exhaustion after routine chores. The anxiety when you're feeling worse and wondering if you'll even pull out of it."

"Jolie! This is cruel," Thea cried.

"No, Thea. He *needs* to face this. Pulmonary edema can be diagnosed in a clinic setting, but I can't determine the exact cause or best treatment without more information."

Lifting a clipboard from the counter, Jolie started writing up his history and physical. "I'm documenting my recommendations—*again*—for an echocardiogram. It's noninvasive and completely safe. I'm also listing the tests I mentioned before. You should be admitted to a hospital."

Robert struggled to sit up, then fell back against the gurney, but this time he didn't start coughing. "I'm fine…just have spells now and then."

"Right. And every one of your Angus cows knows how to fly. Face the truth, Dad. For your own good."

This time he did manage to sit up. The glare he directed

at them all could have melted steel. ''I...don't need anybody telling...me what to do.''

She took a deep breath, then said a silent prayer asking that he listen for once in his life.

''You've been told before, but I'm telling you again—if you don't take care of yourself, you won't be the Maxwell running Walking Stones Ranch. It'll be Thea and Bobby— if he ever straightens out. And you'll be six feet under.''

HE'D REFUSED TRANSFER to a hospital. But he couldn't convince any of the young fools to take him home. Even Bobby and Beth refused when they'd come into the clinic after midnight.

Bobby had looked scared. Beth had looked...deeply worried, her forehead creased and her pretty, brown eyes damp. What nonsense had Jolie told them, for God's sake? That he was about to die?

Maybe Bobby needed something to shake him up a little, but seeing poor Beth upset had made him almost want to reach out to take her hand. *And what would she think of that, you old fool?*

Once the damn diuretic kicked in, he'd had to pee so much that he'd been glad he hadn't tried the thirty-mile trip back to the ranch. Stopping every five minutes at the side of the road with Beth and Thea and Jolie worrying over him would have been unbearable.

So he'd bullied Jolie into letting him stay in the small bedroom at the back of the clinic overnight, though she'd muttered darkly about violating hospital coding regulations the entire time it took to move him.

Robert reached up and punched at the unfamiliar pillow under his head and peered at the clock. Three in the morning, and he still couldn't sleep.

Had to be those damn medications Jolie and Althea had

forced him to take last night. He'd had to pee three times in the last hour, and each time he was just more wide awake. With Jolie coming in to check on him every fifteen minutes he might as well be out of bed and reading that stack of livestock journals out in the waiting room.

Tomorrow he'd be exhausted from lack of sleep and the sheer stress of having someone—his *daughter*—constantly hovering. Taking his vitals. And tending to his most...basic needs.

The humiliation of lying in bed and handing a full urinal to his oldest daughter was beyond anything he'd ever imagined. He had to admit, though, that now he could breathe a hell of a lot easier.

He stared up at the ceiling and counted the flecks in the tiles from north to south, then east to west, trying to figure out why he felt so...adrift. So edgy.

And then he realized. For thirty-five years he'd slept in the same house, same room, same bed. With Helen for nineteen precious years. And then, just with the memories. Except for that damn hospital stay last fall.

And, oh God, he still missed her every single night. After she died, every last bit of joy had left with her, leaving only duty. Responsibility. And four young kids to raise on his own. What had he known about dealing with teenage girls? Or a boy barely out of diapers?

He'd raised the best Angus cattle in the state, but hadn't had a clue how to raise children. They'd probably feared more than loved him, and he'd never known how to change that. Helen had understood his failings, and she'd done a wonderful job raising them.

After she was gone everything just went to hell.

Sometimes, in the darkest hours of night, he welcomed his failing health and imagined Helen awaiting him with open arms and that beautiful smile, made all the more radiant by the passing years.

But he couldn't go yet. Not when their fool son was still making a mess of his life. Not when Bobby didn't show even a fraction of the ability and devotion to Walking Stones that Thea had.

If she'd only been a boy...

CHAPTER FOURTEEN

As JOLIE HAD EXPECTED, her dad still refused transfer to a hospital the next morning. He also firmly declined the blood draw she wanted, which would have provided valuable information.

And when Thea and Jolie refused to take him home, he promptly called Beth at the ranch and ordered her to come immediately.

Robert Maxwell was firmly back in control.

Pale with frustration, exhaustion and anger after a night of staying up with Jolie, Thea gave in, but from the look on her face, she didn't plan to mince words once she got him home.

"He must have been desperate, to let anyone else drive his car," Thea muttered as they watched Robert laboriously transfer from the wheelchair into his dark blue Cadillac, Beth hovering at his side. He'd adamantly refused all assistance. "He's driven it since 1980, and I don't think it has more than twenty thousand miles on it. Every one of them has been to church. Did you call Cassie yet?"

"I talked to her briefly last night to let her know what was going on but told her she didn't need to come. A hundred thirty miles late at night with Zak just didn't seem necessary unless Dad got worse. I'll give her another call."

Thea pursed her lips. "What did she say?"

"Well..." Jolie gave her a rueful smile. "I'm not sure

Cassie wants any suggestions from me, even after all these years. But she said she'd wait to hear from us.''

"If you told her *not* to come, I'm surprised she didn't show up." Thea stepped forward to shut the car door, then rested a hand on Beth's shoulder. "Thanks for coming to get him. He probably thought I'd hog-tie him and haul him to the hospital if he dared get into my pickup."

"He should be at the hospital?" Beth twisted her hands together, her eyes filled with worry and deep affection for her longtime employer. "I wanted to stay longer with him—with all of you last night, but Bobby can't drive, and his mare was on the verge of foaling. Why wouldn't Robert go?"

Thea stepped back, deferring to Jolie.

"Dad has serious congestive heart failure that isn't going to get any better. He doesn't take his meds, he refuses diagnostic tests that would help a cardiologist provide better care. That mild heart attack last winter didn't help."

Beth gave Robert a narrow look, then crossed her arms. "Medications?"

Thea and Jolie exchanged glances. Beth could often do more with their dad than anyone else, and she was one of the few people he listened to. For years, Jolie had wondered if the two might someday fall in love and marry, but Robert never seemed to notice the kindly woman beyond her role as his housekeeper.

Jolie reached into her lab-coat pocket. "Here are his bottles of meds, plus an instruction sheet on the dosages and times he needs to take them. What do you think, can you bully him into cooperating?"

"Bully? That man is more cantankerous than a stallion during breeding season. But I can sure try. Sometimes you've just got to be tougher than they are to get much accomplished.'' She winked, and rounded the front of the car. ''See you later, girls.''

''I'll follow you, Beth.'' Thea briefly laid a hand on Jolie's shoulder. ''Thanks. You may never hear it from Dad, but I'm really glad that you're back in Montana.''

Jolie watched the two vehicles head down Main Street, then walked slowly into the clinic. In a half hour, she had everything in order once again.

Surely there wouldn't be any calls this morning, and going home for a few hours of sleep in her own bed sounded like heaven. She hadn't taken a Saturday off in a long time.

The phone rang just after she pulled on her jacket. Her heart sank. And then it did a slow somersault at the sound of the voice on the line.

''Jolie?'' Matt's voice sounded even lower than usual...almost as if he'd just gotten out of bed. Or was maybe still in it.

Which conjured up a whole train of thought she had no business thinking about. Especially about a man who'd been so angry when she'd tried to help his daughter.

''Is this the clinic?'' he persisted.

''Yes...yes, it is. I was just distracted for a moment.''

''I'm sorry about yesterday.''

''Over anything specific?'' Sheer exhaustion after last night made it easier to resist his sincerity. ''Like the accusations, lack of trust? Thanks for calling, but—''

''Wait.'' He gave a low chuckle that sent a shiver dancing across Jolie's skin. ''I was way out of line.''

That caught her attention. ''Oh?''

''It's no excuse, but I'd had a rough day, and Lily's was much worse. Not being there when she needed me just sent me over the edge. Thanks for all you did to help her.''

He cared so much for his children. He worried and hovered and was tough when he needed to be. "I—I understand."

"Lily and I are meeting the deputy in his office at nine. Will you be seeing patients this morning?"

"I was just heading home, but I'll wait if you or Lily need an appointment afterward."

"No...I just need to talk to you. Alone. Sometime soon."

He was going to talk about transferring Lily to another doctor, probably. Then he would tactfully tell her that he really wasn't interested in a relationship despite that kiss on the trail last weekend. She could feel it in her bones.

He'd probably regretted that intimacy ever since, and now wanted to establish a purely professional medical relationship elsewhere, even if it meant forty miles to Big Timber, or a hundred to Bozeman.

"Barring any emergency calls, I'll be home this afternoon."

"Good. I'll stop by."

She held the receiver long after he'd hung up, wondering why she already felt such a sense of loss, when she'd never really had him at all.

MEGAN MET HER at the cabin door, dressed and glowing with good health. She was at thirty-three weeks now, with none of the problems that plagued a lot of pregnant women. So far. In that baggy sweatshirt and sweatpants she didn't look nearly as unwieldy as some did at this point.

"I figured you'd still be sleeping, since this is your day off."

"It's getting a little harder to sleep," Megan admitted. "I have to get up a lot to go to the bathroom, and that's getting *really* old."

Jolie chuckled. "Mother Nature is training you for all those nighttime feedings." She joined Megan on the porch, and leaned against the railing. "Mmm...it feels so good to get out of that clinic for a while."

"How is your dad?"

"He refused transfer to the hospital, won't go for tests. He thinks he's immortal, I guess. None of us can convince him otherwise."

A startled look flashed across Megan's face.

"What is it? Is something wrong?"

Megan laid a hand over her belly and grinned. "She kicked, really hard. I think she's going to be a soccer player."

"Or...*he* might be a football player."

"Nope, I just know this is a girl. It's a good thing, too, because a girl will be easier to raise on my own. I don't know much about sports, and fixing cars, and all that guy stuff."

To raise on her own. Jolie felt a flash of concern. Megan had no idea just how hard that would be. "Have you talked to Bobby? Tried to work things out?"

"No."

"At least for custody and child support issues?"

Megan stiffened. "No one is taking my baby."

"Of course not," Jolie soothed as she searched for another angle. "Just think about it. It isn't fair if Bobby ignores his responsibility, and the extra money would help you a lot."

"He can jump off a cliff, for all I care." Hurt and anger shimmered in Megan's eyes. "I'm going to move away, and go to school."

Which meant that the tiniest Maxwell probably would be shifted from one day care to the next, away from the extended family that would have showered him—or her—with attention and love.

"Don't forget that you're welcome to stay with me until

the baby is a little older, if you'd like.'' Jolie said slowly. "It wouldn't be charity. You could even bring the baby to work at the clinic, if you wanted to.''

Despite her brave words, there was doubt and a touch of worry in Megan's expression. "Maybe…''

"Hey, did you see the Lamaze flyer that came to the clinic yesterday?''

The change of subject brought a twinkle back into Megan's eyes. "From the hospital in Bozeman? Irene and I looked it over, and she says she'll be my partner. Isn't that cool?''

"Of all the people I know, she would be the very best.'' *Except for Bobby, who should be there.*

"Do you have any friends giving you a baby shower?''

Megan's gaze dropped to the floorboards of the porch. "Umm…no. Not really.'' After a long pause, Megan darted a glance at Jolie, then looked away. "I did have friends. Me and Bobby did, because we were always together. But after the accident…''

"His group of friends blamed him?''

"They got really mad. Especially my best friend, Racey. She's Dan's girlfriend, and she said Bobby wasn't even sorry that he almost killed his friends, and that he only cared about himself. When I tried to stand up for him, she said I wasn't any better than he was.''

"That must have really hurt.''

"I tried calling her once. She never called me back.'' Megan's lip quivered. "Her mom wasn't very nice.''

"What did she say?'' Jolie prompted gently.

"She said Bobby was a—an egotistical jerk, and anyone…anyone who got pregnant by him was either stupid or trying to get her hands on the Maxwell money.''

Jolie took a sharp breath. "Just for the record, I don't believe a word of that.'' Stepping closer, she wrapped an arm around Megan's shoulders. "For that woman to be so cruel to you is simply unconscionable. If Racey is anything like her mother, she's a friend you don't need."

"N-no...she was nice, until this happened."

Jolie gave her a gentle squeeze. "You're a sweet girl, Megan. What matters now is that you take good care of this baby and yourself."

"I will, honest." Megan stepped down the stairs, then looked over her shoulder. "Thanks. For *everything*. No one has ever been nicer to me." She patted her rounded stomach. "And Melissa Jo Wheeler thanks you, too."

Watching her walk toward the barn, Jolie smiled at Megan's optimism. And then she felt a tiny catch in her heart. This might be the only time in her life she'd ever be so close to the excitement and joy of a new generation of Maxwells.

She'd simply have to enjoy it while it lasted, and hope that Megan and her baby didn't move too far away.

MATT STOOD at the bottom of Jolie's porch steps, shielding his eyes against the bright afternoon sun. Megan and Lily had walked over to the edge of the clearing, where Lost Coyote Creek meandered through the rocks.

Charlie, currently on a one-hour time-out, was sitting on the porch swing pushing off with one foot. "How long now?"

Matt folded his arms. "You tell me."

"But it's been *hours* already."

"Twenty minutes."

"I didn't mean to spill that paint, honest."

"You weren't supposed to even *touch* it. It was for a job your uncle Ed and I are doing. Now one of us needs to drive clear to Big Timber to buy more."

"I'm sorry," Charlie said in a small voice. His surreptitious peek at Matt's expression spoiled the effect.

"You have forty minutes to go. I'm going inside to have coffee with Jolie, and expect you to stay on the porch, on that swing. Not staying put is why the time was increased from a half hour, so don't make it worse, okay?"

"What if I have to go to the bathroom?"

"One time."

Charlie's gaze slid over to the box of saltines by the railing. "What if I get really, really hungry?"

"I think you'll last. You ate lunch less than an hour ago."

Charlie fell silent. After a last stern look, Matt knocked on the door and stepped inside the cabin.

It was a cozy place, maybe a quarter the size of his. The timbered walls gave it a rustic, hunting-lodge atmosphere, but there were cheery gingham curtains at the windows, and a framed mountain scene hung over the fireplace.

Piles of colorful pillows on the floor by the fireplace and on the sofa relieved the unrelenting darkness of the heavy pine furniture. Two pillars supported an open loft overhead.

Jolie came out of the kitchen with a tray laden with cookies and two cups of coffee, and tipped her head toward the round oak dining-room table. "Here, or would you rather be on the sofa?"

Taking a cup, he headed for the sofa and settled at one end. After setting the tray on the half-log coffee table, she took her own cup and sat at the other end of the sofa, one leg curved beneath her.

"Did the furniture come with the place?"

"How did you guess?" Her smile brought a flash of sunshine into the room. "The owner—Fred Walters—was here for years and years, and he apparently liked to buy things that would last. It would take a tow truck to drag some of these pieces out of the cabin." She gazed at him uncertainly. "Was there something you needed to talk about?"

This wasn't going to be as easy as he'd thought. And he'd done a lot of thinking on it, before deciding to come here.

"Yeah. Charlie's probably already planning his escape, and heaven knows when the girls will wander in." He took another sip of coffee, then cradled the mug in his hands. "How is your dad?"

Jolie gave him a wry grin. "There are people in this town who would say he's too tough, too mean to ever die."

Matt silently agreed. Ed had told him about Boss Maxwell long ago, but since then Matt had heard a lot of tales around town.

The man had too many connections, too many people who owed him, and crossing Maxwell had spelled disaster for more than one businessman in town. Loan applications failed...zoning proposals didn't go through...subtle, supremely effective retribution that could never be traced back to Robert.

Matt shook off his thoughts. "Thanks again for taking care of my daughter after that incident at the drugstore." *Good move, Dawson. First you talk about furniture, and now this?*

"What did Rafe say?"

Matt gave a rueful chuckle. "The lecture he gave Lily could have blistered paint, but in the end I think he believed her. The store owner couldn't remember ever being suspicious of Lily before, so I think we'll be okay."

"And the other kids?"

"They're talking to the judge this week. I've tried to warn Lily about the dangers of hanging around those kids after school."

Jolie raised an eyebrow. Restrictions on friendships might

work with grade-schoolers, but teens tended to run on hormones and the drive to rebel, and were entirely another matter. "What did she say about that?"

"It didn't go over very well," Matt admitted. "And when I tried to discuss that massive amount of ice cream she ate, she hit the ceiling—said she wasn't going to let some stupid disease ruin her life."

"Diabetic education isn't a one-shot deal," Jolie warned. "Most teens think they're immortal, and have trouble grasping long-term diabetes consequences. But with good support from you and close medical supervision, she should be fine."

"Lord knows I'll do everything I can."

Jolie started talking about something else... Was it Charlie? The llama? He only half heard her words.

It had been so long since he'd been in this situation. A lifetime, it seemed. But looking at Jolie, with just a foot or so between them, he suddenly found himself as tongue-tied as a kid in school.

She'd dressed in a black turtleneck, the color a perfect contrast to the waves of strawberry-blond hair that she'd casually tucked behind her ears. The knit fabric did absolutely nothing to disguise her lush curves, and he found himself wanting to move closer, to—

"Is something wrong?"

"I didn't come to talk about Lily, or Charlie, or Dolly."

She worried her lower lip with her teeth. A full, soft lip that looked all too inviting.

Where words had failed him, instinct was happy to take over. He draped an arm across the sofa, ran his fingers through her hair. Then drew her closer and lowered his mouth to hers.

She stiffened, laid a hand against his chest.

But then, sweet heaven, she softened in his arms, and

suddenly her hand was threading through his hair, cupping his head, drawing him deeper and deeper into a kiss that sent heat spiraling right through him, to places that hadn't responded in a very long time.

At the sudden, uncomfortable pressure, he drew back a little and shifted his weight. And stared down into eyes that had darkened with desire that matched his own.

"*That's* what I remembered," he said softly, brushing a kiss against her forehead. "I'd decided maybe it was just my imagination."

She swallowed. "I'd figured it was just mine."

He rose, gently set her coffee cup aside and pulled her to her feet. With a driving intensity that nearly took his breath away, he backed her against one of the pillars and held her so close that he could feel the warmth of her thighs against his. The beat of her heart. Her ragged breathing.

In her eyes he saw the reflections of past pain, past disappointments—a hesitance born of trust given too freely and relationships gone wrong.

If anyone had ever walked away from this sweet, beautiful, intelligent woman, they must have been completely mad.

With a sense of wonderment, he traced her cheekbone, then curved his arm behind her shoulders and kissed her until he felt dizzy with a far deeper need.

He dropped a hand to her lower back, then lower yet, and cupped her bottom, pulling her even closer. His heartbeat thundered in his ears... It was someone knocking at the door.

Breathless, he felt her step away from his arms. He focused on her swollen lips, on the stunned look in her eyes. If they hadn't been interrupted, he might have had her on the floor in the next heartbeat. With three kids just outside.

And she knew it, too.

What on earth had just happened? He'd *never* allowed himself to be caught up in such intense emotion that he'd lost sense of time and place and sheer responsibility.

"Dad! I need to use the bathroom! And you said I could, one time. Dad?" The pounding grew louder. *"Dad!"*

Matt swallowed, moved to the windows facing the mountains. "Come in, Charlie," he managed to say.

Charlie bounded in the door, looking a great deal less stressed than one would have guessed from his pleas a moment earlier. "So, where's the bathroom?" he called out cheerfully.

Matt looked over his shoulder, but didn't turn around. "Ask Jolie—I think it's the second door on your left."

"Hey, you guys look *weird.*"

Thank God the boy hadn't just walked in the door a few minutes earlier—like a typical ten-year-old boy, he'd been appalled at that simple kiss up on the mountain. This embrace had gone much farther than that.

Matt lowered his voice, infusing it with meaning the boy couldn't possibly misunderstand. *"Charlie.* You know the rules about your time-outs. You have to stay put, and you must be quiet. Go to the bathroom, then go out on the porch."

"But—"

"March!" But even as Matt gave the order, he knew why Charlie still stood at the door, staring.

Jolie did look different. In wild disarray, her hair was a tangled gold cloud around her face. Her cheeks were rosy, her eyes bright. And her twisted turtleneck revealed a sliver of creamy skin at her waist.

"We're just having an…uh…adult conversation," she said. "Your dad is right. Take the second door."

"How much time do I have left on my time-out?" he wheedled.

"I'll double it *again* if you don't do your business and then get back out there." Matt gave him a stern look. "I'm also thinking about taking that paint expense out of your allowance, so don't press your luck."

"Jeez, Dad. It was an accident."

"I know. And you aren't ever supposed to be in that shop unless I'm in there, too. Now *move!*"

Charlie took a sharp left into the bathroom and was back out on the porch swing in less than a minute.

"I don't suppose he washed his hands," Matt sighed.

Jolie nervously adjusted her shirt, then scooped her hair back with both hands. "I just hope he didn't see what was going on in here. In broad daylight! I feel like a...a—"

Matt crossed the room and locked his hands low behind her hips, drawing her closer. "Like an extremely sensuous woman?"

"No...I mean..."

He gave in to the impulse because she was just too close, and too incredibly desirable. He settled his mouth on hers once more, tasting the sweetness. The vulnerability. Her instinctive response kicked his pulse into high gear once again.

But by sheer force of will, he let her go.

"I didn't come over planning to do this," he murmured against her hair. The shimmering mass smelled of flowers, and sunshine, and felt like silk on his cheek. "I came over to ask you for a date."

He could feel her trying to stifle a laugh as she pulled away. "That's funny?"

"No...not at all. Except given what happened here, I think we already got to that last moment on a date. You know, where we try to decide if we ought to kiss or not? And worry about it most of the night?"

Maybe *she* would have worried, but he had no doubt

about what *he* wanted. Not now. The problem would be trying to stop. "Since we've got that part over with, we'll have a low-stress evening. What do you think?"

She tilted her head to study his expression. "There's the strangest glint in your eyes. Would we actually *go* somewhere, or are you just hoping to pounce before I get out the door?"

He held up two fingers. "Dinner, Scout's honor. Maybe down in Big Timber, or one of the resorts up the highway? I can't tell you how long it's been since I've been out with another adult for a nice dinner."

A smile played at her lips. "Me too."

"Dad?" Charlie's plaintive voice filtered in through the front door of the cabin. "Is it time yet?"

"There's never time enough." Matt searched Jolie's face. "Well?"

"Next Friday?"

Next *Friday?* He'd been thinking tonight, but the afternoon shadows were already lengthening, and he had to collect the kids, get home and make them supper. Impulse plans weren't easy to make. "Sure—that's fine."

But Friday night just seemed too far away.

CHAPTER FIFTEEN

FOR THE FIRST TIME in more years than he could count, Robert Maxwell wasn't in church Sunday morning. He'd never come down for breakfast this late, either.

He could imagine what the other church members were saying behind his back. *Did you hear about Maxwell? Bad heart. He sure isn't going to be such a powerful force in these parts anymore—maybe they'll even sell out so he can retire.*

No one was going to be dancing on his grave just yet. But given the worried looks and hovering Beth was doing, she must be thinking that day was close.

"Just go on to town," he urged. "You could make the second service if you want. I'll be fine."

"I've got plenty here to keep me busy. Can I get you something? I made low-fat muffins, and I can scramble up some of those eggs that don't have any cholesterol. I've been reading up on recipes in a heart-healthy cookbook, and—"

"I'd like an omelette, three eggs, with ham, sausage and cheese. Three strips of bacon. White toast, heavy on the butter. Coffee strong enough to take paint off a Chevy. Just the usual."

Beth glanced at the clock, then lifted two of the prescription bottles from the kitchen shelf and drew a glass of water at the kitchen sink. "For starters, here you go. Consider this your first course."

When he didn't take the bottle from her, she folded her arms. "You want breakfast?"

"I can go to town for breakfast."

"Thirty miles? In that time I can have you fed and on your way."

He started to push away from the table, but the powerful drive that had kept him going nonstop for decades didn't seem to be there anymore.

"Please."

"Darn it, Beth, I don't like what those meds do to me."

"Keep you alive? Keep you here for your children and grandchildren? Cassie called last night and said she was bringing young Zak out early today. Ought to be here any minute. If any child ever needed a grandpa, it's him."

He nearly snorted at the thought of his own children truly caring if he lived another decade or not. They felt duty, yes. But he couldn't remember a time when he'd ever laughed with them, or had made any of them smile.

But Zak...the thought of the boy caught him up short. Zak had started to come around a little, on his visits to the ranch. Not much. Having his dad take off had nearly crushed him, and he was still near shy as a fawn. But he was a smart one—a Maxwell to the bone.

When that little guy tagged along behind him, the years rolled back and Robert could imagine the child was Bobby, all innocent eagerness and excitement over every new day. Zak was giving him a second chance to do things *right*.

"Give me the damn pills," Robert growled.

Beth beamed as she watched him take the medication, then handed him a glass of water. "Now, just you relax, and I'll have your breakfast ready in a minute."

From outside came the sound of a car wheezing to a stop. Cassie's old Toyota, a car she should have traded off three years ago.

When she walked in the back door, with Zak hovering at her heels, he scowled at her. "When are you getting rid of that car?"

She peeled off her trim leather jacket, then bent to help Zak with his. "Just as charming as ever, I see," she said under her breath.

"Dammit, Cassandra, one of these days you're going to be stranded on the highway with that boy. I'll give you the money for a car."

Her eyes flashed with the rebellion that had been as much a part of her as her red hair since she was a girl. "No. But thanks anyway. I can manage on my own."

Beth bustled forward, wiping her hands on a towel. "If it isn't Zak! Hi there, Tex. Are you going to ride Smoky today?"

Zak's shoulder twitched.

"Well, I think he's been hoping you would come," Beth said. "And did you know that we have new kittens out in the hay barn? I've been hoping someone could help me tame them a little."

As she watched Beth and Zak, Cassie's expression softened. She lifted her gaze to meet Robert's. "How are you, Dad?"

"Fine."

"You're never in the house this late. And you look tired."

He gave an impatient gesture with a hand. "Your sisters and Beth made too much of that spell. I couldn't be better."

"I would have come home last night, but Jolie said you were stable."

"I wouldn't want you driving a hundred thirty miles in that junker at night. There was no point in coming."

"Dad, I…" Her voice trailed away. "I'm just glad you're home."

Zak slipped his hand in hers and whispered something.

"I guess we're going to go check out those kittens, and maybe the new calves, too."

"Breakfast will be ready in fifteen minutes or so," Beth called out as Cassie and Zak went out the door.

"Breakfast?" Cassie stopped in her tracks and glanced at her watch. "At nine? Now I *know* you aren't feeling as good as you say."

Zak peered around her. The worry etched in that young boy's face doused Robert's heated reply. Did Zak worry that more people in his life were going to disappear?

"Just go on, you two," Robert muttered.

Through the kitchen window he watched them cross the lawn and head for the barns. He'd known Cassie's husband was no good from the minute he laid eyes on him, and he'd warned—no, *demanded* that she quit seeing the bastard. Being Cassie, that had only driven her to marry the guy anyway.

Maybe it was my fault. For the first time, Robert realized that maybe he'd been the one to blame for that marriage...and the sadness of the little boy who shadowed her. His thoughts drifted back to other times...

"Robert! Wake up, it's time to eat." Beth hovered close, shaking his shoulder gently. Her hand held the scent of fresh-cut oranges, and the aroma of good strong coffee filled the air.

Feeling disoriented, he opened his eyes and had to concentrate to focus on the wall clock above the stove. Nine-thirty? "I wasn't sleeping."

"No, of course not." A smile played at the corners of Beth's mouth as she moved to the stove and started filling a plate. With her usual efficiency she set it in front of him, then slipped out of the room.

"Yes, you were," Bobby said blandly.

Startled, Robert swiveled and found his son sprawled in a chair at the end of the table. His face was dark with stubble, his shirt buttoned halfway up. He'd pushed aside an untouched plate of bacon and eggs.

I was dozing at the table like an old man? Images of walkers and wheelchairs and flocks of white-coated doctors flashed through Robert's thoughts. Powerlessness. Loss of control.

The all-too familiar fear snaked into his heart...then took refuge in anger. "Where the hell were you last night? You look like roadkill."

"I'm nineteen. I don't have to answer to you for every minute." Bobby returned his glare, though he wasn't pacing the room and gesturing as he usually did when riled, and his eyes had the glassy appearance of someone fighting either a bad headache or a big hangover. Probably the latter, young fool that he was.

"You're on my ranch, under my roof, and I want to know!" Robert roared. He took little satisfaction in seeing Bobby wince at the noise. *Hangover.*

"Don't worry, *Dad.* I was with—" his gaze slid away "—my friends, and there sure isn't much going on in Paradise Corners. I didn't take my truck."

He *couldn't* have taken it, that much Robert knew. Knowing of the boy's propensity to rebel, Robert had told Herman to park Bobby's truck in a locked barn on one of the distant leased ranches, and now they both kept a much closer eye on the keys to the ranch pickups. But that didn't mean Bobby would stay out of trouble. "If you violate the terms of your probation you'll end up in jail."

"How the hell could I do anything wrong? I can't drive. You have me working every last minute here, or doing that community service. I have a damn *baby-sitter* taking me to town for that."

"Don't you ever, *ever* talk about Beth that way." Anger and a wave of unexpected protectiveness burned through Robert's gut. "After your mom died, she raised you kids and ran this house. You will give her only the *utmost* respect."

Bobby threw up his hands in exasperation—then gingerly lowered them to his sides. "You think I don't? It's sure great seeing how little you think of me."

Robert sighed heavily. "You were going to send away for college information."

"Yeah."

"Well?"

Bobby fell silent.

"I figured as much. I had the bookkeeper do some checking. I figure we'll enroll you at MSU-Bozeman. If you toe the mark, you could get a master's in animal and range science, or applied economics. Either would be good background for operating Walking Stones."

"Good God, Bozeman is less than a hundred miles away!"

"Right. You can be home every weekend, studying." Robert slammed both palms on the table and rose from his chair. "I know about the temptations in college—the parties, the bars. You sure as hell aren't ready to deal with all that."

"Are you going to pick out each class for me, too?" Bobby spat. "And choose my clothes?"

Pressure built in Robert's chest, making it hard to breathe. Turned his knees to jelly. *Easy. This is no big deal.* He sank back in his chair. *You'll be fine.*

After a few seconds he found his voice again. "You have the world at your feet, son. The biggest ranch in the county. One of the biggest, best Angus-breeding programs in the country. Don't blow a chance most ranchers would kill for."

Bobby's eyes narrowed. "It's always just *control* for you. Controlling the land, your livestock, and oh, by the way, your kids. You've dangled the ranch in front of Thea but never let her have the satisfaction of even recognizing her value. She's more dedicated than *anyone*. You drove Cassie and Jolie away. But you aren't pulling my strings forever."

"Dammit, that's uncalled for. I expect you out on your horse in twenty minutes, checking calves in the north meadow, so maybe you'd better get going before we both say things we'll regret."

The triumphant gleam in Bobby's eyes said it all. "See what I mean? And you don't even realize what you're doing. Well, some things you *can't* control."

"I own this ranch, and everything on it. It's…something to be…damn proud of." He might have just wrestled a seven-hundred-pound steer to the ground, for as heavily as he was breathing, Robert realized. *Steady. Take it easy.*

"You sure as hell don't own me. Not Cassie or Jolie either. Ever noticed that Jolie almost never comes home? That Cassie stayed away for years?" Bobby's voice rose.

"That's not your business."

"No? What about family? Being close? *Caring?*" Bobby launched to his feet. "From what I hear, some carpenter is sniffing around Jolie," he sneered. "Maybe he's just another guy after the glorious Maxwell empire, like all those other guys you've always checked out—do you think the girls even know about what you do?"

"Bobby—"

"Don't worry. I'll get to work. But I'm not letting you interfere with my life the way you've tried to interfere in theirs. If I have to borrow every penny, I'm going to college someplace far away. And when I'm done, *then* I'll decide if I'm ever coming back."

Bobby's heavy boots stomped toward the mudroom. The

door squealed open, then slammed shut hard enough to rattle the crystal and china in the dining-room hutch.

You handled that well. As his breathing eased, Robert rolled the tension out of his shoulders. Then picked up his fork and dug into the—

He froze.

One piece of dry toast. A pile of those no-cholesterol eggs, now cold. A strip of something vaguely resembling bacon that had never been within a hundred yards of hog. And he'd bet his best bull that the coffee cup was filled with decaf.

With a growl of displeasure, Robert stalked across the kitchen and headed for his office. After shutting the door firmly behind him, he settled behind his desk, grabbed the phone and hit the autodial code for the private home number of the most senior lawyer of the firm representing Walking Stones.

"Ted? I need you to do some research. Contact that P.I. we used last time—yeah, that's the one. Whatever it takes. I want a background check done on a guy here in Paradise. Matt Dawson. If he missed the school bus in third grade, I want to know. Got it? And I want preliminary information by tomorrow."

There were plenty of people out there who wanted to get their hands on the Walking Stones empire, and they'd preyed on his daughters before in the guise of devoted admirers.

Just hearing about the investigation was often enough to send them packing. A visit by one of the lawyers—finding there would be no chance of receiving even a nickel—usually doused the flames of romance.

But for the determined few, there were always skeletons unearthed during an investigation—unpaid taxes, questionable tax shelters, shady business dealings or illegal-alien employees or any number of secrets. A subtle hint, and a boyfriend with avarice on his mind invariably dropped from sight.

Swiveling in his chair, Robert leaned back and surveyed the snowy peaks of the Crazies, a sense of satisfaction and control seeping into his bones.

"YOU'RE AS NERVOUS as a filly in the starting gate," Irene murmured with an amused waggle of an eyebrow, leaning a shoulder against the door frame of the first exam room. She studied Jolie head to toe. "Hot date tonight?"

"Too much caffeine, I guess." Jolie thumbed through the remaining three patient files on the counter. Three more patients this afternoon, two of them new. She *definitely* was not dwelling on her date with Matt tonight. A quiet dinner with a companionable neighbor—what was there to be nervous about?

Megan looked up from the computer keyboard at the front desk and shook her head. "The coffee in the lab is decaf."

With the two women waiting expectantly, Jolie gave in. "Okay, so I have a date with Matt. No big deal. We're just friends."

Megan grinned. "He's way cool. Those eyes—" she sighed melodramatically "—I'd kill for those sexy eyes of his. Wear something really hot."

"Oh, sure. Like what, a spandex dress?"

"No—something classy. Sexy. You know, the little-black-dress thing you always read about in magazines."

Irene nodded. "She's right. You need something special. What do you have?"

Jolie gave an unladylike snort. "I wear slacks and blouses to work and church. Business suits to medical conferences. I date maybe once every quarter century."

"I could fit two of you in the clothes I've got," Irene muttered. "Megan?"

The light in Megan's eyes dimmed. "I don't have anything either. But wait—" She took a quick glance at the clock on the wall, then bent under the desk to grab her purse and started for the door. "Come with me to Remembered Treasures. It's only a block away. Please?"

"The consignment shop?" Jolie stared after her.

Megan stopped halfway out the front door. "They've got the perfect outfit, and I'll bet it would fit."

"Well—"

"Go on," Irene ordered, shooing Jolie toward the door. "You've got a while until the first afternoon appointment and you could be a few minutes late. I've never known Marge Watkins to be on time a day in her life."

The whirlwind trip to Remembered Treasures, under the youthful guidance of a teenager almost half her age, was an eye-opener.

The dress Jolie returned with was as well.

"Let's see it," Irene ordered, waving them down the hall to Jolie's office. "Mrs. Watkins will need a few minutes to fill out her registration form anyway."

Jolie slid the dress out of the protective plastic bag and held the hanger on one finger. "I think this is just a bit too much for Paradise Corners. What do you think?"

"But you wouldn't be eating here, anyway," Megan pointed out. "I hardly think you'll be going to Grizzly's."

The deep V of the neckline, both front and back, looked deeper than before, now that the dress was on a hanger. Jet black, with thousands of tiny jet beads sparkling in the sunlight streaming through the window, it looked appropriate for New York or Los Angeles.

And it looked awfully, awfully short.

"Are you *sure* this is okay?"

Megan nodded. "Perfect."

"I'll look overdressed." *And desperate.* What if Matt showed up in jeans and a polo shirt?

"Elegant," Irene said firmly.

"It's too short, too tight...and cut too low. It makes my...uh...chest look too big."

Megan reached for the dress and slid the plastic bag back over the hanger. "Even the manager thought it was great on you."

"Given the slow business day she was having, she would have said that if I'd tried on the entry rug."

Irene drew herself to her full height. "She's my sister's mother-in-law, and believe me, she'd never steer you wrong. She says it's bad for business."

Abashed, Jolie gave in. During her years away from Paradise, she'd forgotten the basic rule of thumb in a small town: assume *everyone* is related to, or friends with, everyone else.

She made herself smile despite her misgivings. "Thanks for the advice, you two."

A sharp knock sounded at the back door.

Irene stepped into the hallway and hurried to answer it. A murmur of voices rose, and in a moment she reappeared. "It's your brother, Jolie. Are you free?"

"Send him on in." Alarm slid through Jolie as she moved to the door of her office, her first thoughts on their dad's condition. Was he worse? Had he collapsed?

Bobby sauntered toward her, his black hair rakishly tipped over his forehead and a devilish grin on his face. "Hey, sis, how's it—" The words died on his lips.

Megan, who'd darted toward the front room, came face-to-face with him at the door to Jolie's office. She gasped, curved a protective hand over her belly.

Bobby's gaze flashed between Jolie and Megan, then

down to Megan's swollen waist. He paled. "I—I was just stopping on my way over to the fairgrounds. I didn't realize…"

"How real this pregnancy is?" Jolie asked calmly. "Megan is working here until the baby comes, then she's thinking about moving away for college. Have you two had a chance to talk about this lately?"

Megan whimpered and drew back, but Jolie caught her arm. "I think it's time, don't you? Let's go into my office and get you two settled. And then I need to get to work."

"I don't want to talk," Megan said. "I don't even want to *see* him again. Ever."

Jolie steered her firmly into the room. "Don't let it go any longer, honey. You'll feel better, and so will he."

With the glazed look of someone heading for death row, Bobby followed them in and took a chair. Megan perched on the edge of another one, ready to bolt.

"I tried talking to her twice," Bobby said through his teeth. "She wouldn't talk to me."

Megan's expression changed from wariness to indignation. "You told your father that this baby wasn't yours. I never even *dated* anyone else, and you know it. I once thought I loved you, Bobby."

Bobby shifted uncomfortably in his chair.

"Why did you *lie?*"

Shoving a hand through his hair, he slouched down in the chair and closed his eyes at the painful memory. "You don't know my old man. That night I had no idea that you were…were…"

"You can say it," Megan snapped. "I've had to, for the past seven months. *Pregnant.*"

"After your dad told mine about it, Dad called me into his office. He was in such a rage I didn't even know what he was talking about at first. So of course I denied everything." He shook his head slowly. "And later...well, it just seemed easier to leave it that way."

"Easier?" Megan choked back a sob.

"Why didn't you tell me right away?"

"How could I? After Danny got hurt in that accident last fall, you disappeared into the mountains. That's when I first found out I was pregnant. And after you got home, you never called...you didn't come over..."

"Dad really got on me about responsibility, and the ranch..." A dull flush crept up Bobby's neck. "I didn't get to town for weeks."

"None of this changes the facts. You have a legal responsibility here, Bobby," Jolie said quietly.

Megan stood up abruptly and shoved her forefinger at Bobby's chest. "Well, don't worry. You're off the hook. I don't want your money, and I don't want you. I'll deny that you're the father, and if anyone tries to force me to undergo DNA tests, I'll disappear. *Happy?*" She headed for the door without looking back. "I have to get back to work."

A heavy silence fell after she left.

"I did try to call her a few times. She wouldn't ever come to the phone." Bobby leaned forward and dropped his face in his hands. "I have made such a mess of things."

"You hurt her very badly, Bobby." Jolie moved to shut the door for privacy. Jolie took a deep breath, sending up a silent prayer for the right words. Wondering if she could get through to him. "If you aren't careful, you'll have a son or daughter whom you'll never see. If Megan meets someone else, that man will raise your child. You'll never know if he treats your child well."

Bobby flinched. "Don't I have rights?"

"Parental rights can be settled in a court of law, but it would be much easier if she doesn't try to disappear. For the benefit of the child, you two need to work out a friendly relationship. An adversarial one will be hard on all three of you.''

A soft knock sounded at the door. ''Mrs. Watkins is still waiting,'' Irene said. ''Do you know how long you'll be?''

''Coming.'' Jolie rose as Bobby did, and moved forward to give him a hug. ''Take care. And let me know if there's anything I can do.''

Bobby nodded, then silently walked out the door.

CHAPTER SIXTEEN

"HE'S HERE," Megan called out. "Should I let him in, or should he wait out on the porch?"

"Um…let him in." Jolie struggled with the snug zipper and back hook fastener of the dress, then searched the floor for her high heels while fluffing her hair. A thrill of antic-ipation fluttered through her midsection.

This is just two friendly neighbors, having a sociable night out, she reminded herself.

But memories of that last kiss still had the power to send tremors clear down to her toes, and this date had given her minor anxiety attacks all week long. *Enjoy the night and don't expect anything else. He's just another nice guy, and heaven knows none of them last, anyway.*

The cabin door opened, then shut. Heavy footsteps moved into the great room, and the sound of Matt's deep voice, interspersed with Megan's, filtered down the short hallway.

Jolie swallowed. Took a deep breath. And opened the door.

From the hallway she could see Matt was facing the other way, talking to Megan. He'd worn a navy blazer that fit perfectly, accenting his broad shoulders and narrow waist. Khaki slacks skimmed his slim hips. He looked taller. Big-ger. Far more imposing than he had in jeans and flannel. He laughed at something Megan said, and when he moved, the firelight danced on the dark, deep waves of his hair.

"Hi," she said quietly as she reached the great room. "All set to go?"

As Matt turned toward her, Megan gave Jolie a double thumbs-up and a broad smile from behind him.

Matt simply stared.

"Matt? Is something wrong?" Jolie surveyed the front of her dress. Felt for her earrings.

"Nothing at all." His voice dropped even lower than usual. "You look...wonderful."

As if an overly curvy, five-foot-five, thirty-three-year-old could look wonderful, but she had to give him points for trying. He, on the other hand, looked magnificent. His deep tan only accented the strong lines of his face, the deep dimples of his smile.

"Are we set, then?"

"Absolutely," he murmured, his eyes twinkling.

She grabbed her cell phone from the counter and glanced at its screen—the digital symbols indicated it was half-charged, but that much would last the next few hours—then slipped it into her purse.

At his truck, he opened her door and gave her a hand up, then shut the door and rounded the front of the truck. Once behind the wheel, he turned on the ignition and slid her an easy grin. "It's been so many years, I feel as though I'm on my first date ever."

The reminder of his late wife help calm Jolie's rapid pulse. *Just friends, just neighbors.* "It's been a while for me, too."

He threw the truck into gear, then muttered a soft curse and shifted it back into Park. "There's no room in here for this, but..."

With an inarticulate sound, he slid over a few inches. Slipped his arm around her shoulder and pulled her closer. "That is," he growled, "one incredibly sexy dress."

He stared intently into her eyes as if trying to read her thoughts, his mouth hovering over hers, as if he needed a clear sign from her.

He smelled of soap and faint after-shave and man, a beguiling scent that teased her senses and warmed her blood. The golden highlights in his eyes seemed to flicker, go dark and deep. His mouth settled on hers. Mobile, searching. Hot.

Thankful she hadn't yet buckled up, she turned into his arms and threaded her hands into his hair. Wanting *more*. After weeks of trying to deny the sexual tension she felt between them, he was here, just a breath away.

He withdrew. Rested his forehead against hers. "If this steering wheel wasn't in the way—" He gave her another swift kiss, cupping her face with both hands. "But maybe that's just as well. Let's go, okay?"

Somewhere between the cabin and his truck, she'd lost her ability to speak. Perhaps she'd even lost her mind.

Whatever her reservations had been before, she couldn't even guess at them now.

IF IT HADN'T BEEN such a crazy thought, Matt would have guessed that Jolie was actually *nervous*.

Over the main course he finally set his fork aside and eyed her with concern. "Is anything wrong?"

She looked up from her shrimp and linguini, her fork poised in midair. She'd caught her hair up into some sort of elegant knot on her head, with wavy tendrils framing her face. The candlelight changed it to deep amber, shot with sparks of gold. Her eyes sparkled too, dark and mysterious in the dim light.

"It's all *wonderful*. I can't recall when I had such a lovely dinner. Have you been to Four Pines before?"

He almost smiled at that, imagining Charlie fidgeting in

his chair and Lily dropping her nose in a book. "No. One of my clients mentioned it."

"Tell him that he's got very, very good taste." She savored the next bite of her entrée. "This is almost too delicious for words."

And she had to be the most beautiful woman he'd ever met. "Would you like to dance?"

He stood and held out his hand, not giving her the chance to say no, not wanting to wait another minute to hold her in his arms.

She laughed softly. "Just tell me how much value you place on your feet. I haven't done this in a long while."

The string quartet in the corner eased into "Unforgettable" as she followed him onto the empty dance floor and moved into his arms.

She must have been made just for him. She fit perfectly in his embrace, every curve. Soft, sweet, warm. He reached up and cupped her head, holding it against his chest, and closed his eyes. The dinner had been excellent, but this was sheer heaven.

The faint scent of her perfume—Cashmere Mist, she'd called it—teased at his senses. And the dress, heaven help him, revealed more than it concealed.

Slit way up on one thigh, draped to her lower back and revealing the far-too-enticing shadow between her full breasts, it sparkled and dared him to reach up to slip the slender straps from her shoulders.

He was pretty sure that she wore absolutely nothing but those shimmery black nylons underneath, for the dress clung like a second skin, skimming her breasts and the flare of her hips.

Her warm thighs against his sent heat and desire rushing through him as they moved slowly to the music. Clouded his thoughts. Made him want far more than this dance. Far more than this single night.

She sighed against his chest. "This is wonderful," she breathed. "I think I could go on forever, just like this." She looked up at him, the sensual promise in her eyes lit with a hint of amusement. "Do you think we could pay that quartet to play for the next twenty-four hours nonstop?"

She felt it too, then. The sweep of emotions too powerful to ignore. A tidal wave of possessiveness rushed through him, coupled with deeper feelings he quickly shut away.

He glanced up, found another man approaching who was eyeing Jolie with the keen interest and confidence of one who'd cruised this territory for women before. From the top of his well-cut hair and yacht-club tan, to the tips of his expensive loafers, he was trouble, wanting an introduction.

At Matt's intense warning stare the man's stride faltered, then he veered away.

"Come on. Let's go!" Matt took her hand and started for their table.

"No, wait. Can't we dance just a little longer? Please?"

"Our food will be cold if we stay much longer." He winked at her, slid an arm around her waist as they crossed the floor. Rested a guiding hand at the small of her back as they wound through the tables to their own. "Your shrimp looked excellent, and I hear the chocolate-mousse cheesecake is incredible."

As she slid into her seat, she tilted her head. "What happened out there? One minute I'm in heaven, the next I'm being herded off the floor."

I realized just how much I want you. He lifted a shoulder. "Nothing—it was just getting a little crowded out there."

She glanced at the half-dozen couples slow dancing, then her eyes widened with concern. "Did I crush your toes?"

If that man had so much as touched you, I might have

had to kill him, right on the dance floor at Four Pines Lodge. "No problem." He reaching across the table for her hand. "At least I know a good doctor."

A rosy flush bloomed in her cheeks. "I'm *so* sorry."

Her hand felt soft and cool within his, and he marveled at the delicate bone structure. At all she'd done with these hands—healing, comforting, operating, situations he couldn't even begin to imagine—and regretted that he'd teased her.

"Honey, you didn't step on my feet. You're a wonderful dancer. And I'm very, very glad to be here with you tonight. I don't even want to think about taking you home."

Their eyes met, held.

The need to hold her in his arms, the need to slide that dress right off of her and savor every inch of her smooth creamy skin, warred with stark reality.

The kids were undoubtedly still awake at his house, and a teenage girl awake at hers.

He had an overriding responsibility to Lily and Charlie that precluded looking for a night in a motel room or on a blanket under the stars. There could be no midmorning, bleary-eyed homecomings after dates, not with his children still learning about life from what he did himself.

What he wanted from them—responsibility—he had to demonstrate himself.

Maybe Jolie wasn't even interested in taking this relationship a step further. But right now, the scent of her, the feel of her, and that damn dress were driving him over the edge.

With a growl of frustration, he stood abruptly and threw three twenties on the table. "Let's go."

"But—"

"Please." He took a slow breath. "Come outside with

me, for just a minute. We can come back and dance the rest of the evening if you want to."

She rose, never breaking her gaze from his. "Let's go."

THE PHONE RANG at eleven. Rubbing his face in frustration, Robert reached for the receiver on his desk.

He'd been going over the plans for the Walking Stones' spring production sale for the past hour, proofreading the sales catalog that would be printed and mailed in two weeks to buyers all over the world. There could be no mistakes—not even one small error—that might reflect badly on the ranch or its breeding herd.

"Yeah?"

"The investigator has some of the information you wanted."

The silky, sophisticated voice set his teeth on edge, but Robert didn't pay his lawyers for being likable. "Fax it."

"He says there'll be more, but I'll send along what I've got."

In the background, Robert heard the clinking of crystal, the murmur of voices and the faint sounds of music. "Thanks."

He started to hang up, but the lawyer cleared his throat.

"Thought you'd like to know that the guy is out with your daughter tonight. He…ah…looked as if he wanted to undress her right on the dance floor. When I got a little too close, as if I wanted to cut in, he practically dragged her away by the hair."

Cassie had rebelled and married a no-good hustler. Jolie was not going to make the same mistake, following her blind emotions instead of the Maxwell brains she was born with.

"I want that information on him *tonight*," Robert

growled. "And as soon as it comes through my fax machine, you and I are going to talk."

"Say, Robert, when she's free, I sure wouldn't mind an introduction. That daughter of yours is quite a looker."

Robert slammed down the receiver. Shoved the stack of papers in front of him to one side and reached for the bottom-right desk drawer where he kept a glass and a bottle of Chivas away from Beth's watchful eyes.

After the first tumblerful slid down, he held the glass to the light and tipped it this way and that, watching the last drops slide as he waited for the warmth to bloom in his chest. A soft sound—the subtle creak of that one floorboard near the front entryway—put his senses on alert.

Eleven-fifteen on Friday. Where the hell did the kid think he was going? Anger rushed through him.

"Stop," he roared, shoving his chair away from the desk. He ignored the heavy feeling in his chest and strode out of his office to the center of the darkened great room.

Bobby stood at the front door. His jacket and boots, evidence of his plans, had been tossed to one side of the entryway. Something silver glinted in his right hand.

"Where the hell are you going?" Robert demanded. He marched across the remaining stretch of room, catching Bobby's hand as the boy moved to put the object in his hip pocket.

It was a single truck key. One of the extras Robert had hidden in his desk drawer.

"You were going to sneak out and take one of the trucks," Robert said wearily. "Despite everything—despite the possibility that you could go to jail for defying your probation—you were going to take off like some thief in the night."

The pressure grew stronger in his chest, settling like a hundred-pound anvil right over his heart.

Bobby's chin lifted defiantly. "It's gonna kill me to just sit here, night after night. I can't do it." His gaze slid away, his voice lowered. Something akin to pain glittered in his eyes. "There's someone I gotta see."

The anvil squeezed down harder, making each breath an effort. Cold sweat trickled down Robert's back. "I...can't watch you every minute. I'm not your jailer. But you...drive...if you make any mistakes...that new judge who took LeVay's place is going to crucify you."

Bobby jerked his hand away and reached for his jacket and boots. "You can't buy him off as easily? Too bad LeVay retired." His voice was hard. "That oughta be interesting, seeing what happens if you no longer have half the county in your pocket."

He spun away, jerked open the door and stepped outside, leaving it open behind him.

"Bobby—" The name came out as a whisper, but Bobby had already made it halfway to the trio of ranch trucks parked at the end of the curving driveway in front of the house.

Robert tried again. But this time he couldn't speak the name aloud.

An iron fist grabbed at his heart and crushed it, sending blinding pain rocketing through his chest.

The welcoming darkness enfolded him like a heavy shroud, and he sank into it with relief.

The sound of Beth's anguished cry came like a faint splinter of light that faded before he could even grasp the words.

JOLIE SHIVERED within Matt's arms despite the blazer he'd draped over her shoulders. She leaned her head against his chest and folded her arms over his.

They'd driven to Last Woman Peak, a popular lookout in

the hills above Paradise Corners, parked the truck, then walked the remaining quarter mile. He'd spread a quilt over the grass at their feet.

"It's beautiful, isn't it?"

She felt Matt's answer rumble against her back.

Below them, the lights of town twinkled as the chilly night breeze tossed the branches of the firs and maples lining the streets. The crisp white spires of the four stately churches that had given the town its name, each standing on a corner at Main and Church, gleamed staunchly under the illumination of floodlights. Tradition. Family. Small-town values. *Permanence.* All of the things she'd come home to find.

He brushed a kiss at her temple, then just below her ear. "You smell so good," he murmured, pulling her more firmly against his chest.

The warmth of his mouth was a stark contrast to the chill night air as he dropped another kiss on her exquisitely sensitized nape. She arched her neck, inviting—*needing* more, and when he trailed whisper-soft kisses there she felt a swirl of dark, rich emotions well up inside her.

She moaned, twisted around in his arms. The swift, strong beat of his heart echoed against her own. The heat and raw need in his eyes nearly took her breath away. But it was the hint of vulnerability that stole her heart. *I think I love you.*

A heady thrill of recklessness raced through her as she reached up and pulled him down into a deep kiss, expressing the emotions she didn't dare voice, because she knew from experience that once love came into the equation, relationships always died. *So what are you doing up here?* an inner voice warned. *This is a mistake.*

But right now she could no more listen to her inner voice than she could take flight and soar over the treetops on her own power.

He crushed her against his hard chest, then his hand brushed against her throat and settled there, warm and strong, before snagging the strap of her dress. He slid it gently down, down, until the bodice slid past the peak of one breast.

"You are so beautiful," he murmured. He cupped the weight of her breast in his hand. Gently rubbed at the sensitive tip. "Just so incredibly beautiful."

Sensation rocketed through her, settling deep inside her as he bared the other breast, then bent and took her nipple in his mouth.

At the exquisite pleasure she arched forward, wanting more, offering herself to him without reservation. Wanting the moment to last forever. The gentle suction grew harder, sending ripples of sensation zinging to every part of her. She moaned, dropped her head back. Never had it felt like this. *Never.*

Straightening, he pulled her against his chest with one arm behind her shoulders and the other pressing against her hips, as if he couldn't get close enough. He met her gaze, his eyes filled with molten heat. Desire. And hard-won restraint.

The unspoken question lay between them, but there was no other answer she could give. Not when he possessed every last part of her being with just a touch.

She reached up, caught at the zipper of her dress and released it. The dress fell in a dark, shimmering pool at her feet, leaving just her nylons and a black garter belt, and nothing else.

His breath caught as his gaze swept down, grew darker, more intense as he looked into her eyes once again. "Are you sure?"

She rested a hand against his cheek. Then pulled him toward her, all heat and desire.

"Absolutely," she whispered.

The laugh lines at the corners of his eyes deepened as he searched her face, his lashes lowered and teeth flashing white in the moonlight. "No regrets later?"

He was giving her a second chance she didn't need. "Never."

Like a man who'd been tested beyond his limits, he pulled her close again, and she felt a deep shudder work through him. "Ah, Jolie," he breathed. "You are just so incredible."

Her body responded to the sound of his voice, to his touch, filling her with impatience. She worked his tie loose, flung it aside. Worked at the buttons of his shirt, savoring the warmth of his chest beneath her fingertips.

"Whoa," he chuckled, briefly capturing her wrists. "If my clothes go over the cliff, it's going to be a little hard to walk in the door when we get home."

Home? She didn't want to think about going home. Not when he'd started slowly unbuttoning his shirt, revealing a broad expanse of tanned muscle. Not with his scent and heat surrounding her.

In a heartbeat he stood before her, his skin gleaming in the moonlight, as proud and indomitable as the mountains towering above them. As gentle as the breeze that cooled her heated skin.

When he gave her a wry grin and retrieved a small packet from his jeans, she only loved him more.

Anticipation ran like wildfire through her veins as she pulled him down onto the soft bed of quilt and meadow grass, giving to him everything she had; receiving far more in return.

LONG AFTER MIDNIGHT she lay in his arms. Up in the hills a chorus of coyotes howled at the moon. From somewhere in the towering pines nearby, an owl called, its unearthly, hollow cry echoing on and on.

A faint, high sound rose on the wind from down the trail, the sound of breezes whistling through the pines...almost like the tune on her cellular phone. She lifted her head and listened, but the sound faded away.

She thought Matt might be asleep, but when she raised herself onto one elbow to look at him, he was watching her, his eyes expectant and quietly waiting.

"Are you sorry?" he asked, brushing a tendril of hair away from her face.

Sorry? She'd lived thirty-three years without ever discovering the magic of desire and fulfillment, without ever feeling she'd been well and truly loved.

"Never," she whispered.

And then she moved above him and let him know just how much she meant it.

CHAPTER SEVENTEEN

BACK AT THE TRUCK, Jolie reached for the cell phone in her purse and checked the screen for calls. The battery had gone dead. "Can I use yours to check for any emergency messages?"

Matt reached for the phone clipped to the visor above his head and handed it to her. "Expecting anything?"

"No. But I need to make sure."

The tinny recording on the answering machine at the clinic announced, *You have no new messages.*

"Thank goodness," she breathed. "I envisioned being away for two hours and finding that a dozen people needed me at the clinic."

Matt stroked her cheek with gentle fingertips and settled his mouth on hers for one more kiss, then clipped the phone back up on the visor. "So all is well in Paradise Corners tonight."

Very, *very* well, she thought, watching his large, tanned hand shift the truck into gear.

Over the years she'd been on a lot of dates meant to impress her, but opening night on Broadway, exquisite French restaurants and fifty-yard-line seats didn't even begin to compare with a star-filled night above Paradise Corners, and sitting next to Matt as he maneuvered down this narrow, rocky Montana road.

He turned off the headlights when they reached the edge of the clearing surrounding Jolie's cabin at two in the morning. The wash of moonlight across the meadow turned the meadow to silver, the cabin to dark pewter.

"The lights are all off," Jolie whispered, nestling closer to Matt's side. "At least she's asleep."

"Figure you might receive a lecture?"

Without looking up, she could hear the smile in his voice as he pulled to a slow stop. "No doubt." She straightened, twisted around and rested a palm against his chest, then settled a kiss on his mouth. He tasted like the Pepsi now perched on the dashboard. "Thanks for the lovely evening."

"I'll walk you up."

"Here, in the middle of nowhere? That isn't necessary."

"Here," he said firmly.

At the door of the cabin he stood close, looked down at her. "I don't want this evening to end."

She hiked the strap of her purse higher on her shoulder, then rose on tiptoe for one last kiss. "It was…incredible." *I wish you could stay.*

He tipped his head toward the door. "Want me to come in?"

Oh, yes. "Better not. It's late."

From within the cabin came a small sound, like a child stirring. A faint whimper.

He didn't stop to ask. Taking the key from her hand, he fitted it into the lock and turned it slowly. Eased the door open. "Take it slow," he whispered. "Let me go first."

Someone inside cried out. *Megan?*

Jolie brushed past Matt, flipping the light switch as she entered the room.

She stopped. Looked around. Cupboard doors hung open, kitchen drawers had been pulled out and dumped on the floor. Through the open door of her bedroom it appeared her dresser had been ransacked.

An icy rush of horror flooded through her. "*Oh my God. Megan! Are you okay?*"

A wail rose from a dark corner of the great room, beneath the steps to the loft.

As her eyes adjusted to the dim light, Jolie saw a small figure crouched in the darkness. She hurried toward it while Matt searched the other rooms.

"J-Jolie?" Megan rose slowly, on shaking limbs, her face streaked with tears and one hand held protectively over her belly. "I—I've been so scared. I thought maybe h-he'd come back. The phone was dead and I couldn't call—"

Jolie rushed forward and caught her when she wobbled and nearly fell. Counted weeks of pregnancy as she eased the girl onto the sofa. Thirty-four now, if her original estimate was correct. "Is the baby coming? Are you okay?"

Shivering violently, Megan stared blankly at her. "Someone was *here*. He broke a window. Just like at the clinic." She lifted a trembling arm, pointed toward the windows on the other side of the fireplace where broken glass sparkled on the oval braided rug. "A-and he came inside."

Jolie pulled an afghan from the sofa and snuggled it around Megan's shoulders. "Did he touch you? Did he hurt you in any way?"

"I—I don't think he knew I was here. I hid in the back of my closet and pulled some clothes down around me. He went through every room—I heard him! It was like he was looking for something. Or someone." Her eyes widened. "Your Blazer was here, Jolie. Maybe he was looking for *you.*"

A rush of fear flooded through Jolie's veins. The thought of someone seeking her out in the darkness was nothing less than horrifying.

His jaw clenched, Matt strode into the great room. "Both phones are dead. He must have cut the lines. The bedrooms and loft have been trashed, but I have no idea whether or not things were taken. How is Megan?''

Jolie tried to suppress the trembling of her hands by clasping them behind her back. ''Shaken. Scared. With good reason.''

''I've got to get to my cell phone out in the truck and call home to check on the kids. Then I'll call the deputy as well.'' He grimly scanned the room. ''I want you two to pack a few things and come home with me tonight. *Now.*''

''But—''

''No arguments. This cabin is isolated, you've already got a broken window. The guy could return. And,'' he added, his voice laced with worry, ''I need to get home to my kids.''

Well, that made sense. ''You sit here, honey,'' Jolie soothed. ''I'll grab some of your things.''

Jolie tossed a change of clothes into an overnight bag, then packed some things for Megan. She did a swift survey of her possessions. The intruder hadn't touched the TV, the VCR. Her stereo still sat on the shelf, undisturbed.

Her lingerie drawer had been dumped on the floor, most of its contents kicked across the room. Someone looking for hidden jewelry? Then she saw a black lace bra draped precisely over a lamp shade. Panties laid carefully on her pillow.

Not someone just searching, then…and the alternative made her skin crawl. Not even after a dozen washings would she be able to use clothing that someone had…handled.

She crossed the room to her closet, and lifted a battered cardboard box from the shelf. Untied the twine surrounding it with trembling fingers.

She breathed a sigh of relief as she looked down at the contents. *Untouched.* Small boxes of her few good pieces of jewelry lay inside, along with a larger box containing treasures from her mother—her portion of the jewelry that the three sisters had divided. Most of it was costume jewelry, but each piece held poignant memories. Beneath the boxes lay old report cards from school, papers she'd written in grade school and every birthday card her mother had ever given her.

"Jolie? Are you ready?"

Matt's voice jarred her back to the present. She tied the twine around the box once more, and carried it with the clothes she'd packed. "Coming."

She was nearly out the door when she noticed a piece of ruled notebook paper lying on the floor. She stopped, gingerly lifted the paper by one corner. The words on it were written hastily, in awkward block letters.

Next, I'll have you.

MATT HAD HER CABIN window fixed by six o'clock the next morning. He was still adamant, however, about having Megan and Jolie stay at his house. Rafe agreed.

"I can't just run like a scared rabbit," Jolie insisted, staring at the two men standing in her office two hours later. "I've got a rifle and I've got a cell phone. I'm responsible for Dolly and Sadie. What would poor old Mr. Walters do if something happened to them?"

"This guy wrote a threatening note," Rafe said patiently. "You don't have a security system or a noisy dog. You're a mile from your nearest neighbor."

"I could borrow Jed."

Rafe rolled his eyes heavenward. "He's the most passive dog on the planet."

"But last fall he came through for you, when you had to deal with that poacher."

"*That* was an aberration. There's no guarantee he'd wake up if the roof fell in, much less that he would defend you." Rafe hesitated. "You and Megan could stay at our place, if you'd like. I'm sure Megan would be more comfortable with us than with Robert and Bobby."

"That's sweet of you, but until you build your new place, you hardly have room for two extra people. And I think," she added with a smile, "having us there might cramp your style, you being newlyweds and all."

"Think about Megan's safety, then," Matt growled.

Jolie nodded. "You're absolutely right. You do have extra bedrooms, and she'd be better off at your place."

But I won't. Jolie thought about the night before, when she'd tried to sleep alone in one of those bedrooms, knowing Matt was downstairs in his own. Alone.

Between her anxiety over the break-in and Matt's proximity, she hadn't been able to sleep a wink.

Before either man could say a word, she waved at the chairs in front of her desk. "Please, sit down. The tower-over-her-and-be-intimidating approach isn't going to work. Do you have any leads?"

Rafe settled into a chair, crossed one leg over the opposite knee and settled his tan Stetson on his thigh. "I lifted latent prints, and this afternoon I'll hand deliver them down to the sheriff's office in Big Timber. I figure the prints might match what we took from the doll—nothing that matches our local files, but maybe then we can push for a faster answer on print analyses from the lab in Missoula. A stalker would get higher priority than an isolated incident of vandalism."

"Good. I can't believe how long this takes."

"It's not like you see on TV," Rafe agreed dryly. "Just once I'd like to see things happen that fast in real life."

Matt cleared his throat. "You shouldn't go to the cabin alone, Jolie."

"I appreciate your concern." Jolie rose, braced her hands on her desk. "But I know what I'm doing."

"Do you?"

"I'll just bow out of this one," Rafe said mildly. "I've been on duty all night and I don't have the energy. It never does much good to argue with a Maxwell, anyway." He gestured toward the phone. "Mind if I call the ranch? I tried an hour ago, but no one answered."

"They're probably already moving cattle." Jolie smiled. "Eight o'clock in the morning is practically midday out there."

"I know. Thea usually leaves our house by five."

Rafe's forehead creased the moment someone answered the phone. He waved to Jolie to stay behind her desk, spoke rapidly into the receiver, then hung up, his expression grim. "Your father has had more heart trouble. Beth called for help, and he was airlifted to Bozeman around midnight. He's stable and doing okay, according to one of the hands. I expect we both have phone messages from Thea on our answering machines."

Rafe's words sent a chill through her heart. She'd thought she'd heard a few notes of her cell phone's ring last night, but perhaps the weakened battery disabled the Caller ID. Had Thea tried to call?

"Where is he now? Do they have a diagnosis?"

"He's at St. Andrew's Hospital, but the ranch hand didn't know any more."

"I'll have Irene switch my appointments so I can head up there today."

Matt regarded her with troubled eyes. "I'll go with you. You shouldn't have to go alone."

Which is what I've done all my life, she realized. *Until you.* Warmth bloomed inside her heart.

"Thanks, Matt, but if Dad needs surgery, or if...if he isn't doing well, I could be up there for days. What about your kids?"

"If we need to stay up there, my kids can stay at my brother's place. Megan, too. He's got a big old house. Not fancy, but he has plenty of room."

"But your jobs—"

"We're starting a screened porch for the Sloans this week, and a day or two won't matter. Ed can get it started."

"I still don't think—"

Under Rafe's amused eye, Matt stood, rounded the desk, took Jolie by the shoulders and kissed her. Hard.

"Interesting," Rafe muttered as he slipped out the door. "That always works with Thea, too."

JOLIE WAS THANKFUL for Matt's presence, his amusing stories about the kids and his quiet understanding during the trip to Bozeman.

Alone, she would have worried, dwelt on the past, anticipated a thousand grim scenarios that awaited her at the hospital. She dealt with life-and-death issues every day, but that didn't make her own father's illness any easier.

They arrived by noon, and found Beth and Thea in a waiting room outside intensive care. Both were pale, their faces drawn with tension. "I'm glad you're here," Thea murmured. "I left a message for Rafe, and tried your cell phone—then Dad was airlifted, and we took off in a rush. We were really worried about him."

Jolie hugged Beth, then Thea. "Has the doctor seen him today?"

"Earlier. They said his EKG was consistent with another mild heart attack. He's comfortable now, but they want to do an angiogram before he goes home, and so far he has refused."

"Has Cassie been here? Bobby?"

Thea nodded. "They both were, for most of the night. You just missed them. One of Cassie's friends kept Zak overnight, but she had to go pick him up. Herman came by less than an hour ago to take Bobby home. Bobby's taking this pretty hard. He thinks it's all his fault, because he had a fight with Dad last night."

"Over his ranch duties?"

Thea grimaced. "He *says* he took one of the trucks and went to town to meet his buddies, though I'm not sure that's true. I don't think his friends hang around with him anymore. When he got home, the helicopter had already picked up Dad and we were getting ready to leave for the hospital. So he came with us."

"Maybe this will be the wake-up call he needs." Jolie introduced herself as his daughter—and one of Robert's doctors—to a young nurse, then asked to review her dad's chart.

While being transferred by helicopter, Robert had been given TPA treatment to treat the heart attack. *Good.* He'd shown some brief arrhythmia since then, but he was currently stable. The attending doctors strongly recommended an angiogram, and expected angioplasty and stent placement would be needed.

"I'd like to see him," she said.

The nurse nodded and led her to the open cubicle. "He's been resting. Quite a…spunky gentleman, all things considered."

If you only knew.

"Dad?" Jolie stepped between two IV poles and laid a hand on his arm. His eyes fluttered, then opened. "It's Jolie."

"I know damn well who you are." The words were pure Robert Maxwell, but he sounded tired, sedated.

"How are you feeling?"

"Like hell."

"Good."

His eyes widened.

"Then you have just a taste of how you'll feel if you don't go along with your doctor's advice. And strangely enough," she added with a smile, "most of it's exactly what you were told last Thanksgiving. If you'd listened then, maybe you wouldn't be here now."

"I've got to keep going," he said wearily, "There's too much left to do."

"To do?"

His eyes drifted shut, he turned his head away. After a long moment he opened them again and stared at the partition next to his bed. "I've done some reading. People can die from all that testing—that angio thing. Every one of you kids has made mistakes that have to be fixed. And I've got to run that ranch until Bobby proves man enough to do it."

"What mistakes?"

But Robert's breathing slowed. He was either asleep, or had tuned her out.

"You have to go through with these tests, Dad," she said to his still form, hoping her words might somehow seep into his consciousness. "If you need angioplasty, it could *save* your life. The mortality rate for the procedure is far, far lower than you think."

He didn't respond.

She leaned over him and kissed his stubbled cheek. Emotion clogged her throat as she realized she couldn't remember ever kissing him before.

"Our family has been divided for too long, Dad," she said softly. "You said you have to fix things, but we've *all* got things to say that should have been said long ago. If we don't talk to each other—*listen* to each other—our family will never be whole. Is that the legacy you want to leave? We can't make things right if you decide to die.''

After she left, Robert opened his eyes and stared at the partition for a long, long time.

And for the first time since Helen's death, he whispered a prayer.

ED GLARED at Matt from across the stack of lumber that had been delivered behind the Fosters' house. ''Our plans for this porch were correct. Up to code. Hell, I checked them twice and you did, too. We didn't make a mistake. And while you were gallivanting off to Bozeman, the inspector said we were a half inch off code on the stair risers at the Sloan place....''

Matt had spent two days in Bozeman with Jolie, Beth and Thea, and had come home Tuesday night. The old guy had surprised everyone when he'd finally consented to an angiogram. While he was on the table, the surgeons had gone ahead with angioplasty and a stent to open up a clogged artery.

Thea had figured he'd had brain damage, or he would have checked out against medical advice before reaching the surgical suite. Jolie had just smiled.

Being with Jolie during those long days had filled Matt with a sort of peace that he hadn't felt in a long, long time. It had felt *right*.

And it was getting much harder to remember why he'd ever thought she'd been wrong for him.

The first night they'd all camped in the waiting room, afraid to leave. The second evening, Beth and Thea had reserved a shared room at a nearby motel, and Thea had given Matt a knowing look as they all lingered over a late supper of vending-machine food in the hospital cafeteria.

"Go on, you two," she'd murmured. "We'd have to be blind not to see that's what you'd like to do."

Jolie had blushed. Matt had gone straight to a pay phone and checked in with Ed and the kids, then dialed another number and made reservations.

Alone together, with sheets instead of meadow grass and a blanket, they'd not slept at all.

"Well?" Ed insisted.

His voice slammed Matt back into the present. "Well, what?"

"What are we going to do about this? We can't start construction if we don't have the permit. These people expect their job *done* by next Monday."

Matt shook off his thoughts about the trip to Bozeman. "I'll talk to the inspector."

"And how the hell are you gonna do that? I've called, I've stopped by. I can't get a response—he's always out, in a meeting, or on another line."

"I'll take care of it."

"What, you think you can waltz in and do better?" The anger glittering in Ed's eyes spoke of far deeper issues than just this project delay. "You sure as hell aren't the boss."

Matt stared at him in surprise. "You think I'm trying to take over? I thought this was a straight partnership, all the way."

"You recheck my figures. Question my bids, my scheduling. With you second-guessing every move, it's like having Big Brother watching over my shoulder twenty-four hours a day."

That's because I do find problems, Matt thought grimly. *Too many.* "I never meant it that way. Your craftsmanship is the best I've ever seen. I just happen to have a little more experience on the business side. We aren't playing to our strengths if we don't divide some of the responsibilities.''

The hostility in Ed's eyes slowly faded. ''Maybe.''

''Let's meet at Grizzly's for lunch and work this out. I'll buy.''

After a moment, Ed gave a grudging nod. Then one corner of his mouth lifted into the first smile he'd shown Matt for a good long while. ''Deal.''

On his way into town, Matt thought about the inspector. The code violations that he knew didn't exist. He remembered the one time he'd gone into Robert's room at the hospital with Jolie. The man's mouth had curled with disdain at her introduction, and then he'd turned away without a word.

''Please forgive him,'' she'd said later. ''He hates being in the hospital and is absolutely impossible with everyone.'' But there had been something deeper, more personal in the old man's eyes.

''No one dares cross Robert Maxwell,'' Ed had said last March. And Matt had overheard other stories shared between the old-timers sipping coffee at Grizzly's. Maxwell used his power and connections without hesitation, in whatever way best suited his own best interests. But why would he care about Dawson Brothers Construction?

As Matt pulled up to the county courthouse, the rest of Ed's warning came back to him. *''Stay clear of his daughter.''*

And suddenly everything fell into place.

CHAPTER EIGHTEEN

MATT TRIED CALLING the county building inspector's office from his cell phone before going up. First the secretary offered to connect him, then she abruptly said the man wasn't in.

Phil Nelson might not have been answering his phone, but he certainly was there—and was clearly startled at seeing Matt walk in the door a few minutes later.

The man's wary expression only confirmed Matt's suspicions. "We need to talk about problems with my inspections and building permits," Matt said evenly, baring his teeth in what he hoped would pass for a smile.

"And you are?"

"Matt Dawson." *As if he didn't know.* They'd met a number of times already, over remodeling projects and the plans for the Fosters' home that was to be started in June.

Phil gestured toward the chairs flanking the front door, past the secretary's desk. "Have a seat. I'll be with you in a while."

"A while" stretched into a half hour.

The secretary smiled at him every now and then. "It can't be much longer," she reassured him. "Would you like some coffee?"

"No, thanks." Giving her his most winning smile, he skirted her desk and strode down the hall.

"Wait! You can't go in—he's busy with a *meeting*."

"I should be busy, too," Matt muttered to himself. "Instead of wasting time here."

The lights were off in Phil's office, the door shut. Matt retraced his steps, casually glancing in the other offices. No sign of him.

His anger rising, Matt strode out to the front office. "Do you know when he left?"

"Left?" The young secretary appeared confused. "He's in his office."

"No, he's not. Tell him I'll be back. It's important."

"Yes, sir!"

Matt took the main stairs down, taking two steps at a time. At the first floor, a sixth sense made him turn away from the entrance and head down the hallway leading to the back staircase.

And sure enough, he managed to run into Phil. "Leaving?" he asked softly.

Short, with a gleaming bald spot at the top of his head, Phil looked about as dangerous as Santa Claus, yet he had the power to destroy Matt's career in Paradise Corners. "No—not at all. In just a few minutes I'm due at a meeting with the county attorney."

"You told me to wait upstairs. You implied that you'd be available."

"If you'd like to wait…"

"Maybe I should drop by your house this evening?"

A man in a well-cut suit came out of a doorway a few yards down. "Having any problems, Phil?"

"No—I'll be there in just a moment," Phil called out. He rolled his shoulders as if relieving tension, then lowered his voice. "Look, the safety of our taxpayers is paramount. If your projects aren't up to code—"

"You gave verbal approval for the Sloan project and for

the Fosters' house. You did your inspection and said you found nothing wrong.''

A muscle jerked along Phil's jaw. ''I don't remember saying that at all.''

''Then maybe we need to take this to someone higher up.''

''Like the county attorney? Be my guest.'' His bland smile gave proof that there would be little help from that quarter.

''Just tell me what I need to do,'' Matt said through clenched teeth.

''Rewrite your plans, resubmit with the proper fees. I'll get to it as soon as I can.''

Which might be next month, or the month after that, resulting in angered customers and loss of confidence in the quality of work done by the company. Fighting the delays and subtle interpretations of the building codes would be difficult and time-consuming.

''Is this Robert Maxwell's doing?''

A flicker of uneasiness flashed in Phil's eyes, confirming Matt's suspicions. ''That's ridiculous.''

''You've stepped over the line if you're following Maxwell's orders,'' Matt snarled. ''I'm not going to let this rest.''

A lead weight settled in his stomach as he watched Phil turn and head into the office down the hall.

Matt had gradually managed to forget the gulf between Jolie and himself—the money, the status, the vast difference in their education and careers. Loving her had made anything in the world seem possible, but now her father was proving just how wrong Matt had been.

With a heavy sigh Matt started for the front entrance of the building. Footsteps hurried down the hallway behind him. He turned, and recognized the guy who'd tried to hit on Jolie at the restaurant.

"The secretary upstairs called to tell me that you were here, so I came right over. Can I talk with you a moment—outside?"

"I think here would be just fine with me," Matt growled. "Who the hell are you?"

"One of the attorneys representing the Maxwells."

"So?"

"I'm sure you can appreciate that the Maxwells must protect their interests," he murmured, too low for any passersby to hear. "Jolie Maxwell has a bright professional future, but also stands to inherit a handsome amount upon her father's death."

Matt fought to keep his anger in check. "That's not my business."

"You need to understand that if you were to ever marry her, neither of you would ever receive a nickel. A far smaller amount would be simply put in trust for your children."

"This is crazy. Where are we here—twelfth-century Scotland?"

"When a man sees such financial opportunity, he can work hard to make it happen. Marriages have been built on far less, but they are rarely happy." He raked Matt with a dismissive glance. "Mr. Maxwell simply wants to make sure his daughter doesn't make a mistake. And you might want to consider whether or not a woman with Jolie's professional and family background would ever be content with a *carpenter*." He turned sharply on his heel and walked away.

Matt stared after him, stunned. Then walked slowly out into the sunshine, slid behind the wheel of his pickup and leaned his head against the headrest. He closed his eyes.

Maxwell's money meant nothing to him—he didn't want it. But how could he let Jolie throw away her inheritance? Even if she dismissed the concern now, how would she feel in the future? Would she come to resent him for the loss of that security?

Beyond that, Phil's subtle interference with permits and inspection delays threatened people Matt couldn't place in financial risk—his children, his brother, his brother's family.

He'd never planned to fall in love. Somewhere along the line it had happened, without intention, without a warning— and now it was as much a part of him as the beat of his own heart.

But no matter how much Matt wanted her, he had to admit Jolie's father had brought home a painful truth.

When you came from two different worlds, love wasn't always enough.

ROBERT CAME THROUGH the angioplasty and stent placement with flying colors, though he would likely have to stay in the hospital until at least Sunday. So when Herman, the ranch foreman, came to the hospital for a visit Thursday morning, he gave Jolie a ride back to her cabin.

"You aren't staying here, right?" he asked, his eyebrows lowered with concern. "Rafe told me what happened up here last weekend, and it's just not safe for you to be here alone."

Rafe, Matt, and now Herman, too. Jolie held up her fingers in a Girl Scout salute. "I just need to pick up my Blazer, so I can get to work."

"And afterward?" He folded his arms across his chest.

She wondered if he would throw himself in front of the cabin door if she started in that direction. "I'm checking in with Rafe today, to see what he's found out. And yes, I'll probably go to the neighbor's place tonight. Megan is there already.''

''Matt Dawson's place?'' Herman's eyes twinkled.

So Rafe must have told him about the kiss back at the clinic. ''That's the one.''

''From what I hear you'll be in good hands, then.'' Nodding his approval, Herman climbed back into his pickup. ''I'll call tonight to find out how things go today.''

''You'll be calling to check up on me, you mean,'' Jolie murmured.

He touched the brim of his hat in farewell. ''You betcha.''

Jolie strode for the Blazer, unlocked it and tossed her purse and overnight bag inside, then leaned against the hood and surveyed the peaceful meadow surrounding the cabin.

Dolly and Sadie had looked up from grazing when the pickup pulled in, and were now ambling toward Jolie. ''Beggars,'' she chuckled. ''The soda-cracker brigade.''

Matt had been checking on them every day, and making sure the water tank was full. But he probably hadn't been giving them treats.

Jolie smiled as she started for the cabin to retrieve a box of crackers. But with each step, she felt her amusement fade. The cabin looked dark, deserted. Nothing stirred, but the hairs at her nape prickled as she drew closer and imagined someone crouching in the bushes. Or around the corner.

Someone could have easily found a way inside, and be waiting there for her return.

Her stride faltered. She pulled to a stop ten feet from the porch steps, Megan's fearful cries echoing in her thoughts. There *had* been someone here that night, lurking in the shadows. And God only knew what he might have done if he'd found Megan or Jolie inside.

Rage swept through her at the feeling of violation, at her

lost sense of security in the home she'd come to love. "Damn you, whoever you are," she exploded.

Dolly and Sadie both pulled to an uncertain stop at the harsh sound of her voice echoing through the rocky cliffs up in the hills.

Jolie turned on her heel and forced herself to walk calmly back to the Blazer. She climbed inside...and for the first time since returning to Montana, she locked the doors.

JOLIE HEADED for Matt's place after work. She'd stayed later, for an appointment after five, so Megan had accepted a ride back to Matt's with Irene.

As if staying at his place under the watchful eyes of two teenagers and a kid wasn't hard enough, Jolie noticed something...different in his voice. And in the way he didn't look at her when she walked in the door at seven.

"So everything went okay?" he asked stiffly as she brought in her bags.

"Fine." She looked up at him, surprised. There was no warmth in his eyes, none of the simmering desire she'd seen there only a few days before.

He turned away and walked to the dining area, where several rolls of building plans were partly unfurled, held down by a heavy coffee mug at one end.

"Looks like you're busy," she ventured, wandering over to see what he was working on.

The warning look in his eyes stopped her in her tracks. "Excuse me. I didn't know...didn't realize that all of that might be confidential." She backed away, feeling suddenly lost. "Where are the kids?"

"Megan drove them to school for a fund-raiser carnival tonight. They'll be home around eight-thirty."

A few days ago an hour and a half of privacy would have seemed heaven-sent. Now it felt impossibly awkward. After ten minutes of flipping through magazines and trying to concentrate on a novel, she finally rose and headed back to the dining area and watched Matt from a distance.

He stood over his plans, his hands braced on the desk and an intense look of concentration on his face.

"Tell me what's going on," she asked, leaning against the entryway. "A few days ago we were making love all night. Now, without a word of disagreement, we seem to be on opposite sides of a war. Did I say something? Do something?"

"No." He didn't look up.

"Then what's wrong?"

He straightened. "I'm going over plans for a project. Verifying that everything—our estimates, our materials list, *everything* is absolutely perfect. It has to be turned in tomorrow."

There was something else in his eyes…a weary acceptance. "So…that's all it is? You're stressed over a deadline?"

"Yeah." He bent over the documents again, then gave a soft curse and shoved them all aside. "No."

She stilled—frozen by the terrifying sensation of teetering on the edge of a cliff, knowing that his next words were ones she didn't want to hear.

But she would not give him—or anyone else—the satisfaction of knowing how much it hurt. And she wasn't going to let him off easy.

"We're just too different to work things out."

"Different?"

"Education. Backgrounds. Career."

"If you'd met someone who was, say, a waitress, it could never work—because you had a better job?"

"Of course not. I mean, it wouldn't matter."

"But you think it matters to me."

"It will."

"And if I said it didn't?"

"I'd say you have no idea what you'd be giving up if—" He stopped. Swallowed hard. Then continued, his voice raw. "There are my kids to consider."

"Your *kids?*"

He turned away with a heavy sigh. "When—*if*—I remarry, it has to be to someone who'll be a good mom for them. And someone...I can love."

If he'd slid a knife between her ribs, he couldn't have hurt her more.

FRIDAY MORNING Jolie packed her things as soon as Matt took the kids to school then moved back to her cabin. She hid her rifle in the closet nearest her bed.

Facing the unknown here at the cabin would be easier than having to face Matt again at the end of the day, and *no one* was going to keep her away from her home. Not anymore.

Thankful the telephone lines had been repaired, she called a local electrician about installing motion-detection floodlights on all sides of the cabin.

Once she gave her name, he offered to come right away. There were, on occasion, a few advantages to having the last name of Maxwell.

At eight o'clock, she called Irene and told her not to pick up Megan, then she called Matt's place. Megan answered on the fifth ring.

"I'll be by in a half hour to pick you up for work," Jolie said. "Can you be ready?"

"Where *are* you? I woke up, and everyone was gone."

"We all probably thought the same thing—that you needed your sleep. At thirty-five weeks, you're probably exhausted at the end of the day. Right?"

Megan yawned into the receiver. "I never had any idea pregnancy would be like this. My feet are swollen, my back hurts, my skin is itchy...who said pregnant women are beautiful?"

Jolie tried for a chuckle. "Maybe the husbands who are hoping to be served supper? See you soon."

As she bustled through the cabin, picking up strewn clothing, replacing dresser drawers scattered across the floor, Jolie felt a whisper of longing to know personally what being married and pregnant would be like.

She'd delivered babies and provided pre- and post-natal care. But what would it be like to hold your very own baby, and experience the miracle firsthand? Her thoughts slid to Matt, imagining how tender he would be with a newborn.

And then, to what it might have been like to be his wife.

A truck door slammed. Startled, she spun around and raced to the window, her heart leaping in her throat. *She hadn't even heard the vehicle drive over the cattle guard— who else could drive up the lane like that, without warning?*

Seeing Rafe striding up to the cabin did little to slow her rapid heartbeat.

She unlocked the door to let him in, but he stood outside, his face grim. "I was hoping you'd decided to stay at Matt's place after getting back from Bozeman."

"I thought about it, but I can't just give up my home. How," she added after a moment of thought, "did you even know?"

"Louie."

"Who?"

"When you called the electrician, he told his assistant, Louie, who walked over to the courthouse and told me. If you took a vote, I'd say seventy-five percent of the population thinks you should stay at the Dawson place." One corner of his mouth tipped up. "And at least eighty percent of the women think you two would be a perfect couple. The other twenty want him for themselves.''

''You told the whole town that he kissed me?''

''Of course not.'' Rafe studied the horizon. ''Just Herman. And…maybe Mona Rangel. But only because she heard about the situation at your cabin. She was worried.''

Remembering Mona's cool reception when she and Matt had gone to Grizzly's, that didn't seem likely.

''I'm touched by the concern, given that so many people in Paradise didn't even want me here a few months ago. Have you found out anything more about the break-ins? Any suspects?''

''The preliminary results came on the fingerprints. The same prints were on the doll and found in various places in your cabin. But they didn't match anything on file at the local sheriff's department.''

''Where is the doll?''

''It's in a box in my office, where I'll keep it in case something else turns up. You just never know.''

''Keep me posted, okay?''

''I can't convince you to stay with someone for a while?''

''How long could that be? Days—weeks—months? I appreciate your concern, but I'm staying here. I'm not my father's daughter for nothing.''

''I'll drive up this way now and then. I won't bother you, I'll just blink my lights to let you know it's me, and then be on my way. Okay? I'll call every now and then, too.''

Jolie touched his arm. ''Thanks, Rafe. Maybe this guy made *sure* I wasn't around when he hit the cabin and the clinic. Just wanted to frighten me a little, or something. But if he does come back, I'm ready.''

''I hope you know what you're doing,'' Rafe muttered. ''You'd be much better off at the ranch or with Thea and me, but I can't make that decision for you. Keep safe.''

By THE TIME she got home from the clinic on Friday, the motion-detector floodlights were installed. By midnight Friday, Jolie knew that from now on, Dolly and Sadie would be locked in the barn at night, because the motion sensors worked perfectly whenever the llama or sheep wandered by.

And by eight o'clock the next morning, Megan was knocking on her door.

"I want to stay here with you," she said simply. "I'm not going back, so don't try to make me."

"What's wrong? Did Matt say something to you?"

Megan shook her head. "He was really nice. But I belong here." She brought in her duffel bag and tossed it in the bedroom she'd used before. "He sure doesn't seem very happy, though. This morning he barely spoke to anyone, just grabbed a piece of toast and said that he had to go to work. When I told him I was coming back here, he made the kids get dressed and took them to his sister-in-law's place in town."

"He doesn't usually work on a Saturday."

"He said he had a lot of problems. Somebody called him this morning, and he was even grumpier after that."

Jolie thought about her own sleepless night, and wondered if he'd had the same problem she had. But dwelling on a relationship that was over served no useful purpose.

If he doesn't want me, it's his loss, she'd decided by four in the morning. *I don't need anyone—especially Matt Dawson—telling me that I don't measure up.* And with that came a healthy dose of anger. *I deserve better.*

"We missed your exam this week, Megan. I need to go to the clinic for a while this morning—want to get it over with?"

Megan made a face. "The only good parts are that I get to hear the baby's heartbeat, and that each time means I'm closer to being done."

"We need to go shopping for you, too. You never know about these little guys. Sometimes they decide to come a few weeks early."

"Really? Like the crib, and everything?"

"And everything. This afternoon we could take a drive to Bozeman, if you'd like."

"Wow!" Megan's face glowed with excitement. "You know, it suddenly seems real, like this is really going to happen."

Jolie eyed Megan's maternity top with amusement. "Believe me, no one could doubt it."

Something stirred in her memory as they headed out to the Blazer. "You mentioned that Matt got a phone call this morning, and he wasn't happy. Do you know who it was from?"

"Someone named…" Megan frowned. "Frank? Fred?"

They were both buckled in and Jolie had just turned on the engine, when Megan added, "No, it was some building-inspector guy named Phil. They argued a long time, and Matt kept saying something was unfair—even illegal."

Matt was the last person on the planet Jolie would ever suspect of taking shortcuts or doing substandard work. So why was he having problems?

CHAPTER NINETEEN

"WELL, WHAT DO YOU THINK, Megan? Did we shop well in Bozeman last weekend?" Jolie turned off Coyote Creek Road on Thursday afternoon and headed back to the clinic. They'd gone to the cabin for lunch, and Jolie had had to tear Megan away from the room they'd set up for the baby.

Megan's eyes sparkled and she patted her bulging stomach. "I can't believe it—a beautiful Jenny Lind crib, the changing table, everything! It's all just incredible!"

Maybe she had gone just a little overboard, Jolie thought, but it had been such fun shopping for baby things, for the first—and probably only—time in her life. And seeing Megan's joy had made every cent worthwhile.

It had even lifted Jolie's spirits a little. For the duration of the trip she'd managed to forget about Matt, and what he'd said. Painful words, more painful truths. But what had she expected? She'd known better than to hope for something more than friendship, because she'd been down that road too many times before.

She made herself smile. "Once the baby comes, we'll arrange a shower for you. People will know what color to buy then."

Megan laughed. "But you already know—you could tell everyone but me!"

"Like that would stay a secret in *this* town."

"But the ultrasound report told you, right?"

Megan had been wavering for weeks, first wanting to

know, then deciding she wanted it to be a surprise. "As I told you the *last* six times, the tech said she couldn't be absolutely sure." Jolie grinned. "But if you want me to guess…"

"No! Yes—" Megan threw her hands in the air. "I just don't think the day is ever going to come!"

"It will, believe me." Jolie pulled to a stop at the four-way stop sign by the courthouse. "And then you might think this part was easier—before the night feedings and diapers."

"Hey," Megan cried. "There's Lily with the Heath boy. Isn't he the one who got caught shoplifting? Holy cow! If her dad could see her now!"

Jolie eased forward into the intersection, then had to put on the brakes when someone ahead stopped to pull into a parking space. "What's wrong?"

"She's diabetic. I found out when I stayed with them for a while. I'll bet she isn't supposed to be eating that!"

"Most foods can be part of a diabetic diet, if calculated into the food plan."

Jolie glanced over, and then did a double take. Sitting on the bench with Clint Heath, Lily was giggling and looking up at him with sheer adoration. They were both dipping spoons into what looked like giant chocolate malts.

"Now *that* would be a bit hard to adjust for," Jolie said dryly. "I can't begin to guess at the grams of carbohydrate in something that big. She should know better."

The car ahead moved on, and Jolie stepped on the accelerator, lost in thought.

She hadn't seen or talked to Matt since Thursday. Given the abrupt end of their relationship, he might decide to take Lily to a different doctor. But at this point, Lily was still under her care, and the child was placing herself at serious risk.

Jolie debated, then decided to write a note and send it to

him. Calling would mean talking to him. If Jolie left a message, Lily might intercept it.

As she pulled up to the clinic, Megan turned to her once again. "Remember when someone broke the window here? There was something on the floor, and not knowing what it was has been bothering me." She shuddered. "I keep imagining all sort of *really* gross things."

Jolie had started to open her door, but stopped. "No one was ever told. Rafe figured that someday it might help if that wasn't common knowledge, in case he had some leads. It wasn't so awful, Megan. Really."

"Please? I swear I won't ever tell. It looked like something dead."

Jolie hesitated. "It was only an old doll—one with a china head and bright red hair. Maybe because a lot of the Maxwells have red hair? He—or she—had added slashes of red paint on the body, to make it look scary, I guess."

Megan was silent for a long time. "W-why would anyone do that?"

"Beats me. There have been plenty of people around here who weren't happy when I came to town. Some people resent my family. But why someone would try to scare me is beyond comprehension. I haven't hurt anyone, here. Ever."

"You've been the best thing that ever happened to me," Megan said slowly. "Helping me with the baby…giving me a place to stay, and a job. The deputy doesn't have any clues at all?"

"Nope."

"I'm sure glad there hasn't been any more trouble." Megan looked at her with troubled eyes. "I just want you to know that I'd do anything to help you, if I could."

"I know that, Megan. But we're fine—we're safe. The biggest event coming up is going to be the day that baby of yours decides to come."

DESPERATELY WISHING she'd never gone to the soda fountain with Clint Heath, Lily stared at the note in Dad's hand. The look of disappointment on his face made her feel lower than dirt. "She...um...made it up?"

Matt gave a snort of disbelief. "You think your *doctor* would lie about something like this? She took the time to send a note to me because she was very concerned about your health."

"Maybe..." Lily thought fast. "She's just desperate, or something. And wants you to *like* her again."

A look of pain flashed in Dad's eyes, and it took a few minutes for him to speak. He'd been a lot more quiet since he'd quit seeing Jolie, hadn't been smiling or teasing her and Charlie at all. The change in him filled Lily with a sense of loss.

"You think an adult would lie about a man's children in an effort to save a relationship?" Dad shook his head. "She *cares* about you."

Embarrassed, Lily studied the tips of her Nikes. "I—I just think it's pretty crummy for her to go around spying like that."

"The point is that you were with that boy again—the one who shoplifted. And you were acting irresponsibly. Lily, it's foolish to risk all kinds of health complications just because you want to be like the other kids. You could choose a diet pop, and that wouldn't make you unacceptable to any kids who were real friends."

She could feel her dad giving her The Look, but she refused to meet his gaze. He was right. She knew better. But when Clint had asked her to walk to the drugstore with him, she'd gone all tingly inside, and had felt so special when he'd offered to buy her the malt.

Dad gave a ragged sigh. "Your aunt Betty called today. She mentioned that you've written letters to some of your

Chicago cousins, wanting to stay with anyone who'd take you in.''

The letters. It had been so long, she'd forgotten the letters she'd written those first few weeks in Paradise Corners. From the gravelly sound in Dad's voice, her betrayal must have hurt him a lot.

Dad rested his hand on her shoulder. ''Do you want to go back and live with your aunt, Lily? Are you that unhappy here with me and Charlie?''

With as much trouble as she'd been, maybe he *wanted* her to go. Her eyes burning, she looked up at him. He looked…older, somehow. And as sad as she felt. ''No, I want to stay here, with you. I wrote those letters a long time ago.''

''Are you sure? I know it isn't always easy, being a new girl in town.''

''It isn't so easy for you to deal with me, either, I guess. Maybe things will get better?''

His answering smile seemed to light up his whole face.

MATT STOOD at the site of the Foster house and scowled as he studied the terrain. First Lily, and now this. It had been one heck of a day.

The Fosters' basement should have been dug and poured already, but delays on the approval of the plans had set them back. Now the crew was scheduled for Monday…if the forecast for four days of heavy rain didn't prove true.

The cloudy skies didn't begin to compare to the dark, overwhelming emptiness he felt inside.

Eight days had passed since Jolie had last been in his house, asking what was wrong. He'd struggled for answers, almost unable to go through with what he had to do.

Then he'd delivered a killing blow that she would never forgive. Knowing how much she loved children, he'd told her she wasn't good enough to mother his. And crowned the lie by telling her that he could never love her. That lie had eaten at him, day and night, for the last week. Remembering the stark pain in her eyes made it a thousand times worse.

Maybe there was something he could do about it.

Robert Maxwell had been controlling the lives of people in Paradise Corners too long. The old man had been home from the hospital for a week now. He was surely ready for a little visit.

Settling his cap lower on his head, Matt stalked to his pickup, climbed inside, slammed the door.

And headed for Walking Stones Ranch.

MEGAN BRACED her lower back with one hand as she walked slowly down Main toward the courthouse. The ache still nagged at her, and she felt more tired than she ever had before. Carrying what seemed to be a two-ton baby wasn't much fun, day after day after day.

Shading her eyes against the late-afternoon sun, she looked up at the First Montana Bank clock. The walk—more like a waddle—was taking a whole lot longer than she'd expected, but she still had enough time.

Jolie had gone to the cabin for picnic supplies, but Megan had told her that she'd rather just stay in town. Later, they were meeting Cassie, Zak and Thea at the reservoir for supper.

The familiar sound of a creaky old truck came up Main Street as she neared the courthouse. *Dad.* But he wouldn't bother her here, not on Main Street. Maybe he wouldn't even see her, with the after-school crowd filling the sidewalk.

Some twenty feet ahead of her the truck squealed to a

stop, then took a sharp left at the next corner, backfiring as it accelerated.

Breathing a sigh of relief, she entered the courthouse and found the deputy's office. A small waiting area led to a hallway with several rooms. Sounds of vacuuming came from down the hall. "Hello?"

A Hispanic cleaning lady stepped out of the first door, the vacuum still in her hands.

"I am cleaning his office. He is not here," she said over the whirring noise of the vacuum.

"When will he come back? There's something here—I've got to see it."

"I should have locked that front door." The woman frowned at her, clearly irritated. "He is not here. You can wait outside in the hallway."

At a deep twinge Megan closed her eyes. "Oh, *my*."

The vacuum cleaner stopped. "You okay, miss? You need to sit down?"

"Yes...please." She sank into one of the waiting-area chairs. "I...don't feel so good."

The woman surveyed her, head to foot. "You having that baby soon?"

"Not for a good three weeks."

Clucking her tongue, the woman shook her head. "I had four, and babies don't come when you think. God decides."

"Um...I had a long walk here, and have a long walk back. Could I get some water?"

"The rest room is at the end of the hall." The woman gestured toward the door of the deputy's office. Then she heaved a sigh. "I will go. I remember how it was, being tired and sore."

Rafe might not return for hours. Maybe not until morning. And the walk had been so long. Megan watched the cleaning woman step out into the hallway. Counted to five. Then lumbered to her feet and headed for Rafe's office.

What were the charges for trespassing *here?* She could only imagine. But ever since Jolie had told her about the doll, an image had been racing around in Megan's mind. *It couldn't be, could it? Please, don't let it be true!*

She peered into Rafe's office, disappointment rising in her chest at the clean desk, orderly rows of books on the banks of shelves lining two walls. Piles of manila file folders were stacked on top of the file cabinets lining a third wall, but there were no cardboard boxes in sight that might contain Bonnie.

Holding her breath, Megan glanced back down the hall toward the front door and listened for returning footsteps. Then entered the room.

She tried the file drawers that lined one wall. *Locked.* Then moved behind the deputy's desk. Her toe bumped a cardboard box on the floor by his chair.

She awkwardly bent down and opened the flaps. Inside, something lay in a plastic bag. She held her breath and tugged at it. Pulled it free.

Horror shot through her just as the front door of the deputy's office squealed open. "Miss! Miss—are you here?" The woman's footsteps came closer.

Megan stood frozen.

She held Bonnie, her favorite old doll from childhood— the one with the flaming-red hair and freckles. Red gashes crisscrossed the doll like gaping wounds. In black permanent marker someone had crudely lettered DEAD across her chest.

"What are you doing!" The cleaning lady rushed forward, her eyes flashing anger. "You must not be in here. Put that down!"

Megan looked at her blankly and held out her doll. "It's mine. He used my Bonnie to do this."

The woman recoiled at the sight, crossing herself feverishly. *"Madre de Dios!"*

Waves of nausea rose in Megan's throat. She felt hot...cold. Sank to the floor, trying not to give in to the darkness closing in on her. Then another terrifying thought hit her like a sharp slap in the face. *Jolie.*

Her dad hadn't intended to turn at that corner out on Main a few minutes ago. The way he'd slammed on his brakes at the last moment meant he'd probably seen Megan and then decided to go...where? *The cabin?*

"How do I call the deputy?" Megan cried, struggling up into Rafe's chair. A sharp pain shot through her lower back. With a guttural moan she wrapped her arms around her belly and doubled over.

The cleaning woman's eyes widened.

"Tell me! How do I call Rafe from here?" She pawed through the neat stack of papers on his desk, jerked at one of the desk drawers. *Locked.*

The Rolodex by the phone held no card for *Rafferty*. She tore a phone book off the shelf behind the desk and scrambled through it—no listing there, either.

Closing her eyes tight, she desperately tried to remember his home number. And then she remembered someone who lived much closer. *Matt.* Her fingers shook as she tried to punch the numbers on the handset. *Please, please be home.*

JOLIE PACKED the last of the canned pop into the cooler, then tossed in a package of hot dogs, a pint of potato salad and coleslaw she'd purchased at the store on the way home.

Done.

She set the cooler out on the front porch, then went in for the picnic basket, wishing she could share Megan's excitement over having a picnic. But Matt had left an emptiness in her heart too great to ever fill. How could she have been so wrong about him?

Still…the days at the hospital with Dad had blessed the Maxwells with a silver lining. During the hours in that ICU waiting room, Thea, Cassie and Jolie had begun talking more openly than they ever had before.

They weren't all great friends yet. Cassie, in particular, still seemed to resent Jolie. Maybe they could never be really close. But there was new hope, a new basis for communication. *Family.* With time, perhaps they could regain all they'd thrown away over the years.

Dolly wandered over to the porch, Sadie bumping along at her heels. "Hi, girls," Jolie murmured. "Want some of your favorite crackers?"

The llama's head came up, her ears pricked forward. She snorted. Backed away.

"You don't want your crackers? Just a minute." She bent to retrieve a handful from the box she'd left at the corner of the porch.

Then straightened slowly as a familiar prickle of awareness skittered across the back of her neck.

A shadow fell across her own.

Her hand at her throat, she spun around. And found herself looking into the hard eyes of Abe Wheeler.

"Megan isn't here," she breathed, trying to quiet her racing heart.

"I know." His voice was deceptively soft, slurred. His breath, heavily laden with the sour odor of stale beer and cigarettes, made her eyes burn. "I figured you and me needed a talk, all by ourselves."

He moved closer. Way too close, until she could see the coarse pores on his cheeks and the inflamed capillaries in his eyes.

"I told people about you, you know."

"What?"

"Talk over a few beers, and the whole town hears 'fore you can finish the first bottle. Figured they oughta know better'n to see a doc like you. A Maxwell." He spat out the words as if they tasted bitter.

He'd been the source of the rumors? "But why?"

"Figured you'd wise up and leave town." He gave a harsh laugh. "You'd have been a hell of a lot better off if you had."

She eased back, feeling her way along the porch railing. Another three feet or so and it took a right turn, followed the side of the house. But there were no stairs at the end. She'd be trapped if he made a move.

He leered at her, his hands flexing at his sides. "Did you like what I left you?"

"I don't know what you mean." She eased another few inches farther, but he gained on her even more.

"The present I left, at your office. I figure you owe me, big time. But you were gone the last time I stopped by." He trailed a meaty, callused fingertip down the side of her cheek, sending waves of revulsion clear to her toes.

"Money? I owe you *money?*"

He uttered a curse. "You can't even imagine how much. Maxwell makes sure his precious son gets away with anything he does. Your brother almost killed a few people, but did he serve a day in jail? He got my sweet little girl pregnant—and then lied his way out of paying a nickel."

Abe's voice rose, the rage in his eyes growing with every breath. He shoved a fist in the air. "Who's gonna take care of that kid? Take care of my girl?"

Reaching forward, he caught a handful of Jolie's hair, twisting it painfully until he'd wrapped it around his hand.

"So *you* take her in, pretending to be nice—but it's just a way to avoid paying for what Bobby did, isn't it!"

Trying to ignore the pain, Jolie fought to keep her voice calm. "You're worried about child support? Believe me, I want that for her, too. I'll see that she gets it."

He blinked. Then his voice grew harsh. "What you want is to get off this porch and get away from me, but it ain't happening." He spat at her feet. "I figure the Maxwells have owed me for too many years to even count. They stole my ranch—as if they needed more land. Left me to work at what I could, with no place of my own."

He was referring to the foreclosure of his ranch, when the place had gone up for auction. Walking Stones had placed the highest bid, fair and square, but she knew it would do no good to point that out. "Tell me what you want. M-maybe I can help you get it."

He didn't seem to hear her. "At first, I was gonna take you like Bobby must have taken my girl. I figure he raped her, so that would be fair."

"Abe—we can go talk to my dad, you and me. Get the money—the payments, however you like."

"But then I figured maybe it's time they lost something. Something *real* important." His bleary gaze bored into hers. "Like you."

"If you harm me, they'll track you down like a dog. You'll never get a penny of the money you want."

He yanked her close. "How would they know? That deputy doesn't know I broke into the clinic…he doesn't know I was in your cabin. And who the hell knows I'm here right now?"

He twisted his hand free of her hair. "I think…I want you on your knees."

Jolie's heart crawled up her throat. She fingered the crackers she held. Fisted her hand tighter, crushing them to powder. *Please, let this be enough.* All she needed was a few seconds' head start... He could never catch her if she could just get away. Could he?

At the corner of the cabin she caught a flash of movement. On her other side she caught a glimpse of Dolly, who stood a few yards from the porch with her ears pinned, her jaws working furiously and her head weaving to and fro like a charmed snake. *Come on, Dolly—bite him. Do something!*

Backing up another half step, Jolie felt the corner of the porch railing at her hips. Abe towered over her, a mass of muscle, overpowering strength and pure rage.

This is it.

"On your knees," he roared, lunging for her neck.

She caught the tips of his fingers and lurched forward, forcing all her weight against his fingertips until his fingers cracked. With her other hand she shoved the salty crackers into his eyes, grinding them in with the heel of her hand.

He screamed. And suddenly he was flying backward off the porch, landing in an ungainly heap in the dirt. He'd barely hit the ground at Dolly's feet before she spat a glob of reeking, partly digested grass into his face.

Abe howled, scrubbed at his face with his hands. Then rolled over and retched.

Stunned, Jolie stared down at him. Then she turned and found herself looking up at Matt.

He was breathing hard, and worry etched his face.

"I got here as fast as I could," he growled. "When Megan called, I must have hit eighty in the next breath."

"I...I didn't hear you drive in," she said hoarsely.

He reached up and gently smoothed back her tangled hair. Then pulled her close, tucking her head beneath his chin. "I was afraid he might do something crazy if he saw me coming. The truck is down the lane, around the bend. I ran through the woods and circled behind the house."

Beneath her cheek she could hear his thundering heartbeat and ragged breathing. "But how did she know?"

"She said she went to Rafe's and found the doll Abe hurled through the clinic window. When you mentioned its bright red hair, she started to worry. Sure enough—it was one she'd had as a child."

The distant wail of a siren echoed through the towering peaks above them. "Rafe?"

"I called from my cell phone on the way here. Megan tried to call him—but all she knew was the number to that same office. She was so rattled, it's just lucky she remembered *my* number."

Abe groaned, and tried to lurch to his feet, but his left leg gave out beneath him and he fell again with a cry of pain.

"I guess he won't be running away," Jolie murmured. "But I'm not going near him until Rafe has him in handcuffs."

Matt grimaced. "I'm not sure even Rafe will want to get close. Dolly certainly has unique…gifts."

"Maybe she figured I was one of the lambs she's always guarded." She gave a short laugh. "Or just found it disgusting to have a man like Abe land at her feet."

Jolie pulled away and looked up into Matt's face. The depth of emotion she saw there nearly took her breath away. But then his expression changed—grew distant, reminding her that adrenaline and the aftereffects of danger had drawn them into each other's arms. Nothing more.

"Jolie, I—"

Rafe's truck shot into sight, and came to a brake-slamming halt in the clearing. He was out the door, his gun drawn, a split second later.

"I think Abe might have hurt his leg when he…uh…left the porch," Matt announced.

A corner of Rafe's mouth tipped up. "From the looks of him, he had a little help. What on earth happened here?"

Jolie briefly explained while Rafe bent down and handcuffed Abe's hands behind his back. After Rafe read him his rights, she dropped to her knees and examined Abe's leg.

Though sullenly quiet since his flight off the porch, he cried out, tried to pull away when she got to his ankle. "I think it's probably a sprain, but I'd need to see X rays to be sure. I can immobilize his ankle with bandaging, though. Do you want to bring him into the clinic?"

"Wrap him, and then I'll transfer him the county sheriff's office. They can take care of him there."

After she finished stabilizing Abe's ankle, Rafe and Matt managed to maneuver him into the back seat of the truck.

Rafe's cell phone rang as they shut the door.

"I'm just so thankful you came, Matt." She shuddered, reliving the moment in graphic detail. "I might have managed to get away, but I'm not sure how far."

He gave her a somber smile. "It was all way too close for comfort."

"He planned to *kill* me. I'd recommend a psychiatric evaluation after he's behind bars."

"Hey, Jolie," Rafe called out. "You have a patient waiting at your clinic. I'll give you a ride so you can get back faster."

Dad? "Who is it?"

"Megan. And Irene is worried that she might not make it all the way to the hospital at Bozeman."

"Call the ranch and tell Bobby. I think he ought to be there to welcome the newest little Maxwell into the family, don't you?"

"HI, THERE, trouper," Jolie said. "I hear you've got some contractions going."

Irene had put her in the back room, where there was a comfortable chair and bed, but Megan had been walking up and down the hall since she'd been brought in. She looked pale, frightened and exhausted.

"I'm s-so glad to see you!" Tears welled in her eyes. "I was so s-scared. I thought my dad—I saw him leave town. Are you okay?"

This wasn't the time to go into details. "Everyone is fine. Let's see how you're doing, okay? This will just take a second."

Megan moaned as another contraction hit. "I don't *want* to do this."

"It's a bit late to change your mind," Jolie said with a smile after finishing the exam. "You're dilated to three centimeters."

"But it's too early!"

"Not by much. Based on your last menstrual cycle and my initial exam, I figure you're thirty-seven weeks, but this seems to be a really good-size baby. Maybe our dates are a bit off."

Irene and Jolie both helped Megan sit up.

"Can I have the baby here?"

Jolie tossed her exam gloves in the trash can. "The hospital in Bozeman is less than two hours away. We can make that easily. If there are any complications, you'll be in a hospital where they have the right equipment to care for you and the baby."

"Complications?" Megan's voice rose to a wail. "You think I'll have complications?"

"No. But I'd rather play it safe, wouldn't you? I'll come with you, and Irene will too, right?" Jolie looked over at Irene, who nodded firmly.

"Absolutely. Megan and I are a team. Right, honey?"

Megan offered a wobbly smile. "Thanks."

The flash of sadness in her eyes reminded Jolie that one important person wasn't here. *Bobby.* And all the way to Bozeman, she prayed, for Megan's sake, that he would bother to show up at the hospital.

THERE MUST HAVE BEEN some serious discussion out at the ranch, because not only Bobby came, but Thea and Beth followed right behind him. *So you've finally admitted the baby is yours,* Jolie thought as she gave Bobby an approving nod.

He ducked his head in return.

Not five minutes later, Matt walked in with Lily and Charlie. He headed straight for Jolie. "How is everything? Is she doing okay?"

"Almost five centimeters and a little tired, but Irene is doing a great job of coaching. I've been in there until now, but came out a few minutes ago to take a break."

"Will you help with the delivery?"

"No. I'm not affiliated with this hospital, but there's an obstetrician on staff who's with her right now. She'll be fine."

He smiled. "So you get to wait out here with the nervous masses?"

"It'll probably teach me to be more compassionate in the future." Across the room, Bobby stood up and made his way to Jolie's side through the other groups of waiting relatives.

"I need to talk to you," he whispered. "Someplace private?"

Jolie threaded her arm through his and led him to a small lounge at the end of the hallway. She sank into one of the brightly upholstered chairs flanking a window overlooking downtown Bozeman. Bobby paced the small room in silence.

"Well?" she prompted.

He shoved a hand through his unruly black hair. "Can you get me in to see her?"

"That depends. Are you here to support her, or to make her feel even worse?"

There was a hint of newfound maturity in the way he met her gaze straight-on, without his usual teenage bravado. "I've had a lot of time to think. About a lot of things."

"And?"

A look of misery filled his eyes. "I have screwed up just about everything this past year. Big time. I don't even know where to start on making things right."

"With Megan?"

"And Dan, too." Bobby braced his hands on the windowsill and rested his forehead against the glass, his eyes closed. "I saw him, did you know that?" He gave a harsh laugh. "I went twice. Dad thought I was going out drinking, but I didn't tell him different—he wouldn't have let me go anyway."

"The night of Dad's heart attack?"

"That was the second time. The first time I ran into Dan's mom, and she kicked me off their place so fast my head was spinning. That woman would like to see me rot in hell."

"She's hurting, Bobby. She's seen what her son has gone through."

"The second time I went, I e-mailed him first and then went one night when she was at a meeting in Bozeman. I saw him, Jolie. Oh, God—he's so pale. He used to be this big guy, bigger than me, and now his legs are skinny as pencils. He says he's gonna walk again, but how could he, looking like that?" Bobby took a deep, shuddering breath. "*I* did that to him. I wanted him to slug me in the face, but he said he'd already forgiven me for what happened. How could he?''

Jolie rose to stand next to her brother. "Maybe because it's better to forgive than to let something eat at you, day and night. Some things we just can't change."

"Seeing Dan made me realize how much I've hurt people who mean a lot to me—Megan, too. I want to make things right and ask her to marry me."

"Oh, Bobby..." Jolie rested a hand on his shoulder. "You're awfully young for this sort of decision."

"And she's awfully young to be a mom, but she doesn't have a choice anymore."

"Do you *love* her?"

He set his jaw. "She shouldn't go through all of this alone. Not now, and when she's raising our baby."

Not exactly the answer she'd hoped for. Neither Bobby nor Megan were as mature as they ought to be for such a big decision, but it wasn't Jolie's choice, she realized as she took Bobby into Megan's room. It was up to them.

They found Irene coaching Megan through a contraction, Megan's face sheened with perspiration, her eyes squeezed tight in concentration. Bobby's confident stride faltered just inside the door.

Jolie rested a hand on his shoulder. "Just wait, Bobby. She'll be able to talk to you in a minute."

When Megan relaxed, she opened her eyes. "Whew. This is *hard.*"

"Still five to seven minutes apart," Irene murmured. "Did you see you have a visitor?"

Megan rolled her head against the pillow. Her eyes widened. *"Bobby?"*

He looked at Jolie uncertainly, and she urged him to Megan's side. "He wants to be with you. Matt and the kids are out in the waiting room, plus both Thea and Beth."

"My mom?"

"I understand a neighbor is bringing your mom and little sister."

"I told my family about us, Megan." Bobby reached out, warily avoiding the IV line and the other paraphernalia, and took her hand. "I'm sorry about everything—for lying to my dad about you. Everything." He shifted uncomfortably, then slid a glance between Irene and Jolie. "Could I talk to her alone?"

Irene pursed her lips. "Megan?"

"Yes—it's okay."

A few minutes later he stepped outside and nodded to Irene, who went back in to stand at Megan's side. "Guess that didn't go so well," he muttered.

"You asked her?"

He shoved his hands in his hip pockets. "She didn't believe I loved her. She said neither of us were ready for marriage, and that both of us should go on to school and do some growing up. Jeez. She sounded just like *you*."

A feeling of pride warmed Jolie's heart. *Good girl.* "What next, then?"

Bobby set his jaw in an expression so determined, so *Robert Maxwell*, that she had to hold back a smile. "I'm going back in. I'm going to stick with her." A smile lifted the corners of his mouth. "Maybe someday Megan will decide I'm worth the gamble."

Jolie wrapped him in a quick bear hug. "I love you, Bobby. You're going to make us all proud."

He started for the door to Megan's room, then pivoted back to face Jolie and lowered his voice. "Maybe it doesn't matter since I heard you aren't seeing Dawson anymore, but—" He grinned a little when she cocked an eyebrow. "What can I say? Paradise Corners is a small town."

"But what...?"

Reaching for his inside jacket pocket, he pulled out a folded sheet of paper. ''I found this fax in Dad's office at home while he was in the hospital.''

Jolie slowly unfolded it and read the name of a private-investigation firm at the top. Then in bold print below, the name Matthew James Dawson. A chill settled around her heart. ''What is this?''

''I figured you should know. Dad's always been real suspicious about any guy who dated you girls—I think he ordered background checks on every last one of them. This is what he got on Matt.''

Background checks? She stared blankly at the sheet of paper. Beside her, Bobby fidgeted. ''I should get in to see Megan again, shouldn't I?''

She followed him down the hall, and watched as he slipped into Megan's room with the cautious expression of someone entering a dragon's lair. Then she found a chair in a quiet area and sat down to read the document in her hands.

CHAPTER TWENTY

HOURS LATER, looking ill at ease, Robert hovered at the periphery of the crowd of ecstatic relatives peering at Bobby's tiny daughter through the hospital nursery window. Jolie knew just how much of an effort it had taken for her dad to walk in the door. But, after what she'd just found out, Jolie was in no mood to sympathize with him.

This might not be the best time, but it wouldn't be easy to catch him later. Beth had said Robert had been feeling stronger, and was now in his truck each day, driving all over his vast ranch checking on every last detail of its operation.

"Dad, I need to talk to you." Jolie forced a smile. "Please?"

After a moment of silence he finally gave a grudging nod and followed her to a quiet sitting area down the hall. Even after she was seated, he remained standing, his arms folded firmly in front of his chest. "Well?"

"Something you said when you were in the hospital has been bothering me." His gaze grew wary, and she knew she'd have to talk fast or he wouldn't stay.

"I was sick at the time. Drugged to the teeth with God knows what."

"Yes...well, you were drowsy. But you said that you had to live because we kids all made mistakes you had to fix."

His chin lifted a notch, his mouth settled into a hard, stubborn line as his cold gaze met hers.

"Bobby told me about your background checks on the guys your daughters dated. Tell me, Dad. What did you do with the information? File it, or use it against those guys to drive them off? Did you have a certain criteria for making your decisions?"

She hadn't expected an admission of guilt, but she hadn't expected his anger, either.

A dull red flush crept up his neck. "There've been plenty of lowlifes who would have jumped at the chance for a piece of Walking Stones. They saw available daughters—an easy route to money. I couldn't let that happen."

Jolie gave a bitter laugh. "That's all you saw—guys who lusted after your empire, who couldn't possibly be interested in your *girls?*"

He held his ground, as implacable as ever. "It's my job to protect the interests of the ranch. Background checks were necessary."

"As if these were *job* interviews?" Fury rose in her throat as she considered what he'd done in secret all these years. She'd been too far away in L.A. for him to know about the men she'd dated there. Now she lived far too close. "Do you have any idea how many people you've hurt by playing God?"

"I did what I had to do."

A staggering realization hit her. *"Matt got a phone call this morning,"* Megan had said. *"Some building inspector guy named Phil. Matt kept telling him that something was unfair."* "Tell me about Phil."

"Who?"

"The county building inspector, as you well know." Jolie shot to her feet, her hands clenched at her sides. "I hear he's been giving Matt Dawson trouble over permits and inspections."

"Why would I know about that?"

"If you don't, I'll bet your lawyers do," she said flatly. "Maybe you even called in a few favors at the courthouse. Did you figure you could destroy his business and run him out of town? Do you have *any* idea how illegal this is?"

After a long silence, Robert shook his head slowly. "I knew he was all wrong for you—probably just after your money. Blue-collar, two kids, no college degree. The man has carried a tremendous level of debt for *years*."

"His wife died of cancer, Dad. Did your reports tell you that?" Jolie took a steadying breath. "Did they tell you that he's a wonderful, caring father? That he works hard to support his family, and is as honest a man as you'd ever meet? Did those reports tell you that I've never met a man like him, or that I'd be happy if I could spend the rest of my life with a man like him?"

"Jolie—"

"No, Dad. I'm a grown woman. I have a good career. I love Walking Stones, and almost more than anything, I want to be close to my family after all my years away. But I'm not going to let you run my life. I want my name taken off every document, any will you've filed. You'll have no reason to hurt anyone in my name, ever again. And I want you to repair any damage you caused Matt Dawson. *Immediately*."

The glint in her dad's eyes softened. And, Lord have mercy, one corner of his mouth edged into a faint smile. "Someone else already confronted me about this. He…he made it clear that he intended to prove there'd been interference with the county's inspections. And that he would spend his last nickel to pursue the matter in court.

"However, we resolved the issue without going that far."

She hadn't heard the footsteps approach from the entrance at the other end of the room. But suddenly, awareness shimmered through her and her heart took an extra beat. When a pair of large, warm hands rested on her shoulders, her knees almost buckled and her anger faded. ''Matt?''

She turned in his arms and looked up into his warm brown eyes. Saw the laugh lines crinkling at the corners and the flash of his teeth as he smiled.

He looked over her shoulder at Robert, then lowered his mouth to hers for a kiss that sent sensations rocketing through her. When his arms folded around her and held her close, the world narrowed to his heat, the pounding of her heart.

Matt lifted his head a few inches, his eyes searching hers with such intensity that she nearly melted. ''I went to talk to your dad already, Jolie. He and I…worked things out. He's a decent man, just a little…uh…overprotective at times.''

She stared back at him, speechless.

''I love you, Jolie. I didn't realize how much until you were gone. I want you to be my wife.''

Robert nodded. ''He came out to the ranch and…well…. Guess I might've been wrong about him.''

Stunned, she stared at him. Never, in her thirty-three years, had she ever heard Robert Maxwell admit to being wrong.

At a shuffle of movement, Jolie turned and saw the entire Maxwell clan standing at the door. Lily and Charlie, too, and when Matt beckoned they came forward with shy smiles.

''Will you, Jolie? Will you marry us?'' Charlie's lower lip trembled as he looked up at her.

Lily hung back at first, then she too stepped forward. ''I'm sorry for anything I said. I never meant it, honest.''

Jolie hugged them both, then looked up into Matt's beloved face. Probably from the very first day they'd met,

You won't want to miss
Cassie's story—the final installment
in this exciting family saga.

MY MONTANA HOME
by Ellen James

will be available next month at
your favorite retail store.
Please turn the page for a preview.

CHAPTER ONE

"HUNKS FALLING FROM TREES? Surely, Cassie, even you can think of a better one than that."

"I've already told you, Gwen. *I* was the one who fell out of the damn tree. I landed sort of…well, sort of on top of him. Who knows how badly I've injured him!"

Andrew Morris was getting just a tad…impatient. He'd been sitting in this examination room like an afterthought for the better part of fifteen minutes, waiting for the doctor to show up. Now, it turned out Cassie had rushed him to the office of her son's pediatrician.

"Right, right…you simply happen to fall into the arms of a gorgeous guy. Some girls have all the luck."

"Luck," said Cassie. "I don't think falling on a man and practically killing him is good luck."

Andrew's finger hurt like hell, and he was starting to feel a little light-headed from over-oxygenation—he had always used deep, steady breathing to cope with stress. It wasn't so much the purple color of his finger that bothered him, nor the fact that it was now swollen beyond its normal size. No, what really bothered Andrew was the way his finger looked longer than any of the others, and it just sort of stuck out there on its own at an odd angle.

The doctor, Gwen-something-or-other, who had finally breezed into the examination room a moment ago, slapped up some X rays and perused them. "I mean, if you've made a new gentleman friend," she remarked to Cassie, "why not just come out and say so. No need to make up this fanciful story about falling out of trees.''

Dr. Gwen was definitely getting on Andrew's nerves. Among other things, she had already given him a very painful painkilling shot in his hand. And she insisted on treating him as if he were seven years old.

"Come on, Gwen,'' Cassie urged. "Please just tell me how much damage I've inflicted on him?'' Cassie, unlike the doctor, was not getting on his nerves. She had hazel eyes, and the merest hint of freckles across her cheekbones. And vivid red hair, cascading haphazardly down her back. She was, in sum, beautiful. Too bad that Andrew couldn't truly appreciate her at this moment. Too bad they weren't still alone in the tree house, before the...accident.

He cleared his throat. "Ladies—''

"Not broken. Just dislocated,'' said the doc, giving Andrew an annoyingly cheerful grin. "We can be thankful for that, at least. Now...I am going to have to pop that joint back into place. Not squeamish, are you?''

He gave her a sour look.

"Tell you what,'' she went on imperturbably, rummaging through a supply drawer. "Cassie'll hold your arm steady— *she's* not squeamish.''

Cassie gave Andrew an uncertain look, then glanced toward the door. "I'd better go see how Zak's doing—''

"Your son's fine,'' said Dr. Gwen. "You know how he likes that new game on Lucy's computer. No, you stay here and help me with your...friend. I'm glad to see you getting back into the dating scene. After Jeff—''

Cassie had flushed a bright pink. "Gwen,'' she said in a warning tone.

The doctor came over next to Andrew with gauze, surgical tape and a splint. She gave him a conspiratorial nod. "Surely you've heard all about Jeff by now?''

Andrew stared at the lamentable condition of his finger. "Actually, I haven't," he said.

Now Cassie treated *him* to a warning glance.

"Jeff's Cassie's ex," said Dr. Gwen as he positioned his arm. "Cassie, hold on to him right there…anyway, wouldn't you know she'd marry Jeff even after her dad told her the guy was a flat out loser. Of course, maybe that's why she married him. I mean, what better rebellion can you have? Elope with a man your father despises…"

"Gwen!" Cassie exclaimed, a brighter pink than ever.

"Anyway," Dr. Gwen went on relentlessly as she examined Andrew's finger, "in case you're wondering, I am a very reliable source of information when it comes to Cassie. I grew up in Paradise Corners, went to high school with Jolie…that's Cassie's oldest sister. Of course, Jolie pretty much kept to herself back in those days. It was the longest time before I found out we both had the same dream— becoming doctors. Well, here I am, and Jolie's practicing medicine back in our home town. Now, Andrew, dear, I'm afraid this is going to hurt like hell…and Cassie, get ready to hold as tight as you can. One…two…there! That wasn't so bad, was it?"

Andrew winced. "You forgot to count to three," he said between clenched teeth. But he had to admit the lady was good. His finger was back where it was supposed to be, and Dr. Gwen was now taping it to a small metal splint. Meanwhile, Cassie continued her deathgrip on his arm. He gazed at her, but she seemed to be making a determined effort not to look back.

"Of course you've heard of Cassie's family yourself," Dr. Gwen went on. "The mighty Maxwells, and all."

"Can't say I have," Andrew said.

"Goodness," said Dr. Gwen as she wielded her surgical tape. "I thought everyone in Montana had heard of the Maxwells. They practically wrote the book on ranching. And Cassie's dad…well, *he's* practically written the book on being a patriarch. More than a little overwhelming, if you want to know the truth. I used to be scared to death of him when I was a kid and I'd see him striding down Main Street like he owned it. The look he could give you… No wonder Cassie and Jolie and even Thea ended up rebelling against him… There! All set. I'll put you on an anti-inflammatory and some pain meds. Don't move that finger, and make sure you come back day after tomorrow so I can have a look. Now, Cassie, don't scowl at me like that. I didn't tell him anything he wasn't going to find out eventually.'' Dr. Gwen gave both of them a cocky grin, and vanished out the door.

"She kind of grows on you," Andrew remarked, observing his bandaged hand.

Cassie muttered something under her breath and dropped his arm as if she'd just realized she was holding it. "I'm sorry, I really am," she mumbled.

"Relax. That's about the twentieth time you've apologized. It was an accident. Could've happened to anyone."

She picked up her purse, and fiddled with the strap. "Actually, when I was apologizing just now…it was about Gwen, too. This was the first place I thought to bring you. She's a wonderful doctor, but she does talk a lot—"

"So now I know you're divorced, and you have a rebellious streak when it comes to your father," he said mildly. "Hardly capital offenses."

"I *used* to have a rebellious streak. Not anymore." She sighed. "I don't know why I'm explaining. What do you say we get out of here?"

It seemed an excellent idea to him. A few minutes later they were out on the sidewalk, the brilliant blue sky arching above them. Dr. Gwen's office was in downtown Billings proper, her office a converted Victorian. It was an old-fashioned street, tree-lined, with other old houses that had been turned into offices or duplexes. Cassie's son, seven-year-old Zak, walked ahead of them, his head bowed as if he were deep in thought. Cassie gazed at him worriedly.

"He's an okay kid," Andrew said.

"Yes, he is. He's wonderful. But he's…quiet."

"A lot of kids are quiet," Andrew said.

"He didn't used to be this way," Cassie muttered. "It's only been since…since the divorce."

The infamous divorce. He gathered that it was still a big part of her life. "How long ago?" he asked.

"A while. So, Andrew," she said determinedly, "have *you* ever been married?" She couldn't have made it more clear that she wanted to change the subject.

"Can't say I have. Hannah always told me I was missing out. But, frankly, I never did see how."

"All depends on who you're married to," Cassie said grimly. And then, as if concerned she'd directed the conversation to herself again, she gave him another glance. "How's the finger?"

"I'll live."

"I really am sorry—"

"There you go again," he said. "Apologizing."

She gave an exasperated shake of the head. "You have to admit the whole thing's been highly unfortunate."

He didn't know what to think. It wasn't every day that a beautiful redhead fell into his arms—and dislocated his finger in the process.

"Why are you smiling?" Cassie asked suspiciously.

"No reason." He found, surprisingly, that he was feeling pretty good. He didn't know if it was Cassie Warren, or the unexpected turn of the day. Cassie, however, didn't appear to share his optimism. She gazed at him for another moment, and then her expression grew shuttered. She might as well have put up a warning sign: Keep away. Don't get too close.

She called to her son. "Zak, the car's over here. We're going home." And then she turned to Andrew one more time. "At least—it's home until Zak and I find an apartment. We'll clear out just as soon as we can."

Andrew felt a stirring of disappointment. And that, too, was unexpected.

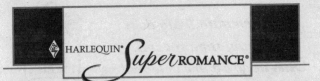

HARLEQUIN *Super*ROMANCE

Welcome to Montana

BIG SKY COUNTRY

Home of the Rocky Mountains,
Yellowstone National Park,
slow-moving glaciers and
the spectacular Going
to the Sun Highway.

Set against this unforgettable background,
Harlequin Superromance introduces the
Maxwells of Montana—a family that's
lived and ranched here for generations.

You won't want to miss this brand-new trilogy—
three exciting romances by three of
your favorite authors.

MARRIED IN MONTANA
by Lynnette Kent on sale August 2001

A MONTANA FAMILY
by Roxanne Rustand on sale September 2001

MY MONTANA HOME
by Ellen James on sale October 2001

Available wherever Harlequin books are sold.

HARLEQUIN®
Makes any time special ®

Harlequin truly does make any time special. . . . This year we are celebrating weddings in style!

A Walk Down the Aisle
WEDDING CELEBRATION

To help us celebrate, we want you to tell us how wearing the Harlequin wedding gown will make your wedding day special. As the grand prize, Harlequin will offer one lucky bride the chance to **"Walk Down the Aisle"** in the Harlequin wedding gown!

There's more...

For her honeymoon, she and her groom will spend five nights at the **Hyatt Regency Maui.** As part of this five-night honeymoon at the hotel renowned for its romantic attractions, the couple will enjoy a candlelit dinner for two in Swan Court, a sunset sail on the hotel's catamaran, and duet spa treatments.

A HYATT RESORT AND SPA   Maui • Molokai • Lanai

To enter, please write, in, 250 words or less, how wearing the Harlequin wedding gown will make your wedding day special. The entry will be judged based on its emotionally compelling nature, its originality and creativity, and its sincerity. This contest is open to Canadian and U.S. residents only and to those who are 18 years of age and older. There is no purchase necessary to enter. Void where prohibited. See further contest rules attached. Please send your entry to:

Walk Down the Aisle Contest

In Canada	In U.S.A.
P.O. Box 637	P.O. Box 9076
Fort Erie, Ontario	3010 Walden Ave.
L2A 5X3	Buffalo, NY 14269-9076

You can also enter by visiting www.eHarlequin.com
Win the Harlequin wedding gown and the vacation of a lifetime!
The deadline for entries is October 1, 2001.

HARLEQUIN®
Makes any time special ®

PHWDACONT1

HARLEQUIN WALK DOWN THE AISLE TO MAUI CONTEST 1197
OFFICIAL RULES
NO PURCHASE NECESSARY TO ENTER

1. To enter, follow directions published in the offer to which you are responding. Contest begins April 2, 2001, and ends on October 1, 2001. Method of entry may vary. Mailed entries must be postmarked by October 1, 2001, and received by October 8, 2001.

2. Contest entry may be, at times, presented via the Internet, but will be restricted solely to residents of certain geographic areas that are disclosed on the Web site. To enter via the Internet, if permissible, access the Harlequin Web site (www.eHarlequin.com) and follow the directions displayed online. Online entries must be received by 11:59 p.m. E.S.T. on October 1, 2001.

   In lieu of submitting an entry online, enter by mail by hand-printing (or typing) on an 8½" x 11" plain piece of paper, your name, address (including zip code), Contest number/name and in 250 words or fewer, why winning a Harlequin wedding dress would make your wedding day special. Mail via first-class mail to: Harlequin Walk Down the Aisle Contest 1197, (in the U.S.) P.O. Box 9076, 3010 Walden Avenue, Buffalo, NY 14269-9076, (in Canada) P.O. Box 637, Fort Erie, Ontario L2A 5X3, Canada.

   Limit one entry per person, household address and e-mail address. Online and/or mailed entries received from persons residing in geographic areas in which Internet entry is not permissible will be disqualified.

3. Contests will be judged by a panel of members of the Harlequin editorial, marketing and public relations staff based on the following criteria:

   - Originality and Creativity—50%
   - Emotionally Compelling—25%
   - Sincerity—25%

   In the event of a tie, duplicate prizes will be awarded. Decisions of the judges are final.

4. All entries become the property of Torstar Corp. and will not be returned. No responsibility is assumed for lost, late, illegible, incomplete, inaccurate, nondelivered or misdirected mail or misdirected e-mail, for technical, hardware or software failures of any kind, lost or unavailable network connections, or failed, incomplete, garbled or delayed computer transmission or any human error which may occur in the receipt or processing of the entries in this Contest.

5. Contest open only to residents of the U.S. (except Puerto Rico) and Canada, who are 18 years of age or older, and is void wherever prohibited by law; all applicable laws and regulations apply. Any litigation within the Province of Quebec respecting the conduct or organization of a publicity contest may be submitted to the Régie des alcools, des courses et des jeux for a ruling. Any litigation respecting the awarding of a prize may be submitted to the Régie des alcools, des courses et des jeux only for the purpose of helping the parties reach a settlement. Employees and immediate family members of Torstar Corp. and D. L. Blair, Inc., their affiliates, subsidiaries and all other agencies, entities and persons connected with the use, marketing or conduct of this Contest are not eligible to enter. Taxes on prizes are the sole responsibility of winners. Acceptance of any prize offered constitutes permission to use winner's name, photograph or other likeness for the purposes of advertising, trade and promotion on behalf of Torstar Corp., its affiliates and subsidiaries without further compensation to the winner, unless prohibited by law.

6. Winners will be determined no later than November 15, 2001, and will be notified by mail. Winners will be required to sign and return an Affidavit of Eligibility form within 15 days after winner notification. Noncompliance within that time period may result in disqualification and an alternative winner may be selected. Winners of trip must execute a Release of Liability prior to ticketing and must possess required travel documents (e.g. passport, photo ID) where applicable. Trip must be completed by November 2002. No substitution of prize permitted by winner. Torstar Corp. and D. L. Blair, Inc., their parents, affiliates, and subsidiaries are not responsible for errors in printing or electronic presentation of Contest, entries and/or game pieces. In the event of printing or other errors which may result in unintended prize values or duplication of prizes, all affected game pieces or entries shall be null and void. If for any reason the Internet portion of the Contest is not capable of running as planned, including infection by computer virus, bugs, tampering, unauthorized intervention, fraud, technical failures, or any other causes beyond the control of Torstar Corp. which corrupt or affect the administration, secrecy, fairness, integrity or proper conduct of the Contest, Torstar Corp. reserves the right, at its sole discretion, to disqualify any individual who tampers with the entry process and to cancel, terminate, modify or suspend the Contest or the Internet portion thereof. In the event of a dispute regarding an online entry, the entry will be deemed submitted by the authorized holder of the e-mail account submitted at the time of entry. Authorized account holder is defined as the natural person who is assigned to an e-mail address by an Internet access provider, online service provider or other organization that is responsible for arranging e-mail address for the domain associated with the submitted e-mail address. **Purchase or acceptance of a product offer does not improve your chances of winning.**

7. Prizes: (1) Grand Prize—A Harlequin wedding dress (approximate retail value: $3,500) and a 5-night/6-day honeymoon trip to Maui, HI, including round-trip air transportation provided by Maui Visitors Bureau from Los Angeles International Airport (winner is responsible for transportation to and from Los Angeles International Airport) and a Harlequin Romance Package, including hotel accomodations (double occupancy) at the Hyatt Regency Maui Resort and Spa, dinner for (2) two at Swan Court, a sunset sail on Kiele V and a spa treatment for the winner (approximate retail value: $4,000); (5) Five runner-up prizes of a $1000 gift certificate to selected retail outlets to be determined by Sponsor (retail value $1000 ea.). Prizes consist of only those items listed as part of the prize. Limit one prize per person. All prizes are valued in U.S. currency.

8. For a list of winners (available after December 17, 2001) send a self-addressed, stamped envelope to: Harlequin Walk Down the Aisle Contest 1197 Winners, P.O. Box 4200 Blair, NE 68009-4200 or you may access the www.eHarlequin.com Web site through January 15, 2002.

Contest sponsored by Torstar Corp., P.O. Box 9042, Buffalo, NY 14269-9042, U.S.A.

PHWDACONT2

HARLEQUIN®

makes any time special—online...

eHARLEQUIN.com

shop eHarlequin

- ♥ Find all the new Harlequin releases at everyday great discounts.
- ♥ Try before you buy! Read an excerpt from the latest Harlequin novels.
- ♥ Write an online review and share your thoughts with others.

reading room

- ♥ Read our Internet exclusive daily and weekly online serials, or vote in our interactive novel.
- ♥ Talk to other readers about your favorite novels in our Reading Groups.
- ♥ Take our Choose-a-Book quiz to find the series that matches you!

authors' alcove

- ♥ Find out interesting tidbits and details about your favorite authors' lives, interests and writing habits.
- ♥ Ever dreamed of being an author? Enter our Writing Round Robin. The Winning Chapter will be published online! Or review our writing guidelines for submitting your novel.

All this and more available at
www.eHarlequin.com
on Women.com Networks

HINTB1R

In October 2001
Look for this
New York Times bestselling author

BARBARA DELINSKY

in

Bronze Mystique

The only men in Sasha's life lived between the covers of her bestselling romances. She wrote about passionate, loving heroes, but no such man existed...til Doug Donohue rescued Sasha the night her motorcycle crashed.

AND award-winning Harlequin Intrigue author

GAYLE WILSON

in

Secrets in Silence

This fantastic 2-in-1 collection will be on sale October 2001.

#1 *New York Times* Bestselling Author

NORA ROBERTS

Will enchant readers with two remarkable tales of timeless love.

Coming in September 2001

TIME AND AGAIN

Two brothers from the future cross centuries to find a love more powerful than time itself in the arms of two beguiling sisters.

Available at your favorite retail outlet.

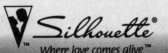